Ana Lydia Vega was born in 1946 in Santuce, Puerto Rico, where she now lives. She is Professor of French and Caribbean literature at the University of Puerto Rico. The author of film-scripts, plays and numerous short stories, Ana Lydia Vega is the winner of the 1984 Juan Rulfo short story prize and the 1989 Guggenheim Fellowship for Literary Creation. In 1982, she was awarded the Casa Las Américas Prize in Havana.

TRUE AND
FALSE ROMANCES

Stories and a novella

ANA LYDIA VEGA

Translated by Andrew Hurley

Library of Congress Catalog Card Number: 93–86123

A catalogue record for this book is available from
the British Library on request

This edition first published by
Serpent's Tail, 4 Blackstock Mews, London N4
and 401 West Broadway #1, New York, NY 10012

Phototypeset in 10½ Palatino by Intype, London
Printed in Finland by Werner Söderström Oy

ISBN: 1-85242-272-6
ISBN:- 13:978-1-85242-272-1

CONTENTS

TRUE ROMANCES

What is drama, after all, but life
with all the dull bits cut out.

– Alfred Hitchcock

I

When Vilma's letter arrived, it was like mouth-to-mouth resuscitation. I'd gotten myself into another one of those iffy situations I was beginning to think I had some kind of perverse calling for, and the life raft Vilma threw me couldn't have come at a better time.

I'd just split up with Manuel. We'd had another fender-bender – our big chrome-plated egos were always getting us into them – but when the time had come to kiss and make up again, I found I had very little desire to pucker. I surprised myself at how unfazed I was by what should have been a classic case of break-up blues. What's even weirder is that I practically wept for joy when I discovered that "the other woman" was none other than his lawfully wedded wife. I don't know which one of us should have won the Oscar, me for faking a fit of tabloid jealousy in order to soften the karate-chop, or him, playing the contrite lover-boy.

Anyway, I packed up my troubles in my very old kit-bag and – *ta-dum!* – I moved to Río Piedras. A closet with delusions of grandeur (it thought it was a bedroom), with its own entrance and a separate bathroom. It wasn't too bad for the price, and considering my miserable per-annum as a school teacher, it would have to do ... It was on Humacao Street, which is a no-woman's land of insurgent university students and the fragrance of overflowing sewers. But what did I care – I had a very Woolfian room of my own where I could finally get some writing done, and that was about the only thing I had any real interest in at the moment. So I felt if not happy at least relatively "at peace."

A peace that was not long to last, of course.

During this time, I was working on a sort of semi-documentary, semi-detective novel about a crime of passion that had taken place not long before in a middle-class condominium in Hato Rey. The victim's name was Malén, so of course every newspaper in the country started calling it the "Malén affair." They loved it, and their readers ate it up – there was sex, nudity, streams of blood, and a reactionary moral to the tale: beware, you girls that are hot to trot. The plot was not particularly novel: a spurned macho catches his ex-squeeze *in flagrante delicto* with his best friend. Through the newspapers' morbose delectation, as the nuns where I went to school called it, and the super-detailed spy-satellite geography of the stab-wounds, you could clearly read between the lines: Women – you just can't trust 'em.

I'd like to think it was the Puritan implications of the newspaper articles that sucked me in and not that morbid curiosity that makes you slow down on the highway to watch some poor mutilated bastard getting scooped up off the pavement with a spatula. But whatever it was, I'd been hooked by Malén ever since that first photo of her appeared cheek-to-cheek with her murderer's on the front page of *El Vocero* – she was a real beauty, with Lola Flores hair, full sensual lips, and that sad-eyed look men go for; he wasn't bad-looking himself, if you liked the type – a serious furrowed brow, the satisfied expression of a man who knows he's done his duty. A miserable, dirty duty, but then somebody had to do it.

Had fate not stuck its fickle finger in, that would have been that: two pictures that deserved better, another run-of-the-mill story of passion. But fate had not just a fickle finger, it had fangs. Or at least a wicked sense of humor, for in its infinite wisdom it saw fit to make the scene of this horrific crime the same condo that the mother of yours truly, a writer who loves a good story, lived in. The killing had turned my poor mother into a veritable wailing wall – all she ever did was moan that somebody had put a spell on the building, because first there'd been that baby that fell down the elevator shaft, and then the couple that did abortions and flushed the fetuses down the toilet, and now this indecent woman roaming the halls stark naked at night, a-different-man-every-day, no wonder what happened to her happened to her. It was my mother's telling of her beads of woe running like a non-stop showing of some B-movie at a 24-hour movie theater that kept me abreast of the juicy updates (and the editorial opinions that went along with them) that the obviously underemployed residents of the building were appending to the merely gruesome newspaper articles that the rest of us had read.

It went like this: Malén and her ex-lover's best friend had been listening to the stereo "full blast" when the murderer, one Salvador, "tried to kick down" the door to the apartment. The stereo probably explained why they also didn't hear the metallic clang when the ex-boyfriend put his fist through the Miami window that opened onto the hall, or hear anything either when in one leap he landed like a cat on his feet in the dark kitchen. They were "naked as jaybirds" on the sofabed in the living room, drinking beer and eating *chicharrones*

– the post-coital munchies, you know. The newly-arrived guest did not come unaccompanied. With him he brought a six-inch switchblade. As Malén was beginning to get a fix on what was about to go down, the back-stabbing best friend ("back-stabbing" in the figurative sense, you understand) high-tails it out the front door, giving new meaning to the expression Wham, bam, thank you ma'am. From the ex: Insults, a little slapping around, then the shower scene from *Psycho* again right there in the living room. Malén plays dead, and it isn't too hard to do. The killer then goes after The Other Man. Malén manages to get up and stagger down the dimly-lit hall, painting the stairs red down to the floor below. Returning from his frustrated search for his erstwhile buddy, Salvador picks up the trail of Malén while the future deceased finds the strength to bang on the deaf doors all along the hallway. – Knock, knock. *Nobody's home*, says Death.

It wasn't for staying home and saying her rosary – that was the epitaph composed by the Condominated Wives' Club, while the Real Men's Society, San Juan Chapter, took for its motto the heroic words of the murderer as he turned himself in at the Hato Rey station the next day: *I cut her up 'cause she tried to cut me out*. Which was the urban lowlife version of the standard macho "Mine or Nobody's."

The funny thing was, it never occurred to anybody to ask why this other guy, who got out while the gettin' was good (and dressed in nothing but his birthday suit), didn't need so much as a Band-Aid. Nor did it ever occur to anybody to question that "none of my business if somebody bleeds to death on my doorstep" crap from the spectators peeking out their peepholes, treating Malén like some magazine-subscription salesman come knocking at the door. *C'etait la vie*, and you can take that any way you want to.

Little by little I collected a respectable stack of clippings and "statements." I would interrogate the gossipers every time I went over to my mother's ill-starred condominium to torture some more clothes in the laundry room. A simple tale of jealous love, I'd tell myself, trying to minimize my sick fixation on the story – no big deal, I'd say. And yet it was a big deal – the world was full of vengeful men and forbidden women, and I found to my dismay that I had a love-hate relationship with that fact.

That was how I started knitting together the story of Malén, and then the novel of Malén, because the skein of loose ends and ravels got more and more tangled every day, and something was always missing, the decisive stitch, the warp that would pull all this woof together. So there I was, knitting away, when another true-crime story, this time brought me by a neighbor of mine, a housewife with bloodhound genes, temporarily made me drop my needles.

A few days ago, it seems, doña Finí had gone on red alert, her optical cannons trained on what she called a "bum" that was roaming the neighborhood, on the prowl for rapable maidens. The disturbing part, according to doña Finí, was that the mysterious stalker, who to make matters worse was motorized, seemed especially fascinated by my bedroom window, which was fatally located directly on the street. He even discreetly slowed down, almost stopped, every time he passed that obscure object of his putative desire.

Doña Finí was driving me crazy. The minute I came home from school, my toes twisted in agony within the four-inch heels prescribed by fashion, dying to stuff a sandwich down that boa constrictor writhing within my gut, she'd start bombarding me with the fruits of her observations: "That guy ought to get a life, I tell you. Today he was around here so much the beans burned on me, because I had to keep going to check the clock, you know, the police the way they are you got to keep records on these guys – I'm going to send you a bill the end of the month, girl. And get this, oh ye of little faith – he came around here this morning at seven, not five minutes after you'd left, and then about ten-thirty when I was changing Charley's diaper out on the porch, and then at twelve o'clock on the dot, I know because *El Show de Mediodía* was just starting, Danny Rivera was on, and he was singing and kind of hopping up and down like he does, that was at twelve, and then apparently he took a little break, had himself some lunch – this guy, I mean, not Danny – because he wasn't back till about one, and then again about two-thirty, not ten minutes ago, you two practically ran into each other, child – ay, Virgen de la Providencia, protect us, because I'll tell you, the way things are going in this country . . ."

I must confess that secretly I was a little flattered. I'd never exactly been overstocked in the boyfriend department, if you know what I mean. In college the *femme fatale* was my best friend Vilma. I was one of those girls that had to work at it, using my brains as much as my boobs. But of course I had to repay my neighbor for her eagle-eyed guard duty, so I put on a grand show of disgust and fear at that threat to my supposed chastity. All week I lived in pleasant suspense, waiting for my clockwork satyr to make his rounds – but I never caught him in the act because the miserable "Activities Month" at school had my schedule totally out of whack. Until Saturday, that is, when my summer vacation made its official debut. That morning I stuck my nose out the window to smell the fresh sewage and found that the phantom stalker was none other than Manuel. *The Return of the Boyfriend*, two thumbs down.

I was more annoyed than disappointed by this turn of events. How the fuck had he found out where I'd made my new nest? What right did he have to spy on me this way? Next thing he'd be rummaging around in my trashcan at midnight looking for icky condoms to paste in his album.

So that was why I was so glad to get Vilma's letter. She was inviting me to spend three weeks with her – free of charge, as they say in the come-ons on TV – in a little village in the French Pyrenees. That, to a *jeune fille triste* from the tropics, was the Platonic ideal of exoticism. How could I say no. The only hair in the soup, she said, is that we're staying at Paul's parents' house. But then she went on to describe, in absolutely paradisal terms, the bucolic locale in which I would be sitting upon the egg of The Great Puerto Rican Novel.

Although she'd been living in France for five years, Vilma suffered from chronic homesickness. She religiously kept in touch with four old classmates of hers, among whom I had been officially designated the favorite. Her letters were in actuality laundry-lists of questions about the national pastime – politics. Since I wasn't particularly interested in palace intrigues, I had a hard time satisfying her draculean thirst for gory detail. Which was why I filled manila envelopes, instead, with clippings about the political goings-on of our dear Isle, sending along issues of *Claridad* for good measure, so she could keep herself, as she herself put it, "linked to The Struggle."

To go or not to go – the question was a snap, which

was a little unusual for me. I took my savings from three years of slaving over a hot classroom full of ungrateful students and invested it in a tourist-class ticket to Wonderland, made a stopover of a week in my mother's apartment to throw my stalker off the track and reassure doña Finí, then finally crossed the pond, my trusty Smith Corona portable slung over my back and the file on the Malén affair under my sweaty armpit.

II

I arrived at night, after a day and a half of trains and planes. My internal thermometer, still set for the eternal Antillean swelter, had trouble with what they called summer over here. My lips trembled, though not with contained emotion, when I greeted Paul in my college-requirement French. Vilma acted like I was the female messiah.

Between the cold, the chitchat, the purring of the car engine, and the curves of the highway, I think I nodded off a couple of times. Paul hardly talked, whether out of shyness or standoffishness I couldn't say, but he did seem to enjoy racing down that dark road covered with fog. Fortunately, Paul's parents were asleep by the time we arrived, so I was spared the receiving line that would have finished the job of zombifying me that the long trip had started. Vilma had a charming room all ready for me, with a stuffed chamois head on the wall and everything. There was even a fireplace (no fire unfortunately) with dazzling copper pots hanging from the mantel for decoration. With great fanfare Vilma pointed out to me her biggest *coup de théâtre* – an antique rolltop desk, smelling of freshly-buffed wax and riddled with unexpected little drawers and nooks. She'd had it restored especially for yours truly, Carola Vidal, writer – with a capital W if you don't mind.

"If you can't get that novel you've been sitting on to hatch *here*," she said, depositing a thick wool blanket on the bed, "we'll have to wonder if it's not addled." With that reminder of my responsibilities still echoing in my head, I fell into the arms of a delightful *ménage trois*: weariness, me, and sleep.

I got up early and threw open the window. Paul's parents' big stone house lorded it over one end of the village, which lay nestled, as they say, in the Aspe Valley between ranges of gray and blue mountains blurred with clouds. I breathed deep, to cleanse my lungs of thirty years of urban pollution in San Juan, went over to pick up the blanket, and threw it over my shoulders for a shawl against the chill. Back at the window, the picture-postcard landscape was still there, but now spotted with folk figures: a flock of black-clad old women was laboring up the hill between the tall narrow houses. A wonderfully synchronized ringing of bells told me they were on their way to church. With the awareness that it was Sunday came that vague anxiety of those olden days of now-discarded pieties.

I looked at my watch, which was still on Puerto Rican time, and cursed the Greenwich Meridian: six hours older. In Puerto Rico it was three o'clock in the morning, and I'd still be snoring – if, that is, some car alarm or a gunshot or students raising hell hadn't come along to disturb the sleep of the just. But here it was nine o'clock of a silent morning in the Pyrenees, where, I had a very clear feeling, time was distinctly different.

I puttered around for a while in my room, unpacking my bag, laying out the paper and other accoutrements of the writer on the desk, opening and closing drawers, until I heard the unmistakable sounds of the rest of the household beginning to emerge from their summer night's hibernation. In a few minutes Vilma burst in, same old Vilma, yelling that the cock had crew and that if I planned to sleep my life away I'd come to the wrong place, so rise and shine, up and at 'em, and other such inspiriting war cries.

"And prepare yourself," she added with a touch of mischievousness, checking her hair in the foursquare mirror of the huge armoire that stood opposite the door, "the old folks are up and about downstairs."

And there indeed they were: him with his black beret and cane, her with her apron on and coffee-pot in hand, the two of them the archetypal French provincial couple by way of Claude Chabrol. I noticed that Vilma gave him but not her that invariable two-pronged buss on the cheeks. Faithful to my feminist instincts, I inverted the ritual, *mwah-mwah* for madame, my hand to monsieur with my most aggressive smile. Both greeted me effusively, gushing in almost-intelligible French over my long black hair with its wealth of split ends, the hepatitis yellow of my Antillean skin, and my other Puerto Rican assets. In that exchange of cross-cultural pleasantries, we breakfasted on *café au lait* and hot *croissants*. Paul was conspicuous by his absence, but Vilma explained that he'd gone out early fishing with some friends. I'd already taken note of the stuffed animals and weapons hung on every wall. *So, a lover of fresh air and a tamer of wild beasts, this Paul*, I thought . . . It seemed like about the right occupation for him, in tune with the paternal beret, the maternal apron, and the stone house on the side of the mountain . . .

To consolidate my gains with the mother, I offered to wash up after breakfast, but (fortunately) my offer was rejected. Vilma dragged me bodily outside, without so much as letting me go upstairs for a sweater, with a song and dance about cool clean air – you'll see, as soon as we start walking you'll warm up . . . And I let myself be dragged outdoors, like one of those soon-to-be-shorn sheep that wandered through the village in the evenings.

My innocence was not fated to last. That first walk nipped my vacation in the bud. Vilma confessed to me what in a way I'd already intuited: her marriage was not in the best of shape and she was even considering divorce, which was why she had wanted her Caribbean Madame Soleil to come to her rescue. A thankless job, that of the confidante. Especially if it was *Vilma*'s confidante – I knew how she was about being "objective" and "keeping a critical distance on things." She was one of those people who can talk for hours, totally oblivious to the exhaustion of that other person lying Gandhi-like on the iron rails of her monologue.

The first two years had been like something out of a movie: the university in Toulouse, the discovery of the "Old World," the romance, the wedding, and the move to Bordeaux. Then things soured a bit when Paul refused to let her work, but that wasn't really so bad. The problems began in earnest when he also declared martial law on her free time – she couldn't even talk to her downstairs neighbor. If she wasn't in the kitchen when he got home, stirring the pot with the copper cooking-spoon the Pyrenean in-laws had given her for a wedding present, he would make a scene worthy of the best of them.

Then and there the roof fell in on my *prêt-à-porter* notions of the Gallic *homme typique*. I'd pictured French men as so sophisticated, so *evolués*, so Sartre and Beauvoir ... Vilma's hubby left our own island machos in the shade. This Caucasian incarnation of the Moor of Venice was suspicious of everything and everybody. That being the case, I asked myself how he'd ever authorized my discreet invasion of his universe. But that wasn't all. The Taino princess locked in the big stone castle by the malevolent boar hunter had also had to suffer the torments of the wicked witch with the apron and the coffee pot (though I must say she'd been super with me that morning).

"Thank your stars you don't live with her the whole year 'round," I said, since some kind of consolation was clearly expected of me.

That was when Vilma, her customary bravado deflated, told me the Hitlerian details of the persecution carried out against her by her mother-in-law: The letters sent to the son, the telephone calls, the unannounced visits to Bordeaux under the pretext of taking the newlyweds some culinary delicacy ... Madame Jocasta had never looked very kindly on Paul's bringing home from the hunt his New World mammal, marrying that plebeian Josephine de Beauharnais of mestizo charm. The old lady had "contacts" in the city, and from the very first, these agents had followed Vilma everywhere she went, filing detailed reports on her movements. These reports the old lady in turn passed on to Paul.

All this sounded so weird, so conspiracy-theory wacko, so Daphne du Maurier, that I started thinking it was some kind of paranoid fantasy that Vilma had caught somewhere. Had homesickness curdled her brain? For obvious reasons, I said nothing – and besides, the story (that's the really sick part of being a writer) absolutely fascinated me. Through my mind passed in parade all the women in French literature and cinema who'd been driven to unfaithfulness by boredom, while Vilma Bovary continued her appalling story.

"Ironically, the least bad part of it is these summers in Paul's parents' house. Here I can more or less move around. I figure they think it's easier to keep an eye on me this way. Plus," she adds with invincible wickedness, "there's nobody under sixty to be found."

"What about your father-in-law?" I asked, remembering the kiss-kiss Vilma had given M. le Beret.

"Poor thing," she sighed, with quiet eloquence.

And we went on strolling along, our arms linked, down the mountain road. Snippets of a brilliant thread of river were scattered below us, on the floor of the valley.

Paul came in very late that afternoon. Or maybe it was night already, who could tell? – because the day's deceptive brightness lasted till ten p.m. I know we were already sitting at the table, fishing vegetables out of our steaming bowls of soup while negotiating international courtesies with the in-laws. I was pretty jittery. I mean, Vilma's confidences weren't calculated to calm a girl's nerves. Either my senses had suddenly gotten extraordinarily sharp or the wine so prodigally poured into my glass by M. le Beret had gone to my head – whatever it was, even the pictures on the walls and the stuffed boar's head in the kitchen seemed almost alive, and filled with secret significance.

When he came in, I was so startled I almost dropped

my soup spoon. Bluebeard said *bonjour* (though I'd have thought *bonsoir* was indicated under the circumstances), kissed his mother, Vilma, his father, and I thought I was going to have the honor, too, but I was wrong. He stretched his leather-gloved hand across the table for me to shake. He then went upstairs, with an excuse I didn't understand – Vilma had told me they sometimes spoke Bearnaise, the neglected language of the region – and the dinner went on tensely but calmly. The *ratatouille* was to die.

This time I did the dishes. Vilma dried and madame swept up. In that *pax domestica* – ah, paradox – I found again the quietness of the morning at the window. The men were out of the picture. It was just us three women working together, and the nine echoing chimes of the church bells (or did I lose count?).

Vilma's good night to me on the stairs was very tender. I took a long hot bath, dried myself off between shivers, and sat down to revise – writing was out of the question – the few pages I'd rewritten.

" . . . *Malén changes the record and lies down. She is naked and her dark skin gleams in the blue lamplight. She is totally naked and the music is punk rock, green hair and safety pins and chains. The telephone rings. It's Rafael, and he's on his way, as soon as he locks up the shop, he won't be long, he's bringing beer and Chinese food,* Don't cook so you won't smell like Mazola, and don't put perfume on your throat 'cause it tastes bad. *Malén whispers not to worry, and don't forget the soy sauce and the egg rolls, punch that time clock fast because her meter's already running, and by the way – Salvador has been following her for three days, trailing her everywhere she goes, marking out his territory in the hall, in front of her apartment, like some tomcat leaving his calling card in piss, sending her messages.* Fuck him, *Rafael inter-*

rupts her, you're not his property – forget it, he's not giving you alimony, he doesn't pay the rent, you don't have to take any shit from him, and anyway I'm prepared, just in case, I bought something to take care of him if he . . . , 'Bye, my sweet, hang on till I get there, *and then there's some masculine heavy breathing that holds a promise of things to come . . . Malén takes off the record, looks at herself, turns on the radio, lies down. She is naked and her dark skin gleams in the red lamplight. She is totally naked, and the music now is an old bolero, a Dipiní bolero of vindictive love . . ."*

In the soft circle of the reading lamp, Malén is gradually clothed in black, like a dream out of François Truffaut.

III

The week passed slowly, in a rhythm of fattening meals, olympic bouts of dish-washing, and clandestine scribbling. Clandestine because Vilma, our friendship rediviva, gave me not a moment's let-up. She would even tag along to the bathroom to tell me the hair-raising details of her private life with Paul. Some of the things she told me were so private I wouldn't have told my own shadow even under threat of torture. She told a good story, though, which meant that I listened, and listened with real interest – and *that* made me feel guilty, as though I were eavesdropping almost against my own will on some grotesquely obscene act. And of course Vilma would see that, and she'd do everything in her power to make a long story longer, pausing at the most strategic moments so that I'd have to ask what happened next and expose my indecent curiosity for all to see.

"The first time he hit me I thought he was playing, so I hit him back. So he hit me harder. That scared me. I tried to get out of the room, but he grabbed me and dragged me over to the bed . . ."

Dot dot dot. I mean, Hitchcock was supposed to be the master of suspense, but he had nothing on Vilma.

And then, she informs me, sure enough, Paul wound up putting it to her, straight out of Freud.

I didn't know whether to be appalled or to congratulate her, because she did tell this with a certain dubious grace, and with the weird enthusiasm of a grown-up that wants to scare a child that wants to be scared.

The discreet charms of Paul paled beside those of his mother. Vilma told – and this was one of her *least* spooky stories – how they'd been staying at her in-laws' house one night, during one of those battles-royal she and Paul now had pretty regularly, and she'd tried to escape from the room. She unlocked the door, but she discovered that something – or *somebody* – was blocking it from the outside. The villainous husband gave a sinister laugh like some modern Gilles de Rais. Vilma swore she heard a snort of laughter, indisputably female, outside the door.

"Carola, I swear on my mother it was the old woman . . ."

The mother-in-law, getting her jollies from what Paul was doing . . .

At the end of a week, my curiosity had shrivelled in inverse proportion to the growing sense of menace produced in me by my friend's spectacular confessions. The worst part was the effect they were having on my perception of immediate reality. Everything was warped. I would stammer when I talked to the old woman. And if The Huntsman should happen into the kitchen, I'd freeze like a scared rabbit. I couldn't look directly at him. My only refuge was M. le Beret – a pretty shaky refuge, since he watched television almost constantly, and when he wasn't watching TV he would sit next to the radiator with a glass of red wine in his hand and doze, head bobbing. Vilma, however, adopted an attitude of almost complete indifference, a kind of controlled calm, in total contrast to the atrocities she brought out for inspection in warehouse lots every time she caught me alone.

On Saturday I broke my own principle of Swiss neutrality and took it upon myself to ask Vilma why in god's name she hadn't gotten out of this. She couldn't answer.

Sunday afternoon we went to Oloron-Sainte-Marie in the family station wagon – Bluebeard driving, Vilma next to him, and in the back seat M. le Beret, the Witch from the Seven Dwarves, yours truly the unholy unvirgin martyr, and the dogs in back. We took a walk, in my honor, through the city, which was so medieval it looked almost like a movie set. There was a burbling river that ran right through the middle of the village, and streets quaintly crossed it like foot-bridges. The town was also full of unexpected steps bordering the steep streets, perfect for a sword-fight. Preceded by gigantic sheep dogs, gala tribes of entire families – aunts, uncles, and grandparents included – strolled, like us, aimlessly, through the village, letting themselves collapse into the open-air cafés where a leisure-class of provincial young people would ignore them with studied fake-urbanity.

We broke our mid-morning fast with *chocolat viennois*

and some incredibly delicious *russes* that Paul's mother
ordered so I could try them. Vilma ate nothing. She
watched me, as though amused, through the steam that
rose from the chocolate. Her mother-in-law gave a long
animated discourse on the excellencies of French pastry
– a wondrous truth, as I was fast proving to my own
satiation. M. le Beret wasn't listening, absorbed as he
was in blithely dunking a *russe* in his huge cup of hot
chocolate. (If the people who invented these wonders
treated them this way, why had my mother told me nice
girls didn't dunk doughnuts in coffee?) Even Paul gave
me a little meek-husband smile from time to time. Under
the trio's implacable eye, I discreetly napkin'd off my
chin dusted with soft white sugar, trying to find something to say in response to so much (and so undeserved)
kindness.

The Sunday ritual ended at seven that non-night. I
mean it was as bright as afternoon, and the sky utterly
cloudless. We squeezed back into the station wagon for
the return to our Pyrenean Wuthering Heights. Vilma
wanted to ride in the back seat, so she traded seats
with her mother-in-law. Her Caribbean beam-breadth
crowded me into the corner. During the ride back, we
chatted like any family returning from an outing anywhere in the world. It was hard for me to connect the
tales of volcanic passions that Vilma wove with Third-
World patience (or like some soap-opera-for-life from a
cable company with a single channel) with those
pleasant, hospitable people that were bending over backward to be nice to me.

On the way back, Paul turned talkative, full of regional
pride. As we drove along he pointed out sites of interest
for my edification. He would catch my eye in the rearview mirror, all very accidentally-on-purpose, so I could

hardly help noticing that his eyes were green, and not without their charm, either. After a certain bridge (Escot), he solemnly announced that we were in Sarrance. The historical Sarrance had been a post station on the old road to the medieval shrine at Santiago de Compostela, Paul pronounced. The new Sarrance, as I saw with my own eyes, was a little village nestled (as they kept saying) in an elbow of the road, and perched precariously above the valley. While Paul rambled on about pilgrimages to Santiago, Vilma clutched my arm and pointed to a sign which my humble French allowed me to decipher as indicating the presence of an inn. I shrugged and gestured, mutely, incomprehension.

"That's where Maité used to live. She left her kids and husband and ran off with a mechanic . . ."

Something in the intensity of her whispering made me turn my head, and there were her eyes, dancing . . .

On Monday came the Deluge, and then there was cold, and a pea-souper straight out of Sherlock Holmes's London. I pulled two sweaters and a military overcoat on, two pairs of thick socks, a pair of wool pants that Vilma had lent me, and I could still feel that numbing wet cold to my very marrow. A certain homesickness for the far-away steambath I had left nibbled at my heart. If not for the fairy-tale fire that Paul lighted to save me, I think I'd have picked up the telephone and moved up my departure for Puerto Rico, which my frostbitten mind had now cast as my true Island of Enchantment.

That day I had a breather. Paul was at home, which meant that Vilma had had to put off our usual woman-to-woman for another day. The flames fed my fancy. I spent hours watching the logs burn down, turning my chill-blighted novel this way and that to catch the warmth. How should I narrate Malén's death? Who should tell it? The frightened next-door neighbor lady that wouldn't open the door? The cop at the police station, who's practically got a hard-on from the admiration he feels for this (ex-)girlfriend-murderer that's in his custody? The scot-free lover, reeking of beer and nicotine, listening to the news of it on the radio? The medical student that lifts the sheet and stands hypnotized over the battered flesh of the woman? Who could tell Malén's story, who could tell the truth? She, who might have, was dead.

That night something strange happened. I remember that it was Vilma who cooked dinner – after a good bit of insisting, given her mother-in-law's culinary monopoly. It was July 25, the dark Puerto Rican (pseudo-) Constitution Day and the even darker anniversary of the Yankee invasion of our peaceful shores. Vilma decreed that the day called for rice and beans, in counter-commemoration of the questionable occasion. She went into the kitchen – a whole percussion section of pots and pans burst into song – and emerged with two huge bowls, one sticky white rice, one beans (Goya – I'd brought them in my suitcase). They're going to love this, she said to me with a twinkle in her eye as she professionally ladled out the Puerto Rican equivalent of the intestinal atomic bomb onto the resigned plates of mother-in-law, father-in-law, and spouse.

Her remark hit some silly chord inside me, and the subsequent attack of laughing made Pyrenean history. With every fatal lift of a fork, the volume of our hilarity increased. There were not gales but hurricanes of laughter. Now, in retrospect, I confess: it was an unpardonable breach of table manners. Vilma choked and had to be whacked on the back several times. The muscles in my throat and belly hurt from the effort it cost me to suppress my shrieking. The in-laws didn't know whether to be surprised or pissed. They just looked at us, and their impassive, confused faces made matters worse. I'd given up all hope of social redemption, when suddenly Paul's *Ça suffit* boomed like the report of an expert marksman's rifle within the room. Silence. I mashed two or three more beans on my fork (so as not to have to look at anybody), excused myself in a tiny voice, and went upstairs to the den, where the fire was. I didn't want to lose a limb in the explosion, if there was going to be one.

In a little while, Paul came up. He sat on the sofa, directly in front of the fire. I pretended I was lost in the dancing of the flames, and the two of us sat in reverent silence at the ritual cremation of the corpse of the evening. The moment was brief but intense. There we were, he and I, two perfect strangers, brought together by another person's will – me with my head full of barbarous stories, him with god only knew what plans in his own, and both of us uncomfortable and unspeaking, the fire the only grounds for our unholy communion.

The next day I started to keep a diary, in a notebook full of old stillborn stories. A substitute for the abandoned novel? A presentiment that something big was about to happen? Blind intuition reads the cards of time in Braille.

IV

July 26

Still raining. Paul has left for Pau. Mission unknown. Madame gave me green beans to snap, a thankless task which nonetheless I enjoyed. She made a wondrous *garbure*, exactly what the doctor ordered for this vile weather and insipid atmosphere. I think she almost likes me.

The cold makes Vilma nervous. She paces and looks for victims. To calm her frazzled soul, I let her into my room after lunch. In this house, time is measured by the gastrointestinal ins and outs (so to speak) of the residents.

She told me the details of Maité's elopement: what an exemplary couple they had been, the husband's dedication to her, the surprise of the entire valley when it was learned that she'd high-tailed it . . . Stuffed as I was with Madame's excellent jugged hare, I had to put myself on autopilot for the rest of the gospel according to St. Vilma. Her stories, whether about herself or other people, weren't that much different from some tacky novel by Mauriac.

Paul brought me two magazines and the *France-Dimanche* from Pau. Had Vilma told him of my passion for the *fait divers*?

July 27

The rain is like a barbed-wire fence around the concentration camp of our daily activities. Last night there arrived the people that live in the apartment that Paul's parents rent out over the garage. He's a doctor in Toulouse. She, quite clearly, is the doctor's wife. They have a six-month-old baby. It's nice to see some new faces.

They had a cup of chamomile tea with us. He speaks Spanish very well – I suspect some secret Spanish fertilizer applied to the roots of his family tree. *Enchantée*, I'm sure. Vilma monopolized him, of course. I got the wife. I picked up the baby and dandled it on my knee, to lend the scene the proper atmosphere. It cried. Paul looked at me, a suspiciously tender smile upon his face.

July 28

A letter from my mother. The island revives in my mind. And with it, Malén – a basket of bananas on her head, a feather skirt. The murderer's in jail. He tried to kill himself, but was prevented. It's been learned that he's from Barrio Jurutungo. I knew it, says my mother, her class prejudices snapping in the wind.

Salvador stalks me. I keep seeing him creep down the hall in the ill-starred condominium. I see him stop before Malén's door. Loud music. The window-shutter is broken – he broke it himself the day Malén refused to let him in. The window-shutter is broken and Felipe Rodríguez is inside singing some spurned-macho lament.

I can hear my mother's voice, all chipper and chirpy: "Rest up and take advantage of the chance to travel around. France must be beautiful. Angela went, and she says it's heavenly. I wish I'd had the chances you have ..."

Sweet sixty-year-old innocence.

July 29

The gods are not so deaf after all. The sun has come out. Shyly, but then ... The Rousseaux (from the garage apartment) have suggested a walk through the mountains. Preparations: sandwiches of fresh bread and sausage, cheese of the region, Bayonne ham, wine, water, fruit. The baby will be left with Paul's parents, fortunately. I feel like a fifth wheel, or like some umpire that's not entirely familiar with the rules of whatever game it is we're playing. My tennis shoes slip and slide on the rocks. Everyone else has boots.

We head up, past the end of the village. At first there's an asphalt road, then a trail that turns steeper and steeper. Bluish-gray roofs crown large whitish houses – color is a shrinking violet here, as though fearful of making a spectacle of itself among these somber people.

In a fissure in the wall of rock we discover (life is stranger than fiction) a nest of vipers. The men, full of braggadocio, poke at them with a stick – to the shrill horror of Vilma and Mme. Rousseau. Not a peep out of me, brother, I'm tough – but I confess, dear diary, that the whole thing gave me the creeps. Vilma scolds Paul and Paul makes fun of her. So I pipe up and the troops are called off. Onward.

The doctor's wife, Paul, and I are in Indian file. From up ahead we can hear Vilma's lilting laughter and Rousseau's virile baritone. They are chattering like children. Paul talks about the fauna, the pathetic chamois and wild boar hunted to the verge of extinction, great bears living a life of absolute independence, a whole French underground of threatened animals running in constant flight through the woods. I ask him why he hunts. He lays down a long explanation of wall-to-wall contradictions – hunting gives man back his instinctual life, it links him to his prey, hunter and hunted communicate on the basis of their shared animality, man is enabled to savor the atavistic pleasures of his DNA, etc., etc., etc. Mme. Rousseau bestows a smile of beatific admiration upon him. I'm unconvinced. Killing for killing's sake.

But the speechifying suits him. It goes with the Paul that Vilma has told me about. Is there such a Paul?

July 30

Rotten luck. The rains have returned. And I'm sick, I've got this stupid cold, my head's stuffed up and my nose is red. I keep myself occupied by writing clichés on the postcards that M. le Beret gave me. They're old photos of hefty women sporting black stockings and beestung lips. I find it strange that Vilma doesn't seize the chance to set up a nursing station in my room. At night I find out *pourquoi* – she went shopping in Oloron with the Rousseaux. She comes back high-energy – like the bright-eyed Vilma of student picket days – singing the praises of the doctor (who's now Jean-Pierre) and criticizing the tight-assed wife. "Can you imagine?" she says to me. "She didn't even know where Puerto Rico was." And then she adds, a touch of pride in her smile: "I think she's jealous."

The thermometer was in my mouth, so I didn't answer. A touch of fever.

July 31

. . . I look out the Miami windows. Malén has returned from the grave, more radiant than ever. Her naked body emits a luminous glow. She is enveloped in its aura. She walks triumphantly along the transfigured hallway, and the doors open to let her enter – Oh Malén, goddess of the passionate shadows. She walks on, imperturbable, disdaining the obvious invitation of the open thresholds that she passes. A man approaches. I can't see his face. Wheezing, as though he had pneumonia, he caresses her backside. She yields, sighs, moans, her hands pull the man to her, her hands rise up the man's back, clutch his shoulders, clutch his neck. And they squeeze, sweetly squeeze . . .

Paul's mother brought me my breakfast in bed. I have a bad case of the flu, as if there were ever a good case of it. I even have a little difficulty breathing – and that takes me back to my childhood sickbed in the wooden house we lived in then. Vilma wants Jean-Pierre to listen to my chest. I resist, the man's on vacation. But she insists, and re-insists, and re-insists again. She finally wins.

Dr. Jekyll asks me if I have asthma, sticks the frigid stethoscope to my chest in two or three places, then my back. Vilma is leaning against the armoire, pubis protuberant, tight sweater, firetruck-red lips. I can spot the symptoms a mile away: she's a professional vamp, boop-boop-be-doop. Jean-Pierre is a professional, too, though, and he gives his professional opinion – it's the weather, he says. He discourses on the consequences of a too-rapid adaptation to a different clime. I've got my antennae out, in spite of my flu, and I catch the unmistakable body-language in the mirror. Vilma sits on the bed beside me, lies back. Jean-Pierre sits on the other side. They massage each other with their eyes. My God, I think, we're about to have an orgy right here, right on top of my sick, defenseless body. My fantasy continues, and it's not far wrong. Vilma takes the stethoscope out of his hands and listens to her own chest, with a stunning display of tropical tits. I close my eyes and then open them again, thinking I must be imagining this.

August 1

The vaporizer helps, but the antibiotics make me feel weak and washed-out. My throat hurts. I'm generally miserable. On the way to the bathroom I run into Paul.

I've got this awful wool nightgown of his mother's on, and apparently the Oedipal vision moves him. *Pauvre petite*, he says, and pats my head. The caress does not go unremarked, *malgré* my condition – goosebumps and a quick retreat.

I spent the whole day in bed asleep. Vilma brought me *crêpes* and yogurt. I've got a week to go. I've begun to count the days. Like prisoners do.

August 2

There's a threat of decent weather. You can see patches of blue.

I've been in bed so long my ass has gone flat, which is no big deal here but would lose me my whole street-corner fan club back in Río Piedras. I'm pale, too, which my mother, the Porcelana Cream queen, would love.

The doctor's wife is downstairs helping Paul's mother. The buckets and buckets of quince jelly perfume the entire house. I sit on the stairs to flirt with a ray of sunshine. I am surprised to find Paul soon sitting cozily beside me. Want to go to the post office? he asks, after the requisite *bonjours*. I politely accept (with just the right degree of shyness, I think). I go upstairs to get my postcards and a jacket. I come down, and Paul is already warming up the car. His mother looks – casually? – out the window.

The ride turns out to have a price. Paul wants to talk about Vilma. He tells me she's changed, she acts as though she's reliving her adolescence. She tells lies, he says, she makes things up. He pumps me – I know you two talk, he says, I know you're old friends, she must have told you something, and so on and so forth. Me, not a peep, my lips are sealed, clitoral solidarity to the end. We mail the letters and cards in Bedous and he says he doesn't want to go back yet, let's have an *apéritif*. I get this inexplicable feeling that I ought to feel guilty, if you know what I mean, riding around like this with Vilma's husband, though something tells me she's got her own hands full playing doctor behind some garden wall somewhere. Paul keeps talking about Vilma – she's never gotten used to living here, she's always nervous, uptight, in a bad mood, and when she's in a good mood it seems forced, strange. . .

Smiling moronically, I look out the window, so I won't have to say anything. A sinister instant replay nags at me: "She tells lies, she makes things up . . ."

August 3

What a *ragoût* of emotions. This *huis clos* would give the Sartre ménage an inferiority complex! Has my old school chum, great head on her lovely shoulders, the first one in the group to learn how to drive, Miss Self-Assured of 1972, has this take-charge person I used to know turned into some kind of pathological liar-slash-Doña Juana cold-bloodedly playing head games with her used-to-be best friend?

This afternoon, while Vilma was having a bubble bath and torturing our tympanums with a Freudian concert of old boleros of unrequited, requited, lost, found, forbidden, and secretly consummated love, the mother-in-law came out into the garden, where I was vainly trying to get some sun, and invited me to have a cup of tea. This kindness had its price, too. A high price. It seems Mme. Rousseau has come to the old lady to complain – there are all these coquettish smiles and winks going on, south-of-the-equator moles discovered (*Tell me, doctor, is it malignant?*), the doctor not getting a moment's sleep at night with all this provocative by-play, and he used to sleep like a baby ... The classical complaints of the jealous wife, in short – except that this time no doubt perfectly justified, because I'd seen some of these goings-on with my own eyes. Madame Jocasta didn't dare accuse Vilma in front of me, and thank goodness for that, because I don't know whether I'd have been able to summon the courage, let alone the histrionic ability, to defend her. So the old lady asked me to talk to her – as though it were my idea, and without mentioning my source, of course ...

Great. An undisciplined writer (with a capital W if you don't mind) recently escaped from her own romantic mess, held hostage in a house with a marriage about to go the way of all flesh, a half-bonkers old school friend who may or may not need saving, a hunter who preys upon visiting female tourists, a doctor with a roving stethoscope, a jealous doctor's wife, and a mother-in-law with interventionist tendencies. Only M. le Beret kept a semblance of mental balance in this free-market commune that Bertrand Blier would've given his left arm to film.

I should have said no. I should have said it was Vilma and Paul's concern. I should have said everybody should keep their nose stuck out of other people's business, or words to that effect. But theory is one thing and practice another, as tennis players and pianists know. So I merely said, with studied meekness, that this was all very deli-cate, I didn't know whether I had the tact for it, let alone the courage, she understood ... And to try to avoid our seductress' bursting unexpectedly out of the bathroom, head wrapped in a big towel à la Carmen Miranda, and discovering me in whispered intercourse with Mrs. Danvers here, I swallowed my tea, not even thinking that it might be poisoned, and returned to the garden before the cock crowed for the third time.

V

I don't know why I stopped writing in my diary. "My life's the book I would have writ, but I could not both live and utter it," or something of the sort, I imagine. (Henry David Thoreau, for you quotation-checkers.) Anyway, that was the end of my notes, and this is me, with the *froid* lent by distance.

That night I went to bed early, thanks to Paul's insistence that I play Scrabble in French with him and Vilma. Feeling like the Puerto Rican defendant in the Yankee Federal Court, I went upstairs and climbed into bed with Stephen King, my favorite antidote to stress. I don't know how late I read. I dozed off for what seemed just minutes, and then my sleep was interrupted by the squeaking of a stair tread. I looked at the clock and saw that it was three o'clock. The Miss Marple inside me noted that the steps were going down, and then in a few seconds there was the rusty creak of the garden door. The dogs didn't bark; the noctambulist was not a stranger. I went over to the window to peek out. Who dared defy the raw Pyrenean summer at this inhospitable hour of the night?

I had no need to apply Rouletabille's implacable logic. A mere glance sufficed to identify the mysterious skulker – it was Vilma, nightwalking in baby-dolls. You had to admire her. What ovaries the woman had – a midnight *rendez-vous* with the *promeneur solitaire*. But that seemed a little far-fetched even for one given to chipping away at establishment taboos. If she was planning to, you know, with the doctor, just steps from her snoring husband and the unsleeping Mme. Rousseau, she was fucked. The river in town would run hemoglobin-red. I could just picture the scene: Vilma and Jean-Pierre, playing stationary leap-frog in the ancestral alleyway between the two houses, or rolling about in garage-dust. Unaware of the serpents in that glacial Eden, illuminated by the indiscreet flares of the lightning-bugs, they didn't notice the reptilian Paul, carbine slung over his shoulder. In super-slowmo, the noble cuckold would raise his weapon and take aim, waiting for the moment the pair uncoiled, while yours truly stood mute at her Hitchcockian window and witnessed The End of Vilma.

But Vilma was not on her way to such a cruel fate. She walked on, stopping beside the forbidden garage, on the slope of the little hill that rose toward the church. Was she going to try to escape in Paul's car? Was she going to flee her husband from his parents' house, just to rub his nose in it? And – the most Machiavellian detail of all – in baby-dolls? I could imagine the five-star scandal when they heard the car engine start.

And what about me? I thought of the possibility of locking myself up *per secula seculorum* in that garret (well, you know) room of mine, vows of silence and hunger strike thrown in for free. Or after a fingernail-biting escape, my fair form hidden under a sheepskin among the anonymous flock of same making their way through the village every afternoon (*Prisoner of Zenda*, for you allusion-checkers), requesting asylum in the Puerto Rican Embassy. *What* Puerto Rican Embassy?

But as though out of Brian de Palma, Vilma did not

flee. She stood a good while in monologue with the stars, did a languid about-face, and returned to Nosferatu's castle.

Two days till I am free. I got up late, the bags under my eyes bulging with the night's booty. I spent an hour in the bathroom leafing through ancient *Nouvel Observateurs* and cursing the reinforced-concrete constipation my quote-vacation-unquote had left me with. Then I tried to cover the war damages with makeup.

I had not the slightest intention of being alone again with either Vilma or her mother-in-law. Not to fucking mention Paul. So I calculated my grand entrance for a few seconds before noon. Like some goddess out of the machinery, I descended to a table groaning with delights, prepared, I suspected, in my honor. The family portrait: Mama Bear, Papa le Beret (ha ha), Baby Bear. Vilma on sick leave. Make that "sick" leave. Only her empty chair and her inverted plate give mute testimony to her existence.

Then, the greetings. The three fairy-tale characters literally throw themselves upon me, welcome me like some heroine of the Resistance, which I guess in a sense I am. That's why I amused myself playing the guest of honor. I am the well-stuffed punching bag for their frustrations. They serve my plate, they fuss over me, they spoil me. With that armor-plated social docility of mine, I am the new daughter-in-law: the spare.

The rebel angel paces her room upstairs. We eat as though we cannot hear the wooden floor's subtle protestations.

This afternoon, the next piece of the jigsaw puzzle falls into place – the doctor's car is missing. In the empty apartment, a gigantic *A LOUER* sign tells me all I need to know.

Vilma refused to come down all day, which would have seemed like a pretty unmistakable snub if I hadn't known better. That night, when I was trying to violate the privacy of the conjugal bedroom, I fell into Paul's clutches. We passed on the stairs – him with a tray loaded with rejected nourishment, and me with this stupid look on my face. Who? *Me?*

"Is she feeling better?" says I, playing the village idiot to perfection.

"She won't eat," says he, playing his own role of concerned husband.

I tried. Could I see her? N-n-n-o, maybe tomorrow. That "maybe" (or *peut-être*, because this scene was played out, after all, in French) was the final straw to my camel of frustration. Did she not intend to come out before I boarded that big silver bird back to America? This stank.

Since we couldn't stand there indefinitely in the middle of the stairs, contemplating that tray as though it were a corpse laid out for a wake, Paul asked me if I wouldn't like to see some snapshots. We could sit in the fireplace room there. I must confess, with all honesty, that if there's one thing I hate above all the other petit-bourgeois rituals that comprise my miserable petit-bourgeois life, it's looking at photograph albums. But curiosity, and perhaps a secret desire to visit again the place of our first ocular idyll, got me in a full-Nelson.

The den was not the same without a fire. The walls looked dirtier, the upholstery more faded by time. The *ambience* was stiff, static, almost hostile in its rustic domesticity. Paul excused himself, then came back with a huge book under his arm. I sighed, preparing myself for the endless parade of round-cheeked babies, virginal *jeunes filles* dressed in white, and family clans trapped forever between the two arm-rests of a sofa. Paul sat beside me, smelling of after shave splashed on in the split-second interim of his absence, and he lay the offering on my lap. Without the slightest surreptitious touch, I might add.

I began turning pages, with the prolonged pauses the occasion called for and the remarks recommended for these occasions by the Photograph Album Martyrs League. But this album was not your garden-variety photograph album. Not content with having his walls covered with dead animals, Paul had taken photos of the wretched victims of his hunting parties – before, during, and after the *coup de grâce*. Chamois, wild boars, vultures, birds of every social rank, and even, ladies and gentlemen, in frank violation of the laws protecting fauna threatened with meeting the dodo in the sweet by-and-by, a bear.

That necrophiliac display scared the shit out of me. I tried not to impose my own morality – after all, it was almost normal that a hunter would want to preserve as trophies the proof of his valiant deeds. They aren't people, they're animals, I kept repeating mentally, trying hard to accept the *fait accompli* of the massacre, but grieved in the deepest regions of my green soul. By the seventh page, my reserves of social niceties were pretty much on the endangered species list themselves, and I asked myself how the hell I was going to be able to survive this zoological attack on my mental health. Oblivious to my squirming, Paul single-mindedly (and in great detail) narrated the paleolithic epic of his adventures. I almost cheered when I turned to the last page.

But I choked on my own rejoicing when I saw what the last picture was. There, in all its glossy 8 X 10 black-and-white glory, a chamois head, and cheek-to-cheek with its fake taxidermy smile, the impish face of Vilma, her eyes bulging and her tongue hanging out.

I didn't dare look at Paul, who kept talking as though nothing had happened. But I wasn't listening anymore. Doubt had slapped me up-side the head again. Who had a lock on truth? Which one was the ringer here?

The last day of my sentence, a Sunday, dawned brutally sunny, with none of that mosquito-netting of fog that the Pyrenean mornings had theretofore been displaying. I could hear Paul talking on the stairs with his mother, and then I heard them go downstairs. I dressed as fast as I could, but I had to take my blouse off and try again. I'd put it on backward – an old habit of mine whenever things got messy in my head. I grabbed a piece of virgin paper and wrote in big block letters

I'M LEAVING TOMORROW.

I folded the piece of paper and went and slid it under Vilma's door, with a soft knock to announce the publication of this most limited edition of my latest work. From Sleeping Beauty, not a peep.

When I went downstairs on the trail of the smell of coffee, I realized that I'd wasted my conspiratorial energies – there was Vilma, live and in person, in all her Puerto Rican splendor, light-years from that depressing duet with the chamois.

The old folks had gone off to mass and Paul, in a fit of filial devotion, had gone with them. Vilma was happy, talkative, sweet, the way she'd been when I arrived that cold night to bring her the fragrances of the tropics. We left the dishes in the sink, made roquefort-and-butter sandwiches, filled a wineskin with red wine, and went out, like two schoolgirls, into the coolness of the morning. My friend was full of energy, full of that unquenchable vitality of my people, a people suckled on misfortune.

"Prepare yourself to stretch your legs," she said. "I've got ants in my pants this morning."

And we walked and we walked and we walked. And then we walked some more, singing songs of the Island, protest songs, patriotic songs, songs to tug at your heartstrings, all in honor of my return (and Vilma's envy of my return) to the balmy shores of Puerto Rico. We went down to the river. We stayed there a while, recalling the years of our wild oats, passing the wineskin back and forth. Vilma and Carola, laughing like crazy, laughing as only people totally irresponsible or totally convinced of tragedy do. But the man-woman violence did seem to have taken a rest, to have hidden its pathetic vampire face from the soft light of the morning.

On an impulse, I suggested that we go back to Puerto Rico together. "That's in the works," she said, "but it'll take some time." The seriousness of what she was saying slowly percolated down into my consciousness. Vilma was calm, with that relentless calm of the person that's made her mind up.

M. le Beret was in charge of the *soirée.* In what had to be his personal best for loquacity, he told me stories of his heroic deeds in the Second World War, while his wife, Paul, and Vilma watched an old Marcel Carné movie.

The night before is always a kick. I packed my bags

like I was leaving out cookies for Santa Claus. That night I dreamed of Frenchwomen with their heads shaved for having consorted with the Nazis.

The farewell was brief. Pinned between two Arab laborers in transit to Morocco via Spain, I said good-bye to Vilma through the window. Paul, always faithful to the precepts contained in the Manual of Western Civilization, waved until the train was out of sight. Vilma was more primitive. She left the platform before the train even started.

I flopped onto the seat. So many emotions.

I scrutinized the ambiguous landscape as though awaiting a sign that would not come.

At the border, I took advantage of the change of cars to buy a Spanish newspaper.

VI

There were no fireworks or parades for my return. It took me a few days to get used to breathing without witnesses again. Classes metronomically marked my days – from school to my room back to school again. The worst-seller of my life continued its boring way. Doña Finí had no new findings to report.

In spite of the hectic back-to-school rat race I was in, I couldn't stop thinking about Vilma. The stylized image of the Latin madonna I'd brought back with me made my sleep a martyrdom. I finally found a few minutes to write – a long letter full of questions, advice, all the things I hadn't had the ovaries to say face to face. I thought the letter would exorcise that nagging and all-too-intrusive guilt complex that had been haunting me since we said good-bye at the train station.

Five, then six weeks passed. Vilma never took so long to answer letters; exile had made her punctual. Was she upset with me? Had my postal unburdenings dejected her? Had she gone back to Bordeaux? But if she had, they'd surely forward her mail ... I sent a note to the address I had for her in Bordeaux, telling her about my other letter and asking her to let me hear from her.

In October my first letter found its way Lassie-like back home. There, among the bills, was the battered envelope, tattooed with self-contradictory stamps. The words *DESTINATAIRE INCONNU*, smeared in red across Vilma's name, made my heart stop.

EDITOR'S NOTE

In early December, 1982, the author brought us this manuscript, which we are proud to publish in our *TEXTIMONIES* collection. On the thirty-first of that month, while she was celebrating New Year's Eve with some friends, the author died. She was killed by a bullet fired through the window of her living room, striking her in the head. The murderer has not been apprehended.

We join the chorus of voices demanding that the authorities carry out a thorough investigation of this case.

Griselda Lugo-Fuentes
Women's Destiny Press

AEROBICS
FOR LOVE

Ce n'est pas la personne de l'autre qui m'est nécessaire, c'est l'espace: la possibilité d'une dialectique de désir, d'une imprévision de la jouissance: que les jeux ne soient pas faits, qu'il y ait un jeu.

– Roland Barthes

It is not the other's being that I need, it is the space: the possibility of a dialectics of desire, of a randomness of jouissance; that the die be not cast, that all remains to be played for.

I

Your head starts nodding during the news at eleven, but you make the effort and keep those eyes open until after the late show so you'll be totally and irremediably zonked.

You toss and turn in the bed, with your rollers digging into your scalp and the alarm clock ticking like a time-bomb in your ear. You close down the shop, count sheep, breathe as deep as you can. You squeeze, relax, squeeze, relax. You repeat the mantra to exorcise tension and keep those stressful thoughts at bay. You relive the boss's nasty remark, the latest fight with the ex over the kid's child-support check, the note from the landlord saying you can't water your plants after dark. You suddenly remember the five gray hairs that subvert the blackness of your hair, the creeping cellulitis, the tiny pain in the breast every time you assert yourself a little more force-fully than usual. And it's good-bye to sweet dreams, hello to those bewitching dark circles under your eyes. You spend another insomniac night. Until exhaustion finally takes over and you faint dead away just as the alarm sounds – not a single Z.

You peel the sheet off you the best you can. You look for those slippers but you can't find them. You walk that chilly floor and try not to think about catching cold. And you turn up your toes because the grit on the floor makes the bottom of your feet prickle. You avoid thinking about the mop.

You wash out the coffee pot, throw out yesterday's grounds, turn on the stove and close the refrigerator that the kid left open as he went off for the weekend with good ol' Dad. You take out the melted margarine. You put the dried out three-day-old bread in the toaster, put the coffee pot on the only burner that works. And you sprint to the bathroom to rinse out your mouth, wipe the cold cream out of the wrinkles with a cotton pad moistened with witch hazel. You throw the obscene nightgown that dates from when you were happily married into the clothes hamper. You fly into the kitchen naked when you smell burnt toast. You don't have time to toast another slice, but it's an ill wind that blows nobody good – a hundred calories less isn't bad. And you go back to the bathroom and brush your teeth and grab your feet and pull them up into the sink so you can save yourself another shower before you put on the new high heels you just bought yourself the other day.

You hook the bra, slip on the panties. The blouse with the drop-dead neckline gets caught on your rollers when you try to pull it on over your head. You yank off the offending roller and discover that your hair isn't dry yet. So you get desperate and try to find the hair dryer that's never where you left it last time and, oh thank god, you find it and plug it in and turn it on. And your hairdo is punk before its time. So now you're dripping with sweat and the bad mood is creeping up on you. That precarious line you tremblingly, breathlessly draw along the crow's-foot at the outside edge of your right eye wavers and takes a detour. And from your soul you dredge up the energy to say Shit.

The mauve skirt is wrinkled. But it's a straight skirt,

so you climb in, wriggling your backside and exercising your triceps, and hoping your curves will put a nice press in it. You grab your purse and are about to be out of there when you remember one last important detail. You stand on the landing and you open your purse, you take out your compact, you pucker up, you aim, and your smile is suddenly wreathed in mauve glory.

This is the moment when you regret having given up the car so you could keep the furniture. Because now you have to take the bus. And Saturday is not a weekday. And the driver takes his own sweet time. And people badmouthing at the bus stop. And you know it's late, you've barely got time, if that bus doesn't come in the next few seconds, your life'll be set back seven days.

The pumpkin-disguised-as-a-bus comes. You grab the life-saving bar. Your perfume fuddles the air. The looks go u-u-u-p, the looks go do-o-o-wn.

But the bell doesn't work. A disgusted passenger has ripped it out. You're obsessed that you'll pass your stop. And the bus goes on, and on . . . You squeeze your way through the people, dancing clumsily toward the door. And naturally you get off at the wrong stop.

You click your way up the street. Walking fast in a straight skirt is excellent exercise. You gain on the bus. And then little by little you slow down. The lines on the sidewalk make you dizzy. You try to synchronize your steps and your breathing.

Deliberately slow, deliberately fabulous, you come to the corner where you're to stake everything. Your feet want to beat it. Your hands turn to ice. Your heart is about to jump out your throat. But you walk, a marvel of mind control, eyes fixed on some distant spot, as indifferent as a duchess, past the door.

And you see without looking – it's the smell, or the sweetness of the air, or that nice warm feeling, or all of it at once, or nothing at all – that He is standing there at the counter, and that today, like every Saturday of the world, you're about to be swept off your feet and into the orbit of those eyes.

II

He gives a blow-by-blow description of the scene – there he stood, like an African king out of *Tarzan*, one foot upon the toilet seat, the other holding the door closed, a wall of wild graffiti at his back, a slave kneeling at his feet, while outside a gang of bearers bearing bursting bladders awaited their chance to drop their loads – and he had had the orgasm of the century, only surpassed in intensity by the more lasting thrill of retelling it.

She proceeds, immediately thereafter, to recall the secret handjob with which one Monday afternoon, in the first row of a moviehouse in Santurce, she had rewarded the patience of her cousin, who sat goggle-eyed in contemplation of the Triple XXX epic *Coitus Uninterrupted*.

To which He counters with a faithful and detailed recounting of the threesome he had with his boss's wife and daughter in the family room (oh yes) of his boss's house one night while that asshole was drunkenly cheering Roberto Durán on to a championship KO, a story She immediately one-ups with another domestic tale – this one taking place in her kitchen one morning when, offering to teach her best girlfriend's husband some special homemaking skills, she had showed him a new way of cookin' with Crisco.

Which evokes from Him the nostalgic recollection of his younger days as a male hustler on the beach in the Condado, the strains of an old-time orchestra playing in the background, the smell of suntan lotion and barbecues in the air, as he knelt in the shadow of one of the most luxurious hotels on the beach and planted his hot dog in a gringo tourist's buns.

Which in turn brings to Her the now-fading memory of the experimental lessons in lesbianism she had so kindly given – a special introductory offer, one time only – to her ex-sister-in-law the day after her divorce.

Which leads Him to remember his German shepherd and Her her palomino pony and Him his soft papayas and Her her green bananas and Him his telepathic orgasms and Her her metaphysical orgies.

And then there is silence, in spontaneous tribute to all that still remains to tell.

He looks at Her. And smiles. And He says, in a voice that tries but fails to be objective and detached:

"Oh baby, thank goodness you and I never tied the knot . . ."

III

Everybody else has either split up or is headed that way. Except, of course, for us. Ten years and counting – a record for domestic stability. Not that I'm against breaking up, when you have to. When things don't work out, it's better to cut your losses, save what can be saved, and get on with your life.

But it's that ... I'm almost embarrassed to say this ... we're, like, *happy.* No, really, I'm not kidding. Perfectly compatible, I'd say – which is really pretty amazing. The same likes and dislikes, the same way of looking at things, the same sense of humor, the same tastes. No kids? We haven't wanted kids. We're busy just trying to get by.

There are people that can't quite cope with how long we've lasted. "Still together?" they'll say, like they expect us to say "Nope, not anymore." People have bets going, there are surveys, estimates – *I'll give 'em one more week. How many is it now?*

Us? Get real, we just laugh. Although it's no joke. A person could begin to feel ... I don't know, *weird.* Is something wrong with us, are we brain-dead, or just bored? Are we stupid, is that it? Or are we too profound? Do you have to be stupid to be happy? But even our complexes don't affect our contentment.

To avoid stress, which everyone's got all they need of anyway, we never go to parties. We don't have any big tragedies to talk about, any traumas we care to discuss. And when we run into some divorced friend of ours, we just wave and keep on going.

We just cross ourselves discreetly and keep on going.

And we don't look back. Hell or high water, come what may – two may be company, but three, so far as we're concerned, three's the only way.

DELIVERANCE FROM EVIL

Elena, Elena,
Elena me dijo a mí . . .

– M. J. Canario

I

Even Madame's voice changed when the spirit of Elena took possession of her. She would turn all sweet and dark and seductive. Her eyes would sparkle. Her face would be young again. She would run her hands down the small of her back, smoothing the ends of her long head of non-existent hair.

Madame warned Violeta – Elena was not just any spirit, oh no, not this one – but Violeta never took the spirit seriously. The way Violeta looked at it, you could hear one or another *espiritista* say just about anything – it all depended on who you wanted to listen to – and when all was said and done, there weren't many people that *didn't* have some miserable ghost trying to move in on them. But with this spirit, there was more than met the eye. The day of Violeta's twentieth birthday, in the midst of the incense and the little bells ringing, Madame had told her so –

"You mind what you're doing, child, because that woman's spirit is going to have its way with you. Don't you let her get on you, because once she does, there's nobody'll ever get her off again – she's one of the bad ones, I'm telling you . . . "

Five years later, and truth to tell, the spirit still hadn't really gotten out of hand. It would appear every so often at the sessions, wanting a place at the table. But that was as far as it went. Violeta had waited so long that by now she almost wished the encounter would just finally happen. Right about then, she met Miguel, fell in love, left her job, and got married.

II

Months went by. She'd stopped coming around here. I thought it was odd, because Violeta was one of the faithful, a true observer of the work, you know. Every Friday evening at seven o'clock, here she'd be, regular as clockwork. She was a good girl. A believer . . . Didn't move a step without consulting me.

Then one day she shows up – six o'clock in the morning. I remember I had a hard time waking up. I'd gone to bed not much more than three hours before. I'd been up setting candles in Keebler cracker cans and lighting them to Santa Marta, to see if Santa Marta couldn't help Belén get that job at the Electric Company. But I let her in and everything, the nicest I knew how. The good work mustn't be denied anybody, no matter what time of the morning it might be.

Her hair looked just awful, and she had her clothes on every which way – a girl that was ordinarily so careful with herself, I mean dressed like a model on television, *ay madre!* I figured it was her husband, you know. I made some coffee and poured her a cup and then I sat down with her and asked her how she was, how things were going for her, whether she was getting used to being married, whether her husband was treating her all right. I was sort of warming up to the problem, see ... Then oh, Great Power of God, what came next! All of a sudden I felt this chill, and my whole body breaks out in goosebumps and my bones start shaking. I thought I had malaria, I'll tell you – I don't even want to think about it. The girl just sitting there like nothing's happening, and me struggling with this evil thing that had come over me like a bat swooping out of the darkness onto me. The table was shaking and everything, oh *virgen María*, and the coffee cups jittering on the shelf. All the strength left my hands, and all I could do was sit there, as floppy as a rag doll. I said a prayer to San Judas Tadeo, that was all I could do, but the cursed thing wouldn't leave me – but it wouldn't come out and manifest itself either, so I could find out what this was all about.

So then Violeta grabs one of my hands and tells me that this thing is for her. She said she was going to take it, said it had been sitting on the foot of her bed now for a long time and she wanted to know who it was. And no sooner said than done – all of sudden there I sat, like nothing had ever happened, just as cool and calm and collected as you please – so calm, I tell you, that I practically fell asleep right there.

III

Mama named me Elena for my aunt, the one a jealous lover stabbed to death out in the cane field.

You've got to be careful with the names you give your children.

I wasn't pretty, though I wasn't ugly either, but I had something that men ... I don't know, it was like it *pulled* them toward me. Every man in the neighborhood – single, married, widowed, or divorced – would be after me one time or another. They'd walk with me down the street. They'd sing under my window. They'd make up songs with my name in them, and sometimes they'd even record them and play them on the radio. None of it made much of an impression on me. I mean I got a little kick out of it, I thought it was funny, you know, but that was all. I wouldn't go out with any of them or anything. They were just ... Until Manuel came along, with that baby face of his and the things he'd learned in the merchant marine.

From the first time he saw me, which was when I was sloshing water on Mama's living room floor and sweeping the water through the cracks in the wood, he started building our house. A big huge house on stilts, sitting high, high up on a hill where the wind blew like forty lashes. When the house was done, he came to get me. And I went with him.

Manuel was never home. I would spend the day cuffing his pants, making mamey-and-pineapple candy, whipping the dust off the furniture with a rag – obeying the holy commandments and shining the bars on my cage.

One day I opened the door and let a man in. Nothing changed. He wanted to carry me off to another cage – bigger, he said, more comfortable, he said, with wider-spaced bars so more sunshine would come in, he said. What was the difference.

What happened next was bound to happen. Manuel sharpened his knife and came home an hour early.

IV

Violeta got real strange. She was always smiling, like she knew something nobody else did. And real absent-minded, like off in space somewhere.

She stopped fighting with me when I got home at two o'clock in the morning. She stopped hiding the keys to the gate. She even quit making faces when I brought the guys from the bar home with me or when I disappeared for two or three days during the town's saint's-day festivities.

It'd have been better if she'd just had it out with me. That stupid smile pissed me off. Any little thing, I'd make a big deal out of it, I'd try to pick a fight, do things to get to her, you know, so she'd blow up. But she wouldn't take the bait. She'd just smile, like some holy virgin martyr in that Catholic Church of hers.

I'd go out on the slightest excuse. Sometimes I'd even go out all by myself, take walks, until the middle of the night. I wanted her to be asleep when I came in. I'd lie there beside her and do it to myself, and I'd enjoy it more than with a woman.

The house stopped sparkling like it used to. The sink would be full of dirty dishes, the floor would be filthy dirty, the bathtub would have this gray ring around it. I thought I'd die the day my mother came over and saw the state that house was in. "This place is a pigsty," she said, "and that wife of yours is a pig." She didn't stay half an hour. Violeta hadn't so much as offered her a cup of coffee.

That's why I got involved with the other woman. I was never at home.

V

Violeta and Elena would have long talks. Elena knew so much – she was very wise, and very entertaining. They didn't need Madame anymore to be able to talk.

At first Violeta didn't want to go out, but Elena was so insistent about it: *Heavens, you've gotta get out once in a while. After all, what's sauce for the goose is sauce for the gander, you can't stay all locked up like this. There's air outside, you can breathe.* Sometimes they would take walks through the town, or they'd take the bus. They never cared much where they were going. Elena would just lead her, and she'd follow. So Violeta got to know lots of places, lots of men. They all looked alike to her. She went into a lot of bars. She lay in a lot of hotel beds. She was always smiling. But nothing particularly *pleased* her. Once in a while she would disappear for days on end. She didn't see much of Miguel – but then he wasn't at home much, either.

The pistol was Elena's idea. You had to protect yourself. Men were unpredictable.

VI

I never saw her again after the day that woman's spirit got inside her. But I had a consultation later with one of my assistants, a spirit of light the likes of which you've never seen – the spirit of the most blessèd Saint Thomas woman that ever lived. She's never let me down – *let her advance in wisdom, Santa Barbara, if it is your will.*

It was that wonderful spirit of light that told me about Elena. I'd warned the girl, I'd told her she had to keep her eyes peeled, I'd told her she had to be careful, had to take her baths with seawater every Sunday and rub her belly with half an apple to wash away the evil influence. Violeta was not a strong woman. I wanted to protect her, bless her heart. Her own mother had asked me to protect her, on her deathbed – "Watch over her for me, Madame. They tried to take her away from me three times when I was carrying her in my womb . . . "

But I never saw such evil as Elena's. She wasn't going to rest till she'd ruined that girl. Spirits that die violent deaths are that way. They'll run right over you. Come to think of it, I'm going to take a few steps with this red rag right now, just in case . . .

You had to be awfully careful, I tell you. So I made up a bath – it had eucalyptus, rue, mint leaves, bicarbonate of soda, honey, alum, and florida water – I followed my guide's directions to the letter. To give it some body, I poured in a capful of King Pine. That mixture was an atomic bomb. And I sat me down to wait for Violeta to come. "Got to come herself, her own foot's got to bring her, got to come of her own accord, don't go get her, don't go looking for her, don't go fetch her to bring here, just let her come, let her come herself, she got to come on her own." That was what my spirit of light kept telling me.

So I waited. But she never came back.

VII

When they opened the bedroom door, the two of them were in bed together. They had their arms all around each other, and they were asleep. The girl's head on Miguel's hairy chest.

Violeta couldn't see. She was sweating and shaking. It was Elena that put the pistol in her hand. She hugged her real sweet, real tenderly. "Go ahead," she said, "you'll see how easy it is."

Violeta stepped into the room, slow, quiet. She wasn't the least bit scared. She wasn't alone. It was . . . it was different now.

Miguel's breathing was strong. The girl's head would rise and fall with his chest.

Elena kept saying, Yes, Yes with her eyes, nodding and pushing Violeta with her eyes. She held one of her hands. Her long fingernails caressed the pistol. Violeta got real close, so she wouldn't miss. She raised the pistol. Elena helped her. Her fingers were cold.

But just seconds from pulling that trigger, Violeta stumbled over a shoe. The girl's eyes flew open – like those dolls' eyes do – her eyes flew open and she raised her head. "Now!" said Elena. "Shoot! Shoot him, don't look at her!"

But Violeta did look at her. They stared into each

other's eyes for a long time. A long time. The pistol fell to the floor. Miguel woke up. Violeta took a deep breath, and she ran out of the room. She ran across the street and up that big avenue and through the whole neighborhood. She was still running when she came to the park. She threw herself onto the first bench she came to. The breeze was cool. There was a little drizzle. She looked around. Elena wasn't there.

VIII

For the first time, I felt real . . . alone.

SOLUTIONS, INC.

Hate oppression; fear the oppressed.

– V. S. Naipaul

I

On December 2, 1990, the lightning in the Corrector-General's eyes set off mood alarms all over the building. Storm clouds brewed in her office, and the defenseless button of the intercom received the brunt of her fury. Her secretary nervously canceled all appointments for the rest of the day and prepared her steno pad for dictation. She took the following letter:

Dear Patroness and friend,

Your letter of November 27 leaves me even more baffled than hurt. I would remind you that in its seven years of uninterrupted operation under my direction, Solutions, Inc. has compiled an enviable record of success: 5,999 cases resolved to the full satisfaction of our clients. Our detailed files on each case testify to this achievement, as do the effusive thanks we constantly receive from our forever grateful clients.

The figures do not lie: 3,995 male spouses regenerated, 1,999 satisfactorily readjusted and/or neutralized. The Board of Adjustors has recommended the Ultimate Solution in only five cases, which represents an insignificant percentage of the total when one takes into account our overwhelming general success. We believe that the

strategies we employ to effect more moderate
solutions are amply justified by our successes.

And that, Patroness, brings me to my point. It is,
as you must know, my fervent desire to clear up
any doubts you might have about our operation and
to remove forever the shadow of incompetence that
now seems to lie over Solutions, Inc. and
consequently over me, its Corrector-General.

Case No. 6000 has monopolized our resources for
the last four months. Virtually our entire
professional staff has been assigned to it. The
complexity and the totally unprecedented nature of
the case have led us to consider the possibility
of technical retraining or reprogramming of at least
a part of our service-delivery staff. In view of the
fact that heretofore unrecognized conditions in
today's society have come to our attention in the
course of this case, we have created a Bureau of
Imponderables to deal with any possible recurrences
of such oversight in the future.

I hope that these initiatives on our part may help
restore the climate of trust that has always
characterized our company's relations with you and
the other members of the Patroness League. I hope
also that we may continue to rely upon your
generous, and to us vital, patronage. Your donations
to our organization make our work possible, and we
are most indebted. And while we fully respect your
desire to remain anonymous, we hope someday we
may be able to thank you in person for your kind
support.

As you requested, I am enclosing copies of all
documents relating to Case No. 6000 for your
review; we believe that a careful examination of these

documents will persuade you of the appropriateness of our handling of the case. We appreciate the special interest you have taken in resolving this complicated matter, and we will be glad to cooperate in any way we can. Should any further information be necessary, please don't hesitate to contact me.

We await your instructions for further action, should that be the indicated course, or for other disposition of this case, and I take this opportunity to send you the sisterly regards of our entire staff.

> Yours most sincerely,
> (signed)
> Barbara Z ——
> Corrector-General
> Solutions, Inc.

APPENDIX 1
CASE NO. 6000
CLIENT'S DEPOSITION

On this __fifteenth__ day of __September,__ 19 90 ,
THERE COMES before this Complaints Section of Solutions, Inc. (hereafter known as "The Agency") a woman – married, of legal age, occupation housewife, and resident of the city of San Juan, Puerto Rico – who shall in this deposition be known as "the Client," and who testifies under oath to the following relation of facts:

1. That she has no reason whatever to complain of her husband's behavior, which up to and

including the date set forth above has been without reproach.

2. That she imagines the great majority of wives in the country would envy the apparent perfection of her marriage, since she believes herself to be the possessor, however unhappy, of what is generally and insistently referred to as the Ideal Husband.

3. That said Ideal Husband (hereafter to be known as "the Actionable") shares the household chores, is a good provider, is responsible, serious, sweet, attentive, polite, affectionate, faithful, and efficient in the functions pertaining to his sex, and that no other defect or flaw may be detected in him except his total and absolute perfection.

4. That the Actionable's said perfection threatens and violates the Client's self-image by emphasizing, underscoring, and otherwise making obvious her own imperfection.

5. That for these reasons, the Client urgently and imperatively seeks legal separation and divorce from the Ideal Husband.

6. That in recognition of the fact that she lacks objectively sufficient grounds for a divorce action, and feeling herself therefore unable to broach the subject to her husband, she comes to the Agency in hopes that the Agency may be able to provide the pretext required by law for said action and that she may be enabled, without further delay, to begin proceedings leading to the dissolution of her marriage.

SWORN before me this <u>15th</u> day of <u>September</u>, 19 <u>90</u> by the Client, whose identity is withheld for her own protection.

_____(signed)_____
Portia M ——
Head Notary
Complaints Section
Solutions, Inc.

APPENDIX 2
CASE NO. 6000
OFFICE OF CASE EVALUATION AND CLIENT ORIENTATION
REPORT: "OPERATION TURN UP THE HEAT"

Preliminary screening indicated that for the full ten years of her marriage Client had been a model wife. Conclusion: Systematic reversal of this exemplary behavior should lead to destabilization of relationship.

Client was advised to attend "Techniques of Vexation I and II," workshops offered to the community free of charge by this office. Client rating in the course: "Outstanding." For four subsequent weeks client carried out "Operation Turn Up the Heat," a program designed especially for her by our experienced program consultants.

This operation consisted of four progressive stages employing the technique of gradual behavioral escalation, and was aimed at creating a crisis in the marital system. These four stages are detailed below, with Client comment:

DOMESTIC SABOTAGE

"I started the program while my husband was away on a business trip. That gave me the chance to stop cleaning house. I let dirty dishes and pots and pans pile up in the sink. I didn't take out the trash, and flies were everywhere. The bathtub got this gray scum around it, and then that hardened into a crust. The sheets started to get that musty smell of old sweat mixed with Vicks Vaporub. I piled dirty clothes in every corner of the house. I unplugged the refrigerator so the meat would thaw and maggots would start breeding in the freezer. I left food out on the counter in the kitchen. The stove turned into a luxury condominium for high-living cockroaches. . ."

PHYSIOLOGICAL TERRORISM

"When he came home, my husband, as expected, put on his rubber gloves and checked bermuda shorts and within two hours he had the house spic-and-span again. Forewarned is forearmed, as they say, so I had been careful to collapse into bed with a case of dizziness, fainting spells, nausea, and other made-up symptoms. I complained of everything, but I refused to see a doctor. My idiot of a husband thought I was pregnant. I could hardly bear his ravings of delight. What perverse pleasure it gave me to show him my blood-soaked panties a week later.

"What came next represented a real sacrifice for me, because I am very careful about personal hygiene. But I stopped bathing every day, in spite of the terrible heat. I didn't brush my teeth even if I ate mangoes and got fibers all between my teeth. I stopped shaving my legs and underarms. I threw out all my combs and brushes so I wouldn't be tempted to do something about the tangled, greasy mess my hair soon turned into. Since I have dry skin, in no time it was as scaly as an iguana's. I had never in my life been so disgustingly, horribly, repulsively filthy – sometimes I almost made myself puke. I don't know how he could stand it . . . "

PSYCHOLOGICAL OFFENSIVE

"My husband was so tender and understanding during this stage of the program that it almost drove me crazy. I didn't have to fake the nervous tics that the program recommended. My eyes blinked, my nose twitched, my lips trembled. What made it worse was that during the whole miserable month Operation Turn Up the Heat lasted, I was totally on my own – I couldn't even go to the Agency for moral support, since we'd agreed that we could give my husband absolutely no cause for suspicion of anything I did during this time.

"By this point in the plan, I found it easy to be in a bad mood. I *loved* following the instructions to be grouchy! At the slightest pleasant word out of my husband's mouth I would bite his head off. I was sarcastic about everything. I showed how much he bored me by openly yawning whenever he tried to make conversation. If he invited me to go out somewhere with him, I would automatically say no. And if he had the nerve to ask why not, I'd unleash a torrent of verbal abuse at him that I'd never before have dreamed myself capable of. Insults, vulgarities, cursing, screaming, fighting – that was the order of the day . . . "

SEXUAL LOCKOUT

"I've never been overly given to the pleasures of the flesh. My main erogenous zone is definitely inside my head. So the final phase was not as hard on me as the first three were. I simply denied him the slightest physical contact—I turned my back on him as soon as we got into bed. This tactic, which would have backfired, so to speak, with any other Puerto Rican husband, was perfectly safe for me. His principled stand on the equal-rights issue kept him from taking the back-door route unless he had my permission.

"A king-size bed never seemed so small to me before. In the state I was in, his breathing, the tiniest movement he made, even his heartbeats sounded like a percussion section – it was deafening, and for days I couldn't sleep. After a month, he looked younger, more rested and handsome than ever. I was on the verge of anorexia nervosa."

DIVISION RECOMMENDATION:
Urgent. Transfer Case No. 6000 to Office of Sting Ops.

> Medea H ——
> Orientations Officer II
> Office of Case Evaluation and
> Client Orientation
> Solutions, Inc.

APPENDIX 3
CASE NO. 6000
OFFICE OF STING OPERATIONS
RE: OPERATION "SPANISH FLY"

Note from Corrector-General: The following transcription of the testimony of provocations agent "Sylvia the Sweet-tart" does not necessarily represent the views of the Agency or its officers, and the deponent is solely responsible for the language and content of the material herein presented.

I was having myself a very well deserved little vacation down on the beach at Boquerón when the Queen reeled me back in for a sting operation she said was priority one. I'd just done my patented Candid-Camera screws on about ten Actionables straight, and I definitely needed a break, but I figured what the hell, a woman's night is never done anyway – and besides, I'm a work-aholic – I always put business before pleasure (if I can't combine 'em) . . . So I pack up my stuff and in two shakes I'm punching in at Orientation. The Queen gave me 24 hours to get my plan of action in. Piece o' cake, I figured – I can usually check out a guy for you and prescribe the right medicine for him in an hour, two max. So I set my scanners on fast-forward, inputted the wife's deposition into the old gray-matter PC, processed it for a nanosecond and a half, and then I did a once-over of the Actionable's photo file. No surprises in the mug shots, so I checked out the full-lengths. Hmm, I said to myself, the dude's do-able, all right, got to hand it to 'im – cute face, a little silver sparkle in the moustache, matching the highlights in the sideburns. Got good hair on his chest, and he's in pretty good shape for his age, although he is definitely *not* my type.

The first thing that occurred to me was that this was gonna be too easy, no challenge for an experienced agent like myself. I mean was this supposed to be some kind of *insult* that the Queen was sending me? These middle-class johns, nice-looking fellas, Clark Kent specs, the whole shebang – gimme a break. Like I say, no sweat processing a mark like that. Ordinarily this kinda guy, he's carryin' around an itch that's needed scratching since he was a kid – gettin' married's more like a hair shirt than a back-scratcher to this dude, and that's where I come in. They may call me Sylvia the Sweet-tart but what I am is calamine lotion for your rash, baby.

The only thing about the look of this guy that didn't seem like it went with the rest of the picture were these three big black rings on all three fingers of his right hand. And I say three because he was missing two. "Vietnam vet," I said to myself, right off. But there was no army stuff in his file, so I let it slide.

One of the girls from Corporal Punishment followed him a couple of days for me, so in case the tail got burned the guy wouldn't connect me with it. The dude was amazing, I'll tell you: from home to work and from work home again, no stop-offs, no detours – no bar, no pool hall, no gym, no liquor store, no girlfriend, no boyfriend, no nothin'. According to the record, once a year he took off on a business trip – strictly business, too, if you could believe his company books. Might've partied a little in New York, but at home the guy was clean, no handle nowhere to catch him by. So if somebody (a girl like I, for example) was to process this dude, she'd have to do it right there in the office. I mean there was no other way, you know?

Meanwhile, one of our undercover agents had infiltrated the company where this guy worked, and that was the break I was looking for. This girl was head of Personnel, so she found some excuse to get rid of the receptionist they had there and she put me in to replace her. Fucked up my budget good, too, buying dresses and getting my hair fixed and buying makeup for that job. I'd never processed a professional type before, mine were usually car mechanics and so on, so Training sent me to a seminar on "How to Dress for Sex-cess in the Modern Office" and another one on "Office Rules of Misconduct." So on November 1 I was all settled in behind the reception desk, with my panoramic neckline and a skirt slit up to where the Decency Police said Hold it right there, miss. Just to finish off my look, I bought a pack of those cigarettes with the holder, like those little cigar things?, and in I went.

Within a week every man in that office, I swear on my dead father, every single one of them, including the janitor, had asked me out. Well, out – what they wanted was *in*, if you know what I mean. All, that is, except for this fucking Actionable whose case I'm on. And it wasn't that he hadn't noticed me, no way he didn't notice me. I mean he had to walk right in front of my desk every morning at eight o'clock – I was the first thing he'd see when he came through that door. I'd have this big bedroom smile on my face and these fake eyelashes would be stirring up Hurricane Honey all over the lobby and I'd bend over real nice for the man, he could see all the way to the Equator, and I'd say good morning so sexy it would've stopped an army of eunuchs in its tracks. The only other thing I could've done would be sit my ass on my desk and show him the rest of the Made in P.R. merchandise. Batteries, by the way, included.

All modesty aside, nature had been kind to me. I mean you can see for yourself, and everybody else saw for themselves. Nobody was ever better than me at bringing in the sheep to the slaughter. But I'll tell you, this son of a bitch had ice cubes for balls. Out to lunch so far as yours truly was concerned. He was nice and all, but I could have been the Coke machine.

But I'm not exactly one to sit around and wait for things to happen, so I didn't let a coffee break or a trip

to the ladies' room go by without giving everybody on
the entire floor the chance to eat their hearts out. The
men that worked there didn't do jack shit – all they did
was sit and wait for my appearances, as I like to call
them. Pencil needed sharpening, stapler needed staples,
any excuse to sashay past the Actionable's desk. Sometimes I'd leave work an hour late, just so I could go
down with him in the elevator, and you better believe
I'd take advantage of the crowd to rub some shine on
that polyester suit of his. But zip, zero, nada – the man
would not rise to the bait, in any sense of the word
"rise."

To make matters worse, I started getting static from
the guy's secretary – this two-legged antique that had
noticed my little crush on her boss and was determined
to pull the plug every time I tuned in to his channel.
One day she ambushed me in the xerox room and came
at me guns a-blazin': he was a decent, serious man, a
happily married man, and what was a cheap gold-digger
like me doing trying to lead the poor man into temptation? Well even if that was my job I wasn't taking no
insults from this dried-up old pruneface, so I told her
what her problem was, she needed somebody to check
her oil for her and give her a nice lube job. She turned
purple, blue, every color you can think of, her jaw trembled, and I thought she was going to choke. Said she
ought to slap some respect into me, so I said "You and
what fucking Girl Scout troop, grannie?" That kind of
took her back, so she cooled it a little bit, and a good
thing she didn't try anything, too, because that fucking
historical monument would've gotten her doors rehung,
and I mean it. She was holding the winning number in
the face-lifting lottery I was about to run – even if
Agency policy does say not to ever get into it with a

woman, no matter how big a fucking pain in the ass she is.

Anyway, to get back to this Actionable I'd been sent out to process, I had a deadline, and even if this old bag had the pressure on me so hard the silicon in my tits was threatening to pop, I had to do something, and quick. So I went directly to the Actionable, I mean, sometimes the direct approach, right? I ran my tongue over my lips in slow motion and I sort of whispered that I needed to see him that afternoon after work. It was urgent, I said. Sure, he says, he'd be happy to talk to me, why didn't I wait for him at five while he finished whatever it was he was doing, look over some accounts past due, I think he said.

At six-fifteen I was still on hold at the reception desk, waiting for Mr. Junior Executive to finish playing tic-tac-toe on that list he was supposedly working on. I surprised myself at my patience. And on top of that, the old mother hen waited and waited and waited to go home – to see what I was up to and try to protect her little chickie if she could – until finally the guy says "That'll be all, doña Thelma, thank you. You can go home now." So all she could do was take the next elevator down. But there was smoke coming out her ears, I'll tell you. 'Bye-bye, doña Thelma, says I, smiling ever so sweetly, See you tomorrow . . . Oh, I loved that.

Anyway, to make a long story short, I batted my eyelashes and smiled and crossed and uncrossed my legs till I practically wore a hole in my nylons, and this guy just sat there like a zombie. I'm good at my work, as anybody that's ever been on the receiving end will tell you, and I might've pulled it off, but when he asked me in that "Now what can I do for you?" voice of his what it was I wanted to "discuss" with him, I couldn't take it anymore, I just jumped him. I was breathing heavy and struggling with his zipper, to see if I couldn't get this guy's engine cranked, get the show on the road. But before I could even get the train's steam up, the dude pushes me off of him, throws it in reverse, and takes off full speed ahead on another track – his little briefcase in his hand and a stupid look on his face. I'll tell you, if I hadn't still had some hope of processing this guy, I'd have planted one of my spike heels in his skull and dyed that dork-o prematurely gray moustache of his red.

The next day they fired me. The asshole had reported me to Personnel and they put me on waivers for sexual harassment. Never in all my years as Provocative Agent III had I had a john like that! There was no way to get to this guy!

As for the Client, in my opinion she's either terminally stupid or one of those women that get off on the rough stuff. I think this case oughtta be hot-potatoed off to Corporal Punishment. They've got Olga the Enforcer over there. She specializes in English stuff, riding-crops and nightsticks and discipline and that kind of shit, she's never denied anybody a little manhandling, so to speak, if they need it . . .

APPENDIX 4
CASE NO. 6000
SEXUAL REHABILITATION DIVISION
REPORT: "OPERATION MOTEL"

The idea of going to a motel with a strange man for the first time in her life, "at her age" (quote from Client) and given the social and personal risks such behavior entailed, was not altogether to the Client's liking. But the case had come to an impasse, we could identify no further options, and her desperation forced her to agree to the plan. With the amount of the retainer that was left (which was very little), we contracted a professional "escort," very popular among the beach crowd, whose *nom de guerre* was Dr. Feelgood. (This is the first and last time we will employ a male agent in helping resolve a case.) We provided transportation and clothing. We chose for the operation an establishment located a short distance from the Caguas highway in an area famous for its feverish motel traffic (hourly, not daily rates). Evaluation had recommended "The Second Coming" for its lower-middle class clientele. Our working hypothesis was that the greater the class displacement, the greater the offense to marital honor.

On November 20, at exactly three p.m., Dr. Feelgood pulled up in front of the Client's house in our car. As per instructions, he honked the horn loudly several times and turned up the radio so that the neighbors would be induced to look out the windows of their respective houses. To increase the sense of expectancy, the Client took her time in responding. When she finally did, wearing a very revealing tight outfit of black silk with platform heels, the escort opened the car door and greeted her with a kiss our observer described as "exploratory surgery."

This scandalous scene culminated in a squealing of tires, as the couple raced off to their rendezvous. At the motel, they were under surveillance by Olga the Enforcer who had been engaged to provide protection to the Client in case any violence should occur.

The Agency, meanwhile, had sent several anonymous letters and made several anonymous telephone calls to the Actionable's office in the days preceding. Olga herself made the last, telling, call. She called from a public telephone and disguised her voice with the aid of the gum she always chewed when she was on duty. She also took the precaution of using a heavy Cuban accent. She courteously asked to speak to the Actionable, and when he picked up the phone she hoarsely whispered (and we quote): "Listen, you stupid meatballs-for-brains, even as we speak your wife's getting her valves rebored by a pimp in a motel out on the Caguas highway, and you can hear her moans all the way to the Shell station . . . "

Olga alleges that just as she was about to tell the Actionable which motel, she heard a click on the other end of the line. We later received confirmation of this fact. Not only had the expected reaction not taken place, but when the Client returned home at seven o'clock that night, her hair tousled, her mascara run and her lipstick smeared, looking as though she had been through a session of sado-masochistic sex therapy, she found the wine uncorked and the table set, down to silver candlesticks. The Actionable did not even ask where she had been; he was too busy putting the finishing touches on the gourmet dinner he had prepared to celebrate their tenth wedding anniversary.

We find it hard to admit that the results we have obtained are inversely proportional to the efforts expended by this division. The infallibility of our operations has been called into question, and my fear is that Case No. 6000 will establish an ominous precedent for future cases brought to Solutions, Inc.

> Circe F ——
> Rehabilitation Officer IV
> Sexual Rehabilitation Division
> Solutions, Inc.

II

The Patroness leafed once more through the documents before slipping them into the manila envelope stamped with the number 6000 in red ink. Then removing the three black rings and setting them carefully on the desk, pulling on rubber gloves with expert elegance, rolling the official-looking paper with its embossed letterhead into the typewriter, and lightly poising eight virtuoso fingers above the keyboard, there was a pause for thought. The Patroness stroked that gray-speckled moustache for just a moment, pushed up the eyeglasses, and smiled, almost tenderly. Then, in the very center of the page, with the greatest care and precision, he typed the following words:

BURN THIS FILE
SILENCE CLIENT
ASSIGN NEXT CASE NO. 6000

JUST ONE
SMALL DETAIL

One generation's nightmare
is the next generation's sociology.

– Stephen King

I

Now that I think back on it, that was one hell of a summer. I lost over ten pounds – and I was as skinny as Mick Jagger to begin with. I started looking like some kind of concentration-camp survivor or something. My parents were convinced I was either into drugs or politics. If they'd found out what it really was, they'd have put their baby boy here on that plane to Georgetown so fast I'd never have known what hit me.

It all began the night I finally got into Dalia's apartment. I was madly in love – I'd just graduated from high school, never "done it," apart from some heavy breathing with two or three girls in the back seat of Vitín's car, and when this incredible older woman came into my life it was like Santa Claus had come to town and I hadn't had to be good or anything . . . And then those two sickos Vitín and Pucho egging me on, telling me to jump her and get it over with . . . Plus they wanted to be the first to hear all about it. . .

Anyway. That night, I decided, I was going to go for broke. And it looked like everything was on my side – the hour, the blue lights down low, the Wilkins album on, the passion-fruit juice with vodka, forget it . . . Oh, I'm no Tom Cruise, I'm the first to admit that, but something told me she didn't woof her cookies when she thought about me, either. In spite of the fact that she was always calling me "kid" and "my dear" and stuff like that, just to be sure we were both fully aware of the fucking difference in our ages. Big deal. I mean, sure, she was thirty, but did that mean I had an Oedipus complex, for god's sake? Even so, the torrid glances were long-play and the silences were electric, not to mention the body heat, I mean body language, which as we all know never lies . . .

I'd gotten tired of waiting for her to make the first move so I could be saved from making an idiot of myself if *I* did it. I mean, how many times did I have to casually mention how perfectly matched biologically a studly eighteen-year-old and a mature woman were, with all the statistics and scientific data I'd picked up in my Human Sexuality class? And Dalia, you'd have thought it was just interesting chitchat, gimme a break. I figured an experienced woman ought to know how to take the bull by the horns a hell of a lot better than a novice like me. So it was pretty obvious she wasn't going to make the first move, even if she was as ready to get it on as yours truly. I figured she didn't want to be responsible for contributing to the delinquency of a minor or some shit along those lines. Or maybe she was afraid I'd want to marry her – which I have to admit, in my sentimental late-night glandular fantasies I'd given some consideration to.

She'd dropped hints about her mental state of the moment – stuff like "I've got to get my head together" and "I don't want to get involved with any man, no matter how great he is." . . . But at the same time she kept lending me books of poetry and taking me to Cine-Art to see those Brazilian movies with Sonia Braga, that kind of thing, which of course meant cold showers for a week for the kid here. Vitín and Pucho kept telling me

I was the Puerto Rican National Jerk(-Off). They'd lost theirs years ago, no big deal, what's to think about?, they said, and they told me if I didn't do something about my "situation" before classes started, one of them was going to butt in line ahead of me, and maybe both of them. That pissed me off more at myself than at them. I'm a pretty civilized young man, appearances notwithstanding, and it chapped me to have to descend to the level of these guys, who all they could think about was It. Why the hell couldn't *she* give a little jump-start to the old jalopy? I mean I wouldn't have needed much encouragement . . . Wasn't women's liberation supposed to be good for something?

But that night was going to be The Night. Picture it: she was lying on her stomach on the couch, with her head on a pillow and her eyes closed and an attitude like if-something-happens-I-wasn't-here . . . Plus she'd just finished telling me that she'd changed the lock so her ex-husband couldn't barge into the apartment at midnight anymore. I was lying suggestively on the floor with the top three or four buttons on my shirt unbuttoned, looking relatively masculine I thought, and I was creeping inch by inch toward the couch, with the idea of offering the reclining Dalia my services as an amateur masseur. I had to keep the emergency brake on because she'd apparently just waxed the floor and it was slippery as hell. My buddy Wilkins was crooning away on the stereo, which provided the ideological scaffolding for me to hang my plan on. The jeans on that favorite divorcée of mine looked particularly edible in the pink light. I chugged the rest of the vodka-and-passion-fruit that was sitting there on the glass coffee table and I gauged the distance to the couch. I stepped back for the leap –

and *bam!*, incredible but true, at the critical moment the lights go out.

Since I was halfway there, all I could do was freeze where I was and make one of those incredibly suave comments that you always make at a time like that, something along the lines of Hey, the lights went out! . . . Dalia said they kept cutting off the electricity to the building because the maintenance people were on some kind of a slow-down strike – the latest synonym for chronic laziness, if you ask me, but she said the blackouts didn't usually last long. If it ain't gonna last then I better make hay while there's still an eclipse, I say to myself. So I creep onward through the darkness. What I'll do is, I'll make it over there and sit on the couch beside her, put out a tentacle very casually, you know, just stretching, lay that arm over the back of the couch, whisper a sweet nothing or two in her ear, in honor of Vitín of course, who always said you had to attack on two fronts, the neck and the ear. So there I go, creeping over toward the couch. You could've heard a pin drop I was so sneaky about it, and when I finally managed to deposit my 130 pounds of skin and bone very gently on the couch, she gives a jump like the last piece of popcorn when you take the lid off the popper.

"Oops," I say, swallowing. And in desperation I throw out a line and hook her hand. Thank goodness it was her hand, too, because I could have hit a more strategic target, and then I'd have been up shit creek for sure.

I started working her hand, as Vitín says, stroking each finger, and then her palm – which was pretty sweaty for a grown woman – and paying special attention to that little web of skin between her thumb and index finger. I'd had quite a bit of flight time as a hand-jockey with the high-school girls. Dalia was still as a little mouse. So

that gave me the courage to bring in the heavier artillery.
And I was just about up to her elbow, ready to give her
the key squeeze and bring out that big kiss I'd been
keeping fresh in the refrigerator now for a good three
weeks, when – *Jesus* Christ! – all this goddamned banging starts.

At first I thought it was the ex-husband. I'm dogmeat,
I thought. The stories Dalia had told me would make an
eel's hair stand on end. I could see myself in Centro
Médico and Dalia at Casa Julia de Burgos for Battered
Women. But then a woman started screaming and yelling
and then a man's voice, sounded pissed as hell, telling
her to shut up, and I realized the war zone was the
apartment next door, not this one.

Then there was all this other banging around and
stuff, but no more yelling. Holy shit, I said, What *is* that
– World Championship Wrestling? I was trying to be
cool after my recent shitting in my pants. Dalia got up
and went out onto the balcony. Me being the curious
type, I got up too, and bumped into every table and
chair in the living room on my way outside to follow
her. I think the phrase is "the silence was deafening."
You couldn't even hear the *coquís*. But she had her ear
cocked anyway, and every time I tried to open my mouth
she put her hand over it and shushed me. Bad time to
follow up on my recent successes, thinks I . . .

About then the lights come back on, and all of a
sudden we hear the grandmother of all thuds, I'm talking serious banging here. And Wilkins warps up to
speed again, singing something about "it's not who
touches her skin, it's who touches her heart," which I
figured was a good sign for me . . . But then Dalia starts
pacing around the living room, muttering Oh my god
right and left and picking up the phone and hanging it

up again and walking to the door and putting her hand out to grab the doorknob and stopping and walking back again . . . She must be thinking about all those fights with her ex, I think, and I decide it's better if I just chill out and let her work out whatever it is for herself.

She went off to the kitchen and started rattling dishes in the sink. I figured that was my cue to split and leave her alone with herself for a while, so I went in to say so long and all, with my tail pretty much between my legs as you can imagine. And what do I find but the girl standing there with tears running down her face and her nose like a W. C. Fields look-alike contest winner. Well, that broke what was left of my broken heart, so I grabbed her and hugged her real tight – no ulterior motives, you understand, I swear it, because all this recent unpleasantness had pretty much put my romantic intentions on ice, you dig what I mean. I mean, I was more freaked out than turned on. I poured her a glass of water for her hiccups and tried a couple of times to make her laugh, but even *I* realized that the jokes I came out with were groaners.

She didn't want to talk about whatever it was, so I didn't push her. Nor did I intend to wait around for her to say "You may be on vacation, but I've got to go to work in the morning." So I split. At that hour, waiting for a bus meant expecting a miracle, so I wore through the last millimeter of my antique hightops hiking home. What with the bummer, the being beat to shit, and this homicidal maniac face Mother Nature pasted on me, I must have looked like one bad dude, because not a single panhandler or mugger fucked with me all the way home.

II

I didn't see her again for a whole week. When you're talking love, you've gotta give things time, take things easy, don't get all ahead of yo'self. *That* I'd learned by the time I was sixteen. Besides, I had this sneaking feeling that between Dalia and me, things weren't ever going to get much beyond first-and-a-half base.

I couch-potatoed so long in front of the VCR checking out Brian de Palma flicks that I began to sprout. I numbed myself out on gore so I wouldn't think of you-know. If Vitín and Pucho came by or called, my sister Teresa had instructions to tell 'em I'd gone to Nicaragua to fight for democracy with the Contras.

My parents were all smiles to have me back on my leash again. They weren't particularly thrilled that their baby boy, a nice white dude that studied with the supposedly sexless priests at a lovely Catholic high school, was hanging out with a bunch of hoodlums from the projects. My mom – I mean was this *obvious* or what – even made me flan, which she hadn't done since about my ninth birthday. And my dad did me the incredible honor of sitting down to see *Blow-out* with me, although he spent the whole fucking movie putting down John Travolta, saying he was a closet queen and making a bunch of other fatherly remarks. Me? Chilled out. I would drift from my bedroom into the family room and back again like some kind of trained ghost, meanwhile in private writing erotic poetry in my old science notebook, which I hid under the mattress with the *Playboys* and *Penthouses* that light up the nights of every decent red-blooded young man. And no, I wasn't going blind yet, smart-ass.

Anyway, after that week of spiritual retreat, during which I put on a couple of pounds and recovered my usual high spirits, I got the itch to see the lovely Dalia again. I decided the best way would be to run into her accidentally-on-purpose in the Parque Central. Didn't want to be too obvious. She went to the park every afternoon to burn off some calories after pressing the upholstery on her secretarial chair all day in the office. That was where I'd first met her, in fact, one afternoon when I went jogging and checking out chicks with Vitín and Pucho. *They* were there to check out the chicks, the lowlifes, because that's not the way I work. But as long as I was there, I started taking note of the scenery, too, I mean what the heck . . . That kind of behavior rubs off on you, as my mother never fails to remind me.

And so it was that I first set eyes on Dalia. And what a sight she was, my man, because that park was full of *very* scenic wonders, but the grandest Teton of them all was Dalia . . . I mean this woman had something in her eyes, I don't know, and the way she walked, and that magnetic kind of smile that you could just look at and look at and look at and couldn't stop looking at. . .

Well, anyway, what happened was that for my romantic come-back I nationalized my sister's bicycle and I took off, dodging the cars flying low on the expressway. If she isn't there after I nearly get myself killed on this bicycle, I said to myself, I'll throw myself in the Martín Peña Canal. But there she was, with a group doing aerobics. And foxier than ever, too, with those sprayed-on jogging shorts that put mere imagination to shame. We saw each other from a distance, and (*Yesss!*) she waved first. When the last stretching exercises were over (*Whew!*) and people began to sort of disperse, I went over to ask her if I could buy her an orange juice at the snack bar with the two or three bills I'd pried loose from the old man at a weak moment. She said she had something important to talk to me about, but not there – too many people. My heart skipped a beat at that – I'm that way, sentimental, call it whatever you want to. All *right*, I thought, she wants to make up for what happened on Sunday. Pay dirt, I also thought.

We wrestled the bicycle into the trunk of her Toyota, which was not easy, and headed out. I was expecting us to turn off for Hato Rey, where her apartment was, and slip straight into something more comfortable. Imagine my surprise to see that she was taking the exit for Old San Juan and heading down toward the harbor, down by where the Cataño Ferry docks. I sort of had other plans, you know, but I had to admit that this wasn't a bad place to start – a nice romantic bench on the waterfront, the soft street lights, the cobblestones. Very appropriate, all things considered, for having a little heart-to-heart.

And we had a little heart-to-heart, all right, but not exactly the kind I had in mind. What Dalia told me was so nutty that at first I thought she was putting me on. It seems she'd gotten it into her head that this neighbor of hers, the guy that was doing all the yelling and banging around that night, had wasted his old lady. Off'd his live-in. *Killed his wife.* However you sliced it, it sounded pretty unlikely to me.

"Where'd you get such a crazy idea, huh?" I put it to her a little more gruffly than I ordinarily would have, but I had to cover up the growling that was coming from my stomach – I hadn't even grabbed a sandwich before I absconded for the park with Teresa's bicycle.

"Well, because doña Lucrecia" (can you believe that

name?) "hasn't watered her plants all week," she says, like how much more obvious could it be?

"Maybe she's sick," I said.

Stupid me, trying to be logical.

"No," she replied with that smile she smiles every time she thinks she's got you, "because Wednesday when I went over to ask about her, don Danilo" (and there's another one for your collection) "told me she was spending a few days at her sister's house."

"Well, there you are," I said.

I guess I should have known it wouldn't be that easy, though.

"No," she said again, with that same adorably irritating smirk on her face, "because there's just one small detail, my dear – doña Lucrecia is an only child. I called every Santoni in the book – Santoni being doña Lucrecia's maiden name – and I told 'em I was doing a study at the university on the Corsican population of Puerto Rico. I interviewed every single one of them, asked them about all their brothers and sisters and aunts and uncles and everything. How about *that*, Mr. Logical? So she has neither a sister *nor* a brother . . . "

That blew me away. What *resourcefulness* this woman had! But I wasn't buying her magazines that easy. I figured she was exaggerating things just a leetle beet, as Desi used to say to Lucy, not to mention making Olympic record long-jumps to conclusions. She kept piling on details, trying to convince me – don Danilo had taken forever to answer the door, and when he did he'd opened it just the tiniest little crack, like when the Jehovah's Rollers come around early Saturday morning to sell you *To the Lighthouse* or whatever it is. And she said that was weird as hell because this don Danilo usually flirted with her like crazy . . . But this time he'd been stiff – stiff and pale and his voice had shaken, she said. And so far as Dalia was concerned, that was enough to go to the grand jury with.

I was just about to give her the whole sermon about how in a democratic system of government a person is presumed innocent until proven guilty and all that, which I had just done a report on for my U.S. History class – which if I may say so myself wasn't bad – but she beat me to it with the last nail in ol' don Danilo's coffin – Sunday night, that is to say "the evening of the crime," she hadn't been able to sleep one minute because of all the strange noises coming from don Danilo and doña Lucrecia's apartment. It sounded, she said, like they were scraping the floor with a spatula and rearranging all the furniture.

"And I'll have you know, my dear," (god, that drove me crazy!) "that don Danilo is not the sort of man to help out around the house . . . much less at that hour of the morning."

I had to admit that things looked kind of suspicious, and even believable, if you consider what you read about every day in the newspaper. But if all this was true, what could we do about it? Did she really want to get mixed up in a big police investigation and all the bullshit that went with it, just for the sake of law and order? And if so, *what* law and order, might I ask?

"I recommend you just forget about this," I told her, "and look the other way."

"Yeah, like since this murderer doesn't live next door to *you*, you think we ought to just forget about the whole thing . . . "

I had nothing more to say.

"Jesus, he could have taken the body out to Lake Carraízo by now in a plastic bag and dumped it!"

I had nothing more to say, I said.

"In your nice white middle-class life these things don't happen, right?"

I still had nothing more to say.

The look she gave me after this if-we-don't-give-a-shit-then-the-whole-society-is-doomed routine could've sent *me* to prison – for life, no chance for parole.

"And what about doña Lucrecia? Is she *nobody?*" she finally said.

It was like I could still hear the priests at school when they would remind us that not doing anything about a crime was as good as being an accomplice to it. That is, you could fry not only by thought, word, and deed but also by omission. I don't know what it was in my genes, but that argument *always* fucking worked on me. But I must say, in my own defense, that the following moving scene (played out in my own personal Penthouse Letters column in that dirty mind of mine) also had something to do with my caving in: While we were investigating this case, Dalia would plead with me to stay with her in her apartment to protect her from the bloodthirsty don Danilo, and I'd stay there and put my arms around her while guiding her protectively toward that gently-swaying waterbed of hers . . .

III

Dalia had made up her mind to get into don Danilo's apartment, one way or another. And come hell or high water, nothing and nobody was going to change her mind. That night I lay awake all night trying to come up with a plan. It didn't look easy. This dude was a retired art teacher that drank like a fish, and he almost never left his apartment. Aside from knockout drops in his drink or something, I couldn't think of any way to get by him.

But while my brain was giving off the smell of burned brake linings, Dalia had already figured it all out. She called me from work the next day to tell me this guy went out every afternoon about six to buy cigarettes and whisky at the liquor store on Piñero. That would give us a good twenty minutes to get in and get out, she said cheerfully. I could be the lookout while she checked the place out.

So at exactly five-thirty I'm standing in front of the elevators in her building. Dalia was late, probably stuck in the traffic jam over on Muñoz Rivera, and I was beginning to get a little steamed. To kill time, I found a public telephone and called Pucho.

"Hey, how's it goin' with Mrs. Robinson?" he says the minute he hears my voice. I was instantly sorry I'd called him. But my skin was tough, so I let it pass. The horny fuck was obsessed with my virginity. For a second I was tempted to tell him about the "crime," but I figured he already thought I was stupid enough without me convincing him once and for all. Anyway, he proceeded to tell me for about the ninth time about the first time he did it with a gringa, this girl staying a few days at the Hotel Palace. Just as I was about to hang up on him, though, I got this weird feeling, like I was getting into some deep doo-doo here. All of a sudden, as he says, "Okay, my brother, we'll see you around. I'm off to the pizza parlor, but anything happen, you know, you let me know," my eyes kind of teared up on me, and I had this impulse to be real nice to Pucho even if he was nothing but a horny lowlife ... Under the circumstances, that "anything happen" sounded real, I don't know, meaningful to me.

But just then, fortunately, Dalia shows up. Real office getup – pantyhose, straight skirt, high heels, a purse to match the shoes, nothing like that sex-symbol health nut I knew from the Parque Central. I had to look twice to be sure it was the same lady. Then all of a sudden the elevator doors open and this older guy gets off – glasses, bald spot, tall, pretty good gut on 'im – and he says hello to Dalia. She immediately gets all nervous, drops her keys, the whole thing. I mean, you didn't have to be a Hercule Poirot to see that this was the guy. He bent down to pick up Dalia's keys, a very polite dude, this guy, and they kind of smile these nerdy smiles at each other. Finally Dalia takes off and this son-of-a-bitch stands there checking her out from the rear until she gets on the elevator. I let her go up by herself, just in case, and I caught the next one.

I got upstairs as she was opening her apartment door. I sort of sneaked up behind her and slipped my arms around her waist. The shriek she gave out nipped the flower that was blooming in my bluejeans in the bud. Then she grabbed my arm and dragged me real fast out onto the balcony.

"He's gone," she whispered, her eyes glittering. "How'll we do this? Me go in while you watch?"

The question put my masculinity on the line. There was no way – I had to go in myself. So we decided she'd wait downstairs to warn me when this dude came back – three buzzes on the intercom.

It was easy to climb from one balcony to the other because the builders had saved themselves a couple of million dollars by building just these low walls between them. Fortunately or unfortunately, depending on your perspective, the sliding door was locked. My twelve years of Catholic education weighed heavy on me. But since I was there, the least I could do was cup my hand to the glass and have a peep.

Everything looked pretty kosher to me. No rotting body lying in the living room, for example. Not even a possible murder weapon with nice clear fingerprints all over it waiting to be discovered by Philip Marlowe Junior here. Just antique furniture all made in the old days in Puerto Rico, wood and cane stuff like you see in the old houses in Miramar and whatnot, a monster grand piano, don't know how they ever got it in there, posters from the Institute of Culture, lots of books on the shelves, and a whole jungle of houseplants all bunched around this big white statue lying like a Roman empress or something (but without the grapes, ha ha) on a wooden pedestal. The ultramodern stereo components and TV clashed with the rest of that typical Puerto Rican middle-class ex-avant-garde intellectual décor. Don Danilo and doña Lucrecia were obviously members of the culture club that went to concerts at Bellas Artes and watched the educational programs on the government TV station.

That peek at the couple's private life through the keyhole, as it were, convinced me once and for all how stupid these suspicions of ours were. If you traded the antique stuff for rattan, that place could have been my own living room, for god's sake, except for the punk litter all over the place that Teresa and I contributed. I stood there a long time taking mental snapshots of the place, figuring I'd pick up big points with Dalia. I was pretty impressed with how neat and clean everything

was. Not that there wasn't a little of that lived in look –
an empty bottle and a glass half-full of some yellow
liquid that I figured could be whisky (among other more
exotic possibilities – I wanted to give the guy a little
credit, you know). I got eyestrain trying to read the titles
of some of the books over by the front door. I recognized
the big volume of Edgar Allan Poe stories translated by
Cortázar because my parents had one in their bedroom.

And then I almost shit in my pants. The buzzer buzzed
three times: The Return of The Bad Dude. I mentally
crossed myself, like in school before a big test, and turbo-
charged by the adrenalin kicking in, I jumped over that
balcony so fast I was lucky I didn't break my ass. I barely
had time to strike a nonchalant pose before Dalia got
back upstairs.

My heroism earned me a big hug I couldn't really
enjoy and the best I could hope for in the way of apology:
"Oh, kiddo, he almost caught you, I didn't see him till
he was already in the elevator." I could feel my stomach
turn over at that.

I gave her my report on the investigation (real FBI
stuff, huh?) and told her my inescapable conclusion –
her neighbors were not going to be making the front
page of *El Vocero*. She didn't even bother to answer. With
that sarcastic smile of hers, she told me to give her a
playback of the whole scene through the looking glass,
I mean the sliding glass door. Practically before I got
going, she stopped me and started asking questions like
a DA.

"This statue, was it bronze or marble or plaster?"

"Not bronze, because it was white . . . "

"Male or female?"

"Well, it had . . . "

"Tits. How big?"

"The tits?"

"Very funny. The statue."

"About your size, more or less."

"Standing or lying down?"

"Equestrian."

"Hilarious."

"Lying down. Very sexy."

"Dressed or nude?"

"Nude."

"Thin or, you know, hefty?"

"Pretty nice figure."

"Young or old?"

"I didn't see any wrinkles."

Dalia thought for a while, staring at me with a look like a Kate Fansler without a cigarette. I kind of liked that. I controlled myself as long as I could but finally I said I gave up.

"That statue, my dear, could be the key to the whole thing. Don't ask me why, but I've got a funny feeling about that statue."

That freaked me out. The same gruesome idea must have been uncoiling like an arthritic snake in both our minds. Were those the noises that Dalia had heard Sunday night? Had he beaten her to death first or strangled her before he embalmed her like some poor mummy? Or had he plastered her in alive, like in those Poe stories, a big volume of which he just happened to have in his living room? I could picture him buying the big sack of plaster of Paris, mixing it with water, putting newspaper on the floor so as not to make a mess, carefully covering the corpse with the wet plaster, smoothing it out, giving it the shape of the corpse with that spatula, then spraying it with some kind of special spray to give it that antique look . . .

Dalia read my mind. "You see how it all fits in," she said, twisting the knife of sarcasm in my back.

I tried to save the last remnants of rationality I had left. "But do you honestly think that he'd have her lying around in the living room like that, where anybody that walked in could see her, d . . . ?"

"First," she cut me off, "nobody goes in there, because I never see anybody paying a visit to those people. And second, that's probably exactly what he'd like, to turn her into a statue, part of the décor . . . " And she detoured into all this stuff about the "reification" of women in art and I don't know what else, which reminded me of my parents when they decided the craze for electroboogie had to do with the mechanization of human beings by industrialized societies. Where do they *get* this stuff?

Anyway, my head felt like I had a cold and had just taken a Contac. Dalia didn't look so hot herself. And to cap it all, I thought how remote the possibility of making it with her was now, and that *totally* bummed me out. Why hadn't I fallen in love with Maritza, Pucho's cousin, who had this real thing for me, not to mention a reputation for spreading her affections, so to speak, around? Why was I so determined to have my world premiere with this very weird lady who'd obviously been reading too many Agatha Christie novels? And if one more thing was lacking to fuck my life up totally, that thing was not long in coming. In fact, at this very moment it was banging like crazy on the door.

Imagine the whispers and big eyes:

"Don't open it, don't open it . . . "

"What if it's important?"

"So just open it a crack."

"Idiot, like they can't tell."

The banging continued. And this deep voice calls out *Dalia! Open up, I know you're in there!*

"Oh my God! It's José Manuel."

"Who?"

"My ex."

"And you're going to let him in?"

"He saw the car!"

"If you open the door, I'm leaving."

"If you leave, I'll never speak to you again."

And the ex out there yelling *If you don't open up, I'm going to break the door down!*

Dalia looks at me, wavers, wavers some more, then she opens the door. And the girlish little voice that came out of her sounded like something from a Fifties sit-com.

"Oh, hi, José Manuel. We didn't hear you . . . "

This José Manuel dude is tall and, depending on your taste, pretty good-looking. He's got a moustache, that is. He's wearing a sort of young-bank-executive guayabera and carrying this very contemporary soft-sided brief-case, no fuddy-duddy Samsonite for this dude. He comes in, sees me, and gives Dalia a pitying sort of look. "If I've come at a bad time . . . " he says.

"No, no, I was just leaving," says yours truly. And with that, I'm out that door with my best chilly indifference act. I was so cool (i.e., pissed off), I practically broke my neck stumbling over doña Lucrecia's dried-out plants out there in the hall.

When I got home, a case of serious rejection neurosis on my hands, Teresa was in the living room. Thank god she was fixated momentarily on Michael Jackson's ripping shirt, so I avoided the third-degree. The Honorable Parents—where else? Locked up in their bedroom with the air-conditioner on Sno-Cone, reading the *San*

Juan Star and blaming the ills of the world on *independentistas*, drug addicts, and Cubans.

I recall being glad there were only two weeks left before I went off to school.

IV

I met Pucho and Vitín in front of the pizzería. I'd just gotten my allowance, and I was in the mood to spend it all in one place, so I told them the pizza was on me. The pizza and the beer opened me up. First I told them about the ex-husband. Pucho shook his head and Vitín said what ought to be done with this guy was jump him in some dark alley . . . I tried to stay cool and calm these guys down, since god knew they were capable of doing just that. But it wasn't easy.

Since they kept talking about cleaning this guy's clock and teaching this guy not to fuck with their bro' and stuff like that, and also so as not to look like a perfect jerk-off to them – which is exactly what I did look like, and I knew it – I had to tell them the rest of the story. To my surprise, they listened to it all without a word, and then they agreed with Dalia's interpretation of things. "The guy wasted her," says Vitín, like somebody else would say It's raining, and then "I'd be careful he doesn't plaster you two into artwork, too, for sticking your wiseass nose into it." . . . Pucho, who loves those blood-and-guts epics like *The Texas Chainsaw Massacre*, says he read in *El Vocero* about this guy that had stuffed his wife into the closet in the family room and poured cement over her . . .

So we were sitting there discussing the pros and cons of cement versus plaster of Paris for getting rid of troublesome spouses while we ate our pizza and drank our beers when (and you're not going to believe this, either, but what the hell) I raise my head and just very casually happen to look out the window and what do I see but Danilo the Ripper, man, stopped at the stoplight in a black Mitsubishi with this incredible-looking chick sitting beside him.

"There he is!" I say, gulping down the mouthful of pizza I'd just stuffed in, and pointing out the window like a madman.

Vitín and Pucho jumped up to look. I threw some money on the table (with a pretty big unintentional tip that got left in the rush) and we ran outside and jumped into Vitín's broken-down Chevy just as the light changed and don Danilo pulled away, headed apparently for the freeway.

"Here we go!" yells Vitín, putting the pedal to the metal as Pucho and I resigned ourselves to an early grave. Don Danilo and his lovely companion, who turned out to be a young dark-skinned thing with about fourteen dollars' worth of makeup on her face, turned off for Santurce and then drove all the way down Ponce de León to Stop Fifteen, which is totally Dominican and the nation's capital for consensual sin. They turned down Serra and we almost lost them. But Pucho's trained eye caught them turning down an alley where Pucho thought there was, and where there in fact turned out to be, a $5-a-night hotel.

"Ooo-weee, so the dude still gets it up," says Vitín,

and he stops the car a little ways away so we could keep our eye on the old roué.

First, thinking this was just going to be a lunchtime quickie, we waited with the engine running. Vitín turned on the radio and started tapping on the steering wheel with his comb to keep time with Marvin Santiago's latest salsa smash. I was already in a pretty dark mood, so when I saw that a half-hour had gone by and then an hour, and this horny bastard hadn't come out yet, I said, "Let's go, looks like this could take a while . . . "

"So the old man gets a little on the side, huh . . . "

"Why do you think he wasted his old lady, asshole?"

I kept my mouth shut, thinking at least this way I'd have an excuse to call Dalia without seeming to be absolutely desperate to make things up between us and finally get in her pants. In front of my house, I gave my buddies the high-five and told them to be on stand-by, I was probably going to need them. Thumbs up. Then they burned rubber.

There was nobody home at my house. I called Dalia's office but they told me she hadn't come to work. That really freaked me out – I could just picture all this melodramatic shit that might have happened to her, like her ex slapping her around and her having to be taken to the hospital, that kind of stuff. I called her house. The phone rang about ten times, but just when I was about to hang up and start calling the hospitals, I heard that bored-receptionist "hello" of hers.

"Uh, you mean you didn't go to work today," I said, being the master of repartee I am. To which she, equally inspired, replied that she was tired.

"Oh," says I. Then I thought fuck it, no more beating around the bush. And I told her I had something new on her favorite next-door neighbor. She perked up immediately and started asking questions, wanting me to give her a preview, but I wanted her to beg – oh no, I says, not on the phone, until she finally told me to come over when I could. Since I just happened to be free, I hot-footed it to the bus stop. And I practically started collecting Social Security before the fucking bus came.

I got there about five. Not even hello – she grabbed my hand (which naturally was sweaty) and pulled me inside and started yelling "Oh, god, I've done something awful!"

Awful wasn't the word for it. She'd gotten this brilliant idea to go through don Danilo's trash, and naturally he'd caught her red-handed.

"What'd you do?"

"What was I supposed to do? I freaked out. But I told him the bag had ripped and I was picking the stuff up ... "

I just looked at her. Pretty weak, I thought. But anyway, then I told her about don Danilo and his tootsie. You could see the lightbulbs come on in her eyes, and she ran off into the bedroom. She was back in about three seconds carrying something. It was a black-and-white picture ripped up and the pieces all taped together with Scotch tape.

"She look familiar?"

She didn't have any makeup on, or clothes either, so it took me a couple of seconds to recognize her, but it was the same mouth, the same naturally curly hair. "Looks like her," I said, pretty impressed with Dalia's professionalism. She'd found the pieces in don Danilo's trash and hidden them in her bra so she could tape them together later. I confess that the second detail impressed me more than the first. . .

"So, do we have a case or don't we?" she finally asked, and you could hear the gloating in her voice.

I thought for a while before I answered. I was getting this wild idea about how to find out the truth, the whole truth, and a little more than the truth . . .

V

We were busy all the next day making preparations. Pucho got together all this weird-looking stuff for picking locks with. He borrowed it from some of his homeboys that were into that kind of thing part time. Vitín brought us each a pair of plastic gloves and a pair of panty-hose. The gloves were so we wouldn't leave any finger prints, of course, and the panty-hose to pull over our heads and disguise ourselves, bank-robber style. I was an honor student from a good Catholic school, and I wasn't exactly used to this shit, so my bowels went into overdrive.

About five-fifteen we were in Puerto Nuevo listening to José Feliciano in Vitín's room and drinking Hawaiian Punch. Vitín lit a joint and offered us a hit but Pucho said he didn't fuck with his head during working hours, and I passed because I'd just read this article on the horrifying effects of grass on the memory. "All the more for me," says Vitín, holding in another big hit.

I was supposed to call Dalia to see whether she'd done her part. The conversation was short:

"Ready?"

"Ready."

"What time's he supposed to be there?"

"Seven."

"Give 'im plenty of gas."

"Not to worry."

Vitín and Pucho were as excited as a couple of kids with a new toy. And I was too, to tell the truth, because something told me that if we didn't get this shit settled pretty soon, I'd never get past first base with Dalia, in this life or the next. And the worst part of it is that I had decided it was her or nobody. The prospect of a life of celibacy made solving this little mystery pretty appealing.

At a quarter to seven we got to Dalia's building. We were suffocating. It must have been ninety-five muggy degrees and we were dressed in black from head to foot – plus we were lugging all our housebreaking equipment in Pueblo bags. We took the elevator up to the seventh floor and made a run for Dalia's apartment. She was waiting for us with the door open.

"You idiots almost didn't make it," she said, and she pushed us out onto the balcony.

It was twenty minutes, but it seemed like hours. We were hiding behind the curtain that covered the sliding glass door. When the doorbell rang, we pulled on our gloves and pantyhose ski masks and we could hear Dalia click-clicking to the door. I could just imagine don Danilo standing there at the door, his bald spot shining like a disco mirror-ball in the fluorescent light of the hall.

Dalia led him into the living room and sat him down very strategically with his back to the balcony as far away from the sliding glass door as she could manage. She put a drink in his hand so fast it'd have made anybody else suspicious, but don Danilo had already had a few, you could tell from the way he slurred his words a little. I waited for Dalia to put on the Daniel Santos album we'd agreed on – just to create a little atmosphere, you know – and I gave Vitín and Pucho the high sign. One by one, we jumped over the balcony wall onto the other side.

Vitín was pissed. After all our planning, he didn't have to force the door – don Danilo had left it standing wide open. The kitchen light was on, too, and the statue was practically glowing in the semi-dark living room.

"Is this it?" Vitín says, feeling it up. That horny bastard would've fondled the Venus de Milo, especially since she couldn't slap his hand away.

"Must be," I said, giving it a good look – because seeing it up close like that, it didn't look much like it had the other day from the balcony. Vitín motioned to us, and the three of us lifted it.

"There's no way there's a dead body in here, man," Pucho said. "This mother don't weigh nothin'." And he was right. The statue didn't weigh as much as a store mannequin.

"Let's go check out the bedroom," said Vitín in his best Commander Zero voice.

"The bedroom" was *two* bedrooms. Apparently they slept in separate rooms. We decided to divide up the house to speed things up, and I got doña Lucrecia's room, Vitín got don Danilo's, and Pucho got the bathroom and kitchen.

The wife's bedroom was totally different from the living room. Frilly curtains, little skirts on everything, flowered wallpaper, real feminine. All it needed was the stuffed animals and the Barbie dolls to make it look like my kid sister's room. What really blew me away was seeing all of doña Lucrecia's clothes and stuff in the closet and the chest of drawers. If she's really dead, I thought, this dude is a sicko. I mean, with all this stuff of hers, I saw doña Lucrecia as a flesh-and-blood person for the first time.

You couldn't say clues were falling out of the sky exactly, and the same held true for Vitín and Pucho. We went back to the living room a little stumped.

"Should we take the statue and break it open later?" Vitín suggested. He was ready to solve this case, you know, like damn the torpedoes kind of thing. But we decided that wasn't such a great idea. It was pretty risky to try to rip off something that big without anybody seeing us.

All of a sudden we heard Dalia's voice – she was yelling at us in this real tight whisper from the balcony. "Come back!" she was screaming, but real quietly. "Come back! He's on his way over there! He forgot his cigarettes!"

It was like the Keystone Kops, I swear to god. We had to put the statue back, turn out the lights, and grab the bag of housebreaking tools before the old man came back in, then jump the balcony wall back into the free world. We all hunkered down on Dalia's balcony again, scared shitless and me for one hyperventilating. Dalia pulled the door closed a little more so don Danilo wouldn't hear Pucho gasping and wheezing, since he was asthmatic. Then she just went right on serving dinner, like nothing had happened. I tell you, that woman had ice water for blood.

In a couple of minutes, don Danilo comes back. Without his cigarettes. "Funny," he says, "I'm sure I left 'em on the night stand, but I couldn't find 'em." I gave Vitín a dirty look, but he looked back at me like Who? Me? and Pucho gets a fit of laughing, so we had to stuff his mouth with a snotty Kleenex so he wouldn't give us away.

They ate for about half an hour. You could hear the clinking of the silverware and the glasses and stuff. The smell of that *asopao de camarones* about drove us crazy, since in the excitement to do the Rambo thing we'd forgotten to eat all day. Finally, that part of the torture was over and they went to sit in the living room. All that ice clinking all the time in don Danilo's glass was driving me up the wall. My nerves had just about had it with all this cloak and dagger shit – and my stomach and lower intestines were worse.

Then suddenly things took a turn nobody had bargained for. To give you a rough idea of why what happened happened, just listen to this conversation:

"Dalia, have you ever posed in the nude for an artist?"

"Oh no, don Danilo, I'm too shy ... "

"Well, I'd love to do a statue of you. Your body is so sculptural, you know ... "

"Are you serious?"

"Of course I'm serious ... If you wanted to, we could do some photos at first, so you could get used to the idea, you know ... "

My arm was covered with bruises from the punches Pucho and Vitín were giving me. But this shit was so unbelievable that I was sort of stunned. I mean I was getting pissed, but at the same time I couldn't believe my own ears, you know? Anyway, he kept on like that trying to brainwash Dalia into taking her clothes off, and me getting madder and madder by the minute. Maybe if things hadn't gone any farther I'd have controlled myself, although I was having to put up with a lot of horseshit not only from Michelangelo in there but from my so-called buddies as well ... This guy kept pushing and pushing and pushing, and he started sort of crossing the line, if you know what I mean, going just a little bit too far with this artist's-model bullshit. He probably thought since she was divorced and all, she lost all her decency, like that chick in the picture. But besides that, I kept remembering, I don't know why, I kept remembering all that lace and ruffles and flowers and stuff in doña Lucrecia's room. And all of a sudden I practically couldn't see straight anymore – my mouth got dry and my heart started going a mile a minute. That was when we heard the sound of a chair sort of scraping across the floor and Dalia saying "No, don Danilo, no, now stop that . . . ," and I realized the filthy bastard was in there probably pawing her, and that was the last straw. I jumped up – still wearing black from head to toe, rubber gloves, and a pair of pantyhose to smush my nose into my face so nobody could recognize me, or maybe so they'd think I was some kind of punk Dracula – and before Vitín and Pucho could stop me I flung that sliding glass door open and ran for that filthy son-of-a-bitch like some rabies-infected cat burglar.

Don Danilo, who was sitting beside Dalia on the couch of my dreams and trying to get somewhere fast with her, just froze when he saw me. But then he reacted pretty good. He raised his arms to defend himself. I grabbed him by that statehooder-blue guayabera he had on, lifted him straight up off the couch, and gave him the roundhouse right of his life – of my life, too. I don't know if it was the hard floor or me, but he was out cold. Pucho ran in and grabbed me when it looked safe to do so. Dalia kept saying Oh my god, oh my god, what a crazy thing to do, oh my god . . . Vitín's face was about a yard long. And inside that pair of pantyhose it looked worse yet.

Dalia ran over to where don Danilo was lying on the floor and checked his pulse. "He's alive," she said, and Pucho finally stopped holding his breath.

"We've got to get him to a hospital," I said, beginning to come out of shock.

"Hospital, fuck," said Vitín, "how you going to explain this, man?"

"But what if he dies on us, man?" says Pucho, and we all freaked out. Dalia, who'd been strangely calm through all this, all of a sudden started giving orders. And thank goodness she did, because that was what kind of snapped us all out of it.

While Dalia opened don Danilo's door with the key we found in his pocket, I watched to make sure nobody was coming down the hall. The four of us carried him in and put him on his bed. The asshole Pucho thought it'd be funny to cross his hands over his chest, but Vitín put a stop to that shit with a well-placed elbow to the ribs.

Then Dalia got real serious and told Vitín and Pucho she was going to call an ambulance, so they had to get out of there. They didn't like that, but they knew she was right. If anybody saw us in that get-up we had on, they'd throw us in jail automatically, man. I told 'em to at least take off the pantyhose and the gloves before they left. As they were leaving, Vitín turns around all of a sudden, sticks out his hand, and as I'm about to slap it what do I find but a pack of Winstons.

"Give it to 'im," he grins, "so he can have himself a smoke when his headache goes away . . . "

When they'd gone I felt, just between you and me, pretty hung out to dry. Dalia was talking on the phone in the living room and don Danilo looked whiter than ever in the light of his bedroom.

"Now take it easy, okay?" she said when she came in, "Because José Manuel is coming over."

This time she didn't have to remind me who he was. The twinge from the knife in my back was reminder enough. Jesus, after all we'd been through, after the mini-brawl I'd gotten into to defend her honor, she goes and calls that asshole. That struck me as just about the most unfair thing I'd ever heard of, double-crossing with a capital DC. But I didn't say anything. I was afraid if I opened my mouth I'd start crying.

Just then, thank goodness, don Danilo starts moaning – "Ooh, aah, oh my god, my head," he says, and we run to roll some ice cubes in a towel to put on it. Dalia threw a bedspread over him.

"What happened?" he says, looking up at Dalia like a hurt baby, and you would've felt sorry for him if you hadn't known better.

"You fell down and hit your head," she said, a little too tenderly for my own taste. He turned his eyes away (when he turned his head, he winced, so he just turned his eyes), looked at me, and smiled stupidly. Between the alcohol, the bump on the head, and his advanced years, he couldn't even remember what day it was.

The doorbell rang and Dalia went to the door. In a couple of seconds the ex-husband comes into the bed-room carrying that same yuppie-asshole soft-sided brief-case he was carrying the day of our fatal encounter, but this time in a checked shirt à la thirty-something instead of the guayabera. If looks could kill.

"Who's the wounded man?" he asked, I hope uncon-scious of the double entendre. It wasn't until he opened the bag that I began to see the light. When he took out the stethoscope, I looked at Dalia, whose eyes were boring a hole through my head, and breathed deep, like it was me whose lungs were getting checked out.

What was wrong with don Danilo came down to a big knot on his head and an overdose of whisky. "Let 'im sleep," the world-famous diagnostician says, "and give him a look now and then. Aspirin every four hours for that headache." And call him in the morning, I thought.

I noticed he signalled to Dalia, and they went into the living room together. What they said, I don't know and couldn't care less. Plus with the asshole don Danilo snoring over there, you couldn't hear a thing.

I went over to the window and stood there and let the lights of the city hypnotize me. Dogged by bad luck, that's what I was. And to top things off, I remembered how few days I had left in Puerto Rico before the gun went off on the university marathon I had ahead of me. Losing my cherry meant a lot less to me now than it had before, I swear to you. But the idea of not seeing Dalia again kind of choked me up. This is goodbye, Dalia, I thought, with a suspicious wetness in my eyes.

When I felt a pair of arms around my waist I jumped like Dalia had when I did the same thing to her. And once more my man-about-town alter ego leaped to my rescue:

"What, did he leave?" I said. Duh.

She smiled, took me by the hand, and tenderly said, "Want to go back to my apartment for a while?"

We went out into the hall with our arms around each other like two newlyweds. And just as she was about to put the key in the lock – I swear on the Bible, the Koran, and the Talmud – the lights went out.

VI

I will not give details of my first night with Dalia.
I'm not that kind of boy. Suffice it to say that it was
great, and that I surprised myself at my inventiveness.
Nor did I feel like some student driver, or that Dalia
was the Driver's Ed teacher. I proved *empirically*, as my
chemistry teacher always said, that that thing about teen-
age guys and mature women was not just so much
mythology . . .

Between the love-making and the nursing in the apartment next door, we never slept a wink. We took turns
changing the icepack and checking don Danilo's pulse
and respiration, just like the doctor ordered. Don Danilo
would open his eyes when we shined the flashlight in
his face, mutter two or three stupid things, probably
from some dream he was having, and turn over and go
back to sleep.

One time while I was tucking the sheet in so he
wouldn't fall out of the bed, I touched something under
the mattress. Look at this, Dalia, I said, turning the flashlight on a very nice collection of dirty pictures of naked
young women. Oh, what Vitín missed, I thought to
myself.

"Jesus," said Dalia, probably thinking That could've
been me . . .

I looked down at that poor old man lying there, and
I thought Shit, do appearances ever lie, and I tucked
the manila envelope back under the mattress where I
found it.

About four in the morning we were so zonked out
that we couldn't take it anymore. Good intentions were
out the door, and we crashed. I'd never slept in a water-

bed before. It's like floating in the middle of the ocean without worrying about the fucking sharks swimming up and nibbling at your toes. And with Dalia as the fabulous mermaid (but without the fish tail, ha ha) swimming sensually beside me . . .

She was out. I had all these little short dreams. Every few minutes I'd wake up and look over to see if it was true. There was a lot of water under the bridge since that first night with the banging and screaming next door. Although if you thought about it, there'd been a little banging tonight, too, ha ha.

The sun came in through the Miami windows and the room was striped with light. Dalia looked excellent lying there with her super-black hair and her dark skin on the white sheets. I must have fallen asleep without realizing it, because when I looked at the clock it was almost nine. She'll be lucky not to get fired, I thought. But I didn't have the heart to wake her up.

I got up without making any noise, although the bed moved like Jell-O, and I went into the kitchen to fix breakfast (which was one of the things I really shined at) and take it in to her in bed. I knew my way around a sunny morning kitchen because my mother stopped cooking breakfast for me when I was five years old – so I'd know how to take care of myself and not depend on somebody else the rest of my life, as she never tired of saying.

I had the stove on and the milk in a pan and was putting coffee in the coffee pot when I heard the water. I checked the sink, but the faucet wasn't on. More noise of water. It sounded closer. Could it be the fucking water-bed that had sprung a leak from all the jumping around on it? Nope. The noise was coming from outside. Then it hit me. Somebody was watering the plants with a hose.

And it was right next door, at don Danilo's apartment. I peeked out the window onto the hallway, expecting to see don Danilo. Wow, I thought, watering the plants with that lump on his head and the hangover he must have . . .

But of course it wasn't don Danilo. Or if it was, the guy was a cross-dresser. Whoever it was watering the plants, they had on one of those housedresses with African designs all over it, and high heels. Like whoever it was had thrown the housedress on over their clothes as soon as they walked in the door. The phantom waterer turned around, gave a couple more swashes, turned off the hose, and came towards Dalia's door. I jumped back, so whoever it was wouldn't see in through the window and catch me in my altogether . . .

The doorbell rang three times, and I didn't dare move. Just about the time whoever it was was practically convinced nobody was at home, Dalia's voice piped up. "*Com*-ing." Still half-asleep and wrapped up in a sheet like some Roman empress in the movies, the Woman of My Life was walking to the door. Hard as I tried to motion her not to answer, she was going to have it her own way.

"Oh, my goodness," says this voice, "I'm sorry to wake you up so early, but I heard you in the kitchen . . . "

Dalia muttered something, Don't worry, I was already up, that sort of thing. And so this lady doesn't worry, she just blasts right ahead – "I just wanted to thank you, sweetheart, for what you did for poor 'Nilo. He told me, bless his heart – what a thing to happen, why you're not safe in your own house anymore . . . "

Frankly, I don't know how Dalia could handle it without at least a half a cup of coffee after the hard night (if you know what I mean, ha ha) we'd had. But she did. I couldn't have handled the interview better myself if I'd studied a week for it. You had to take your hat off to Dalia. Finally this lady leaves, wagging her tail in contentment. Too content, says I to myself, for somebody that finds her husband in bed with a nuclear-war hangover and an ostrich egg growing out the side of his head. . .

The door slammed from the wind coming in off the balcony. Dalia collapsed against the wall and we gave each other the mother of all long looks.

"So does she have a sister or not?" was all I could think of to say.

"Why don't you go ask her," Dalia says, and she turns and plops full-length on the couch, like a bag of potatoes – sweet potatoes.

All of a sudden I heard the volcanic sounds of the milk boiling over on the stove, and I had to run to the rescue. You could hear the news from Radio Reloj machine-gunning next door as clear as if it were in your own kitchen. That was why I dropped the coffee pot – when I heard the news about the naked body of a woman the Dominican maid had found in the closet of a certain hotel at Stop Fifteen.

"What was that?"

Dalia's voice sounded far off, and not attached to the footsteps I heard approaching. And me like some idiot looking for the fucking sponge and not being able to find it, so trying to hold back with my hands that black river slowly running across the kitchen floor . . .

SÉRIE NOIRE

I was only trying to cheat death.

– Cornell Woolrich (William Irish)

I

CRIME WITHOUT A BODY

I take my time. I work noiselessly. I wash the dishes, I scrub the pans, I put the things in the drainer to dry. I sweep the crumbs off the table. I dry the silverware carefully so it won't tarnish. I dry the glasses so they won't spot.

From the hall I listen quietly. The pages are not turning. There is no light under the door. I concentrate. The doorknob turns effortlessly. The fibers of the carpet yield under my bare feet. I wince; I cringe; I resist. If I turn back now, everything will remain as it is. But it is time.

A blind force controls the objects of the room. The bed slides toward the door. The walls lean inward, into the room. The floor rises, lifting me away. I can read the quiet eyelids. The sound of breathing drowns the hammering of my heart. My lover's breast is a sail in the unexpected wind of my rage.

A finger of moonlight tests the thin blade upraised by my vengeful hand. The sheet is in flames, like a shoreline under the foreordained tide of his blood . . .

An icy wind awakes me. The pillow is moving under the lash of my hair. It is he, looking down upon me, it is his upraised hand that is about to fall. His teeth are silvered in the light of the knife that seeks my throat . . .

I scream. He screams. We both awake – our flesh crawling, bathed in sweat, seized with terror. Tired of living, night after night, through this shared nightmare.

II

THIS SIDE THE GRAVE

Still tearful from the funeral, the widow lies back on the couch. Her thighs flutter open like wings in the first second of flight. Her fingers search, search, within the nest, the door within . . .

The Mysterious Stranger approaches. This time he is dressed as a postman. The shadows of the room feed the magic, the sweet anonymity of the couple. And the widow opens herself to the solitary vice, as she inaugurates her new life of celibacy.

"Come 'ere, baby, come and get it. I've got a special delivery for you," he whispers, pulling her toward him, rubbing deliciously against her flank.

Her skirt rises, his zipper falls, and they slide to the floor. He takes her artfully from behind. His mail pouch rubs against her haunch.

And "Give it to me, give it to me, give it to me," she moans, every inch the lady of the house.

And "Here you go, here you go, here you go," he replies, in syncopation.

He forges ahead, then pulls back; back, then forth; thrust, then parry. The unbearable pleasure of it mounts. The widow now pleads with him – "Please, Mr. Postman, GIVE ME THAT LETTER!"

"Kiss me, sweetheart, come here and kiss me and I'll give it to you," he says, his rough words wounding her soft cheek.

She makes herself hold back. But the force of the pleasure at last turns her head. And the price of curiosity is dear. The widow looks, and she sees. Her cry of terror rips her breast.

Brushing away the flies from his lips, the dead man drily remarks:

"I told you you were mine forever. When will you ever learn that when I say something, I mean it?"

III

SAVED

The building is an old, beautiful one, framed by a sky of indigo blue. Such a day doesn't deserve this. The firemen shift position, hold their nets tight. Some people move back a little. Others crowd closer in, and the police have to push them back. Ungodly hot today. I lean back against the wall. Little black spots before my eyes.

The siren's shrill wail cuts through the noise of honking – the traffic jam the police have created with their barricades. A breeze comes up, and it's cooler now. My dizziness passes. A man in a nice suit gets out of a black Volvo – serious-looking, mid-forties. He asks for a loudspeaker and somebody hands him one. Psychiatrist – you can spot 'em a mile away. My name? Sure. My age? No problem. My address? You must be kidding. They try to distract you, the old "just a few details, please, for the record" trick. The shrink pleads with me, orders me, reasons with me. Every time he starts talking again I lean out over the ledge. People scream. The firemen run back and forth with their nets. I'm crawling along the very edge. I nudge off my shoes. The breeze comes up again and blows my hair. Must be pretty from down below. I can feel the fear leaving me.

The police are on the roof now. People pointing at them. I turn my head and I see them, just getting ready to jump down onto the ledge. I crawl along a little, stalling for time, and the firemen down below move along with me.

Then somebody down there yells up at me, but I can't see, my hair is in my eyes. It's a kid, though, I know because his voice breaks – he doesn't really mean any harm, he's just showing off.

"Eeeh, will you just get it over with? – my bus is leaving!"

Just as I get ready to make his day, the cops grab me by the legs. The curtain comes down, the audience applauds. The shrink smugly gives statements to the reporters that got there late. There's probably a bored kid down there walking off kicking a bottle cap.

And here I am again. Ah well, there's always another day.

CONSOLATION
PRIZE

*Si on juge de l'amour par la plupart
de ses effets, il ressemble plus
la haine qu'à l'amitié.*

If one judges love by most of its effects,
it resembles hatred
more than friendship.

– La Rochefoucauld, *Maximes*

This is a true story, historical fact, and not some eye-opener made up to entertain the professional do-nothings sitting around on the benches in the town plaza of some bored-to-death little burg out on the Island. In deference to those that suffered through the events about to be recounted here, the name of the town the events took place in will not be revealed, nor will the true names or occupations (if any) of the sufferers, or any of the other miracles that might identify the saints in question. We will only say that this story took place in the faraway Sixties of this now moribund twentieth century, and that we are relating it upon the authority of a near-eyewitness: doña Yamila, that same well-known doña Yamila who lives in Maunabo and makes the finest, chewiest *dulce de coco* of all the candy-makers on the south coast.

To satisfy the doubters, those men and women that distrust even the Pope and the United States Federal Court, we will quote without cuts or editorial comment the deposition given by the above-mentioned doña Yamila – the text, the whole text, and nothing but the text. And though the events narrated by doña Yamila seem strange, we are assured that in certain parts of the Island this sort of thing happens with alarming regularity. But perhaps that word "alarming" shows our bias: in this age of freedom of information we will present the evidence and allow our readers to judge for themselves . . .

Back then I was living over in Patillas, like I said. I had lost my husband about a year before, so I remember clearly when it was. My husband Cirilo, may God rest his soul, was a good man mostly, in spite of the way he carried on when he came home under the influence, but he left me with five orphans – two from the first wife and three of our own. And so that was when I started making my candy, although of course selling candy didn't bring in enough for breakfast, let alone the rest of our daily bread, so I made up the rest cooking and cleaning wherever I could find work.

But to get back to what happened – the girl you were asking me about wasn't from Patillas. Her papa had moved there from Aguirre to work at the Lafayette Sugar Company, and he'd gotten her a job as a secretary to some bigwig over there. He had some kind of connections, as I recall. She was real light-skinned, real elegant this girl, not pretty but what you might call cute, and she had that backside, and those nice firm ankles that you couldn't get your two hands around, the kind of ankles men like – she came with what you might call good recommendations, you know . . .

The boy, now, the boy *was* from Patillas – his whole family for generations had been from Patillas – and his daddy had a store that brought in plenty, *plenty*. Plus his mother had five or six acres out around El Real. He didn't do a thing – lived off his folks. The old man had tried to put him to work in the store but the kid was kind of wild, he drank a lot and ran around with the girls – you know the type, Mr. Romeo. Sweet Dick, everybody called him in Patillas.

Unfortunately for the girl, they fell in love. He was a

smooth operator – any little excuse, and he'd be bringing her flowers, chocolate candy. Saturday nights he'd be at her house strumming his guitar and singing under her window, and Sundays they'd go for a drive out to Guardarraya and have champagne with their *salmorejo de jueyes*. That's the way, of course. No girl can resist it. But to tell the truth, he'd have swept anybody off their feet – he was good-looking, suave, and as attentive as any girl in her right mind could want. I'll give him that.

Her friends tried to tell her, they warned her about that fairy-tale prince of hers. But she was either stupid or she didn't want to believe it, or she may have thought – the way we all think, of course – that love can change men. Oh, lordy – as the branch is bent, so the tree grows, and you can't make a leopard change his spots, either. Just old proverbs, you may say – but every one of them has its grain of truth. And he was one of those men that thought women are the ones that get married and stay true, not men. He still thought, I swear, that a woman ought to be barefoot, pregnant, and in the kitchen stirring the pot and spraying spray starch on his clean white shirts.

The girl's mother was against it, she said Puerto Rican men made bad husbands, the best thing to do was find herself an American from the sugar plant to marry – not that they were any better in the long run, but at least they were more discreet about it.

Anyway, what happened next was bound to happen – he managed to talk her into it (assuming it was talking he did, if you get my drift), they got married, and they came to live in a house that belonged to her daddy, down on Muñoz Rivera Street, next door practically to where I lived at the time. She was already pregnant, according to some people. Heaven forbid I should ever repeat a thing like that. What I do know is that within a few months she had an abortion – that news I got straight from doña Petrín the midwife, who was famous for being able to solve certain problems of that kind with a clothes hanger and *alcoholado*. And so far as I know, the girl never got pregnant again – heaven knows, all that poking and pushing around in there may've made her sterile.

From the very beginning, what's-his-name was up to his old tricks. Why imagine – they say the day of the wedding he was fondling the bridesmaids right under his mother-in-law's nose.

The first few months weren't so bad, though. He at least kept up the appearances, and whatever he might have been doing, he did it far enough away from home that we didn't hear about it. What you don't know can't hurt you, so they say . . . He would drive that new wife of his to the plant at seven and at five he'd pick her up and they'd come by to pick up the dinner I had waiting for them – because I would cook for them in my house and they'd take it home with them to eat, that was the arrangement we had. On weekends he'd always take her somewhere, and she'd iron her a dress and paint her face like – well, there's just no describing it – and off they'd go. They'd be in that car all lovey-dovey sitting right beside each other – people say that's how you can tell if a couple is getting along. By this time, he'd even found himself a little part-time job as an exterminator. I remember he'd have this big huge contraption slung over his back and be carrying a sack of rat poison. Certain people said that contraption gave him an excuse to be in just about anybody's house any time, and that mostly he serviced the maids, not the houses he went to. But I'm not saying that.

Things started to get what you might call interesting
about two years into the marriage, as I recall, when he
decided to bring his women home to his own house –
to save money on the motel rooms, I imagine, or so as
not to be so uncomfortable back there in the back seat
of that car . . . Women were in and out of that house
like it was a beauty parlor – they were every shape and
color, I tell you, and I ought to know, because many was
the day I'd spend the whole morning out on my porch
ironing – because in the morning with that sun coming
in, the heat in my kitchen would melt the curlers in your
hair . . . The one that came the most was a kind of albino-
looking freckle-faced black woman with her hair hen-
naed a neon red, and she stuck out in front like this and
behind even farther, the woman was something to see,
and she lived out there in a place called the Bottom.
Those two were shameless – he'd drive his wife to work
and then in that very car he'd pick up the other one and
drive her to his house. They'd drive up all cootchy-
cootchy with their arms around each other, then he'd go
in first, open the back door for her (why not the front
door you might well ask) and bam – off to bed. How do
I know? Well, what are windows for? I never saw two
people more brazen – they'd leave the windows half
open, and what you couldn't see you could hear. There
were even times – oh *Virgen Santa*, the way some people
will betray you – that that hussy would come to the
house in a *público*. And she wouldn't get out two or
three blocks away and walk, either, she'd get out of that
público right there in front of the house, she'd tell the
driver to just let her out right here, please sir. And there
he'd be, waiting for her, with his eyes just sparkling and
that horniness of his (excuse my French, but that's

exactly what it was, just pure horniness) coming out all over him.

The neighbors talked, of course. How could they not, if that good-for-nothing sport was in there at batting practice all day every day? Oh, not that there were any saints along Muñoz Rivera – I doubt you'd find a man in the neighborhood that hadn't played around at least once, just to keep in practice, you know. But nobody flaunted it that way – everybody else could be discreet and respectful about it, but not him . . . The women on that street were fuming. It was like they'd all sat down and had a meeting – nobody spoke to him, not so much as a good morning, and if he tried to say good morning to *them* (him being the smooth-talking thing he was), they'd give him the coldest shoulder this side of the North Pole. I bet you're asking yourself why it took so long for the girl to find out. Good question – but you know what they say, the wronged woman's always the last to know. I don't know, being wronged that way must be like being a vampire – you can't see yourself in the mirror. Poor thing, everybody felt sorry for her, but nobody had the nerve – or the heart, maybe it was – to sit her down and tell her what was going on.

But the dirt that doesn't blow in the window sooner or later blows in the door, and every Judas has his Good Friday.

One day she got sick at work. She'd get bad every month when her special friend came for his visit, and there wasn't an aspirin or a hot pad that'd do anything for it. And this particular month her belly was being twisted and ripped so bad that she asked one of the girls that worked with her to drive her home to Patillas. At twelve o'clock on the dot (I know because of the soap opera I was watching at the time) she was opening her front door. She'd seen the car in the carport, so she knew her husband was at home. She'd no more than walked in the door when she hears the bedsprings squeaking and somebody in there moaning and breathing hard enough for even *her* to finally hear it. Pain or no pain, she tiptoes over to the bedroom door, sticks just the end of her nose inside, and comes upon that scene. Her husband had that yellow-skinned redhead on all fours and he was taking her from behind, great god, and the redhead was in heaven, wiggling her backside six ways from Sunday! The things men like these days . . . Thank goodness I was widowed when I was.

I don't know where to start telling you what came next. I'd been holding my breath since I saw the girl drive up, of course, to see whether I ought to call the police or not, so I was an eyewitness when that yellow-skinned tramp came shooting out the front door with a towel wrapped around her. Running down the street like that, the shameless jezebel! And since she was the nearest thing to naked you ever saw without seeing Paris itself, the men started following after her – and she was as cool as a cucumber, couldn't have cared less, I swear to you on the memory of my dead husband. Meanwhile, back at the love nest, you could hear the plates smashing and skillets banging and the flower pots bashing. He'd locked himself up in the bathroom and she was trying to break down the door. Who'd ever have thought that mousy little thing had it in her!

Anyway, quite a while passes, and you couldn't hear anything anymore. I was concerned, you know, nervous as I could be, thinking something awful had happened. Happened to *her*, I mean, because I couldn't have cared less what happened to him . . . I peeked in the window of their bedroom, and I couldn't believe my eyes. I just stood there with my mouth open, I tell you. It was . . . it was something. After all the smashed crockery and screaming and yelling, there the two of them were, up in that bed like two turtledoves, him lying all sprawled out on his stomach, her going over his back for pimples.

The day after that, the porch of that house was literally filled with flowers, big huge arrangements, must have cost him a fortune. When the news got out that things had settled back to normal with them, nobody could believe their ears. From then on, nobody had a good word to say about *her*, either.

No need for me to mention that he went on just like before, except of course that now he was having his fun on the sly, like at the beginning, instead of in broad daylight. She learned to drive, and she bought herself a second-hand car so she could come home anytime she wanted to and check up on him – thinking she could keep him on the straight and narrow that way, poor thing. One day when she was making her rounds, patrolling the neighborhood, you might say, she had the misfortune to catch that henna-haired redhead walking past the house in a pair of jeans that looked like they'd been sewn on her. And there was Mr. Romeo, who just happened to be standing out on the porch, without a shirt on so his muscles would show, watering the plants. That girl got out of the car with smoke coming out of her ears – like the devil herself, I'll tell you – and she grabbed that hose out of her husband's hands and she turns it on that yellow-skinned woman full force. The other woman by this time had turned tail, but she hadn't had time to so much as *think* about running, so she caught the water right up her ass, if you'll pardon my French again, but you couldn't call what that woman had for a backside anything else if you had every word in the dictionary.

Well at that, the husband begins to get a little upset. He hadn't been doing nothing bad, he says, he says it was that woman that had been out of line if anybody had, so then the girl, *bam!* – she turns the hose on *him.* That really made him mad, so he slapped her, and she slapped him, and there they went. I was about to call doña Nelida and tell her to call her brother, who's a policeman at the police station down the street there, so we could restore some order to that house, but before I could get to the phone the girl threw down the hose and shot out to the car and took off.

She didn't come back till that night. Doña Nelida, who was over at my house at the time, said she figured she had come back for her suitcase. I agreed, said she'd probably be going to her mother's, which is what they recommend in situations like that – we both thought the case would be closed right then and there. But anyway, we went out to sit on the porch so as not to miss the last installment. A little bit later, the two of them come out together, holding hands and smiling and just as natural as can be. Hi, they say. Us speechless, as you can well imagine. You won't believe where they were going. To the movies! Zampayo and doña Berta saw them there, buying popcorn.

There's a lot more to this story. I'm just telling more or less the high spots, you know – if you've got any questions, I'd be happy to fill out the details for you ... You just ask. So anyway, things did not end there, the way we'd all expected. There were fights like you never saw before. He'd leave the house nights to go out tomcatting around, come in at daybreak stewed as a hen. She sat for it the first couple of times, but the third time she went out looking for him, went to every bar in Patillas, and that's saying a lot. When she found him – he was coming out of The Bar None, which is a two-bit hooker bar – she practically runs him over with that car. Neither one of them had any use for the other by this time. He was never at home, hardly ever set foot inside the house, and she never did anything but wait for him to come home or go out trying to find him. That was no life for a young woman, in my opinion. The situation was stretched tighter than that redhead's jeans, and something was bound to give. In the end, it was her. And you be the judge of whether she was right or not.

One night, it must have been about ten o'clock because my last TV show was over and the news was coming on, guess who shows up? The yellow-skinned she devil, that henna-haired redhead who's been one of the stars of this real-life soap opera that's been going on next door to me now for what? two or three years? Anyway, there she is, big as life. Swinging that backside in those tight blue-jeans and her tits bouncing like two twins on a trampoline. And before anybody knew what was happening, she was standing there in the middle of the street yelling *I'm pregnant! I'm pregnant! Can you hear me, you son-of-a-bitch? You knocked me up!* This is it, thinks I, and I grab the rosary that's hanging around my neck and get inside as quick as I can, just in case there's shooting. Inside the other house, not a peep, and that crazy woman standing out there in the middle of the street yelling *I'm pregnant! I'm pregnant!*

Finally the door opens over there and the girl comes out real calmly. All of a sudden the redhead shuts her mouth, but her eyes open like two washtubs. "Go home," the girl says to her, real politely. And when the redhead didn't move, she says it again. "Go home," she says. "Go on home. He's not here." I'd have sworn they were going to scratch each other's eyes out, but thank God and the Virgin nothing happened. The girl goes back in the house, the redhead goes on back home, and everybody lived happily ever after.

Just kidding. But the truth is, he wasn't there. About two o'clock in the morning he comes home weaving back and forth and singing boleros. I watched him from my bedroom window. He couldn't even get the key in the lock. The girl didn't make the slightest fuss, didn't even turn on the light. She let him stumble over every piece of furniture in that house. Poor thing's finally given up, I say to myself, she's broken, she's accepted the cross she's given to bear. And with that, I put my asafetida bag around my neck and I went to bed.

Santa Barbara, how wrong a woman can be! In the darkness of that bedroom, the girl was weaving her web. She didn't move a muscle. She just pretended she was asleep while he tried to crawl into bed without waking her up. What happened then only she and God know, because the window was closed, but you could have heard the screaming all the way to Arroyo.

That was what woke me up – the screaming. It was like an animal that knows its time has come. Everybody up and down the street jumped out of bed, and every one of us, in pajamas and pulling on pants and all, every one of us ran out to see what was happening. We banged on the door, but they didn't open it. Lights did go on inside the house, but nobody opened the door. Zampayo and doña Nelida's brother, who were big men – fat as pigs, actually, the both of them – they pushed and shoved on that door, but they couldn't open it.

In a little while the police came. The two policemen shot the doorknob off and stormed in the house, and us right behind them. You could hear these moans coming from the bedroom. We should have stayed outside, I tell you. The bed was soaked with blood. Even the pillows were sopping wet, and red red red. There are things a person ought never to have to see.

Doña Yamila's deposition ends there. The epilogue to the story comes from another source, a person equally trustworthy in spite of (or perhaps because of) her incarceration in the Vega Alta Women's Prison, for the deponent is the cell-mate of the perpetrator of the crime. I will leave the *dénouement* of this story in this source's own irreverent yet sincere words:

Was it her? Of course it was her -- who else could it be? They were the only two people in the bedroom, for god's sake. They couldn't arrest her then and there because by the time the cops got to the house she'd snuck out the kitchen door and made a run for the car, which she'd parked on the street behind the house after that lowlife whore came around yelling that she'd gotten knocked up. Anyway, when she got to the car she headed for the Bottom, where that other woman lived. She was carrying the box on the seat there, like a birthday present all wrapped up with a pretty bow and everything. She went straight there. She'd known the address for a long time, 'cause she'd been planning to find somebody and give 'im a contract to slap some sense into that fucking whore. Anyway, she came to the house, and she leaves that pretty package, with a gift card and everything, just like your birthday, you know?, right in front of the door, where the bitch would have to find it when she came out. Then she gets back in the car, no rush, real quiet-like, and she drives over to turn herself in at the police station in Patillas.

Can you picture the face on that bitch when she takes off that bow, tears off the wrapping paper, and opens that box? I tell you, it's a pity the stupid whore didn't know how to read, so she could have gotten the full fucking enjoyment out of that present.

Readers will doubtlessly want to know the message on that card. The sender has understandably not revealed it, and in solidarity with her secret, her cell-mate has also refused to speak. But the good gossips of Patillas say that the redhead did in fact know how to read, and did not have her rival's discretion. There are those who question the reliability of what she said, since she said it during the attack of hysteria that wound up getting her sent to the psychiatric ward at Centro Médico – but the option of faith is always open to us, is it not? According to the recipient of the message, the block letters, written in suspiciously red ink, read as follows:

CONGRATULATIONS. YOU WON THEM.

EYE-OPENERS

And for to make you the more merry,
I myself will gladly ride with you.

– Geoffrey Chaucer, *Canterbury Tales*

An explosion of red clouds lighted the sky and the shadows of yagrumo trees lay in long slanting lines across the Guavate Forest when our driver made the disturbing confession that he could barely keep his eyes open. "Talk, ask riddles, tell jokes," he entreated, rubbing the merry eyes that looked at each of us in turn in the rearview mirror. The radio, that last resort of drivers lulled in the arms of Morpheus, was broken. It was life or death: we either gave him his dose of Eye-Opener Tonic or the *público* would take a short-cut to eternity.

There was a brief silence that seemed to drag on for-ever while one of us could screw up our courage to break the ice. Fortunately, the passenger from Maunabo, loose-tongued even under less demanding circum-stances, moistened his lips and took the plunge:

"In the town where I live, out near the lighthouse, down by Cape Malapascua, there once lived a man that had thirty-seven children, all of them by different mothers. I don't know what that man had between his legs, but whatever it was, apparently the Virgin Mother herself couldn't have resisted it."

The narrator paused, to await his audience's reaction. You could have cut the silence with a knife, and the faces looked as though they'd been cast in cement. I turned my head toward the window to hide my sinful

grin. When the driver gave a good hearty laugh to celebrate the minor sacrilege, the storyteller plucked up his
courage and continued on:

"Yessir. *BIG* family this guy had himself. And a good
husband and father he was, too. So nobody would get
their feelings hurt, he took turns sleeping one night in
each different house."

The driver snickered again, but this time he had company – a retired schoolteacher type in a dark suit coat.

"But the best part was that this man's wives were all
just as happy as could be with this arrangement, and it
was them that worked out the calendar for where this
man would sleep each night. Why, if one of them had
to run some errand or something, one of the other ones
would take care of the children for her. You'd've thought
they were Mormons!"

The driver's hilarity was irresistible. The other passengers laughed just to hear the driver's asthmatic
wheezes. I must confess that I personally didn't think
that last part was so funny.

"Things were going just fine for this fellow. He worked
hard farming and such, and he'd do part-time jobs in
town whenever he got a chance to, and with the help of
God and that flock of wives of his and his Uncle Sam's
food stamp program, he pretty much kept food on the
tables and clothes on the backs of everybody in those
thirty-seven houses."

A charismatic lady wearing a white habit tied at the
waist by a rope with red balls on the end couldn't contain
her indignation.

"Very nice! He didn't have to change the dirty diapers
or peel the plantains for the *tostones* . . ."

"Now don't get yourself all worked up there, ma'am,"
the Maunabo man said gently. "You'll see what hap-

pened to this gentleman in a minute. Good things don't last, and when they do . . . well, as the old saying goes, It's a mighty good wind that blows nobody ill. As I was saying: Like any good citizen, this man filled out his income-tax form every year and paid his taxes. And every year the list of dependents this fellow claimed on his tax form got longer and longer. At first, the income-tax people let it slide, but when things in the government started getting bad economically speaking – or started getting worse, rather – one of the inspectors they've got there, a real little hornet of a fellow that had ambitions to rise in the government as a reward for the way he squeezed the good honest hardworking folks out of their hard-earned money, this little inspector-fellow sent this man a letter. 'You must present,' read the letter, or words to that effect, 'a birth certificate or evidence of baptism and social security number for each dependent claimed.' What a problem, ladies and gentlemen, because neither he nor his wives had ever bothered to register those children – not in town at the Registry Office and not at the church. And can you imagine what that man would've had to go through at this stage of the game to get that flock of thirty-seven Christian children all registered at once – and with two weeks to go before April 15 at midnight, when that income-tax form has to be postmarked or else? I'll tell you, if it was me, I'd take out a loan even if I had to be in debt up to my ears for the rest of my life before I'd voluntarily get myself into such a mess of red tape as that . . . "

"So what did he do?" the kid with the Walkman asked. When he'd seen everybody laughing he'd taken off his earphones, and now he was hooked on reality.

"A lawyer-friend of his told him to obey the law, that was the best thing he could do, but this fellow had neither the time nor the patience for that route. Several nights he lay in his bed cogitating, and then all of a sudden the light dawned. The next day he went over to this car dealer's place in Maunabo – the dealer it seems owed him a favor – and he reserved himself three vans – those big ones they're using these days to ferry kids to school in, with the doors that slide on the outside? He reserved himself three of those vans and he found himself two out-of-work *público* drivers, and him driving one van and these two other guys driving the others, they went from house to house picking up children of all sizes and colors. There were kids in those vans from little tykes two years old to big husky eighteen-year-olds. The kids, imagine, they had themselves a ball. They rode along singing songs and yelling dirty words out the windows at people along the highway. The other two drivers drove through the mountains like a bat out of hell – they couldn't wait to get rid of those holy terrors they had for passengers. But this fellow I'm telling you about just drove along like he was out for a Sunday drive in the country, smiling to himself and humming.

"When they came in sight of that big new Treasury Building, there at the entrance to Old San Juan, this fellow motioned the vans over to the side of the road, got out, and went from van to van with their instructions: 'When we get there, I want you children to get out of the vans with me, and then I want you to get up those stairs you're going to see inside there, and I want you to make all the racket you can . . . I want you to make the biggest fuss these people ever saw, and if anybody says a word to you about hushing or behaving yourselves, you tell them to talk to your daddy – I'll be right there with you. Everybody understand?' Did they understand? Is the pope Catholic? Those poor people in the Treasury Department didn't know what hit 'em. When that flock of kids erupted through the front door of the building, it was a wonder the roof didn't cave in. You'd have thought it was an earthquake. And their daddy behind them, just smiling to himself."

The driver's belly was rising and falling, brushing the steering wheel with every new gale of hilarity. We passengers couldn't wait to hear what. . .

"Yessir, ladies and gentlemen – this man walks up to that little inspector-fellow's desk as calm as you please, and that gang of young heathens right behind him. Those kids were into everything, opening and closing drawers, poking around in the wastebaskets, picking up telephones, sharpening pencils, everything they could think of, and you could hear the noise all the way to the Plaza Colón.

"So anyway, the man says to that inspector, as meek as can be, 'Here are those thirty-seven dependents you were asking me about, mister. If you want to get a piece of paper we can write their names down for you . . . '

"The little inspector-fellow looked at him a minute. He didn't know what to say. And those children still opening and closing drawers and stapling papers together and playing tag around the desks in the office . . . Finally the inspector stands up, straightens his tie a little, and goes off to find his supervisor, to see if he couldn't get him out of this fix. And those kids running after him, jumping around and doing cartwheels and pinching him on the rear. The supervisor comes out about then, and he goes berserk – within ten minutes he'd lost his voice from yelling at those infidels to keep quiet and settle down, and finally he threatened to call security if this fellow didn't get out of there that minute, himself and his thirty-seven wild animals. No sooner said than done, don't you know. Still yelling and jumping around and screaming like a pack of banshees, they were down those stairs and out of the building.

"As a reward for how well his kids had behaved themselves, this fellow took 'em all to McDonald's in Puerta de Tierra before he trucked 'em back to Maunabo. That was ten years ago. And this fellow is still making out his list of dependents every March, and to this day the Treasury Department hasn't even *thought* about bothering him again. As the saying goes, 'You want to be real careful what you ask for, because you might get it.' "

There was applause from the driver and the retired schoolteacher. The storyteller from Maunabo smiled contentedly, and said now it was somebody else's turn.

Surprisingly, it was the kid with the Walkman that stepped in next.

"In Arroyo, where my grandmother lives, there's been all these fires. There's been businesses, cane fields, houses burned to the ground, and there's even been some women that've poured gasoline all over themselves and set themselves afire. My grandmother says it's the curse of this sailor that got sick on a boat one time, he got sick with something real contagious, I don't remember exactly what she said it was, and the crew put him off in a little boat and set him on fire."

"When he died?" the Maunabo man, a little confused by this last part, asked.

"That's the point, dude, they *torched him*, get it? They. Burned. Him. Alive." The kid pronounced each word separately and very, very carefully, as though he were talking to a lip-reader. He was a little upset that nobody had gotten the point of the story.

The brevity of the story was a disappointment to the

driver; again he threatened to fall asleep if we couldn't do better than that. The charismatic lady took up the challenge next.

"I'm from Arroyo too, and it's a fact – you'd think fire had something against my poor hometown. This story I'm about to tell happened quite some time ago. I'm not going to mention any names, in case some of you know the people – down in Arroyo, everybody is related to everybody else, or about to be.

"What happened was that sometime around the turn of the century a widow lady from the Canary Islands came to Arroyo to live. This woman had a grown son and a lot of money. Pretty soon what was bound to happen happened, and this son fell in love. He fell in love with a nice girl from there that he'd met in town, and he decided he wanted to get married. Only problem was, the girl's skin was a little darker than his. Well the mother wouldn't hear of it, and not only because of the girl's color – truth was, no girl was going to be good enough for her boy. And in order to keep 'em from having that wedding she even got sick and everything. But the son stood his ground, and since he was of legal age there wasn't much the mother could do about it. Finally one day he gets tired of waiting for his mother to change her mind, and he grabs that dark-skinned girl and they go talk to the priest and the next day she had a wedding ring on her finger. They went off to live in a little house he'd rented right there in town. Now this young man was a good son, and he would visit his mother every week, regular as rain. She'd open the door to him, but she wouldn't let her daughter-in-law so much as set foot on her porch. She wouldn't give that girl the time of day.

"Well, as time went on, the son and his new wife

discovered that with the blessing of God they were going to have a baby. It was born as white as the father, but even so, the grandmother refused to even look at it.

"Then about a year after the baby was born, strange things started happening in the son and daughter-in-law's house – keys would disappear, the water would turn itself on and off, smoke would come up out of the toilet . . . One night a pack of big black dogs got into the yard and barked all night. Things were getting ugly. So finally the girl sent for the priest. The priest said two or three *dominus vobiscums* in the living room, the bathroom, and each bedroom and sprinkled holy water all through the house. But that same night those black dogs were back again, and the bed shook, and all the shutters in the front room opened and closed all by themselves."

The narrator had lowered her voice, which accentuated the sinister atmosphere of her story. All of us, including the driver, were leaning toward her, not wanting to miss a word of the tale. Night had fallen now, and the air on the highway through the forest was cool. I surreptitiously rolled up the window beside me, in case some venturesome spirit should take a mind to join us.

"The girl then sent for her aunt, who had the understanding. And that black *espiritista* no more than walked through the front door into the living room when the light fixture came crashing down from the ceiling and landed practically on top of her. '*Ay Santa Marta!*' she says, looking around warily, 'the evil work is in this house,' and she starts trying to find it. She looked high and low – she practically turned that house upside down hunting for the thing that was causing all this trouble. But she looked and she looked and she still couldn't find the lock of hair or whatever it was anywhere. So she took up one of those spirits that's loose just about anywhere and she took it up and it began to speak out of her mouth. 'Your mother-in-law has done this,' the spirit says to the girl, 'she's the one that's doing this to you, and until you find the thing that's doing it, the spirits she's set on you will never leave you in peace.'"

"What they ought to have done is send a couple of guys over to that mother-in-law's house to teach her not to meddle in other folks' business," pronounced the driver, though he had his fingers crossed, just in case.

"Or put a spell on her that was bigger than the one she put on *them*," said the retired schoolteacher type, who not for nothing was from Guayama, which anyone will tell you is the witching capital of Puerto Rico.

"Anyway, that night, when the widow's son found out about all this, naturally he refused to believe it. How could such a thing be? His mother, such an upright, Catholic woman . . . But his wife was convinced, and she refused to sleep another night in that house until the spell had been found and undone. She stood her ground, too, so finally her husband promised her that the next day he'd find them another place to live. Meanwhile, they went to bed, scared to death, and it took them hours to ever get to sleep. Along about morning, they suddenly woke up to the smell of something burning. The smell was strong, too. He ran to find out where the fire was, and she had her housedress about halfway pulled on, when they heard the baby crying. So the girl, dressed in nothing but her nightgown, ran into the child's room. And there – *ay Virgen del Carmen*, it gives me goosebumps just to think about it – she found her baby on fire, like some human torch lying there under the mosquito net."

Thank goodness we'd gotten onto the expressway by now, so the lights of the cars helped not only light the way but dispel our fears a bit as well.

"What happened to the widow? Did they get her for it?" the driver demanded, unconsciously taking out his vengeance on the accelerator.

"What happened to somebody didn't happen to the widow, it happened to the poor daughter-in-law. The widow accused her of murdering the child, and since the old lady had money and lots of connections, she fixed things so her daughter-in-law was carried off to San Juan and locked up in the lunatic asylum."

The retired schoolteacher then asked the question we had all been silently asking:

"And what about the husband? Didn't he do anything?"

"Yes, of course he did," she said, with a gesture of disgust. "He went back to the Canary Islands with his mother . . . just so you'll see how false and cowardly some men are."

The moral of the story aroused protests from some quarters – the four representatives of the male sex, who were in the majority in the car. The retired schoolteacher was determined to save the honor of his sex, and no better way could he find than to take up the challenge with a further tale:

"In a town on the south coast whose name I do not wish to remember, there was a businessman with a great big elegant house sitting beside his store, which was right near a fire station. His wife was elegant, also – a tall, white-skinned foreign lady with blue eyes. She was very lovely, but she was a little, you know . . . "

The charismatic lady pursed her lips in preparation

for the expected offense to her modesty; the driver, as was his wont, noisily greeted the possibility.

" . . . too hot to handle . . . One man was not enough for her, shall we say. Or two. Or three. Or four. Her poor husband had horns growing every which way out of his head – he looked like one of Santa Claus's reindeer. Of course, he didn't even realize he was being . . . *cuckolded*, I believe, is the polite name for it, since he was a little . . . you know . . . slow on the uptake himself."

The driver now was choking with laughter, the Maunabo gentleman joined in, and the lady from Arroyo opened her eyes and took a deep breath. The kid with the Walkman winked at me enigmatically; I had no idea how to take that.

"The wife's taste leaned to firemen, of all things. And since she had them right there at hand, you see, why every night she'd give her husband a cup of linden tea sugared with two or three sleeping pills, and while he lay there snoring she'd spend the night putting out fires."

"Good god!" the charismatic lady muttered softly, and looking for moral reinforcements she cast her irate eye on me. I didn't know whether to look serious or just get it over with and laugh out loud, so I sat there with a sort of half-smile on my face, looking wholly idiotic.

"The husband's friends found out what was going on, of course, and they alerted the guy so he could take patriotic action. The fellow thought about it a good long time, because it was hard for him to believe that his beloved wife was cheating on him with half a battalion of firefighters. One night he decided to just *pretend* he was drinking the linden tea his wife always fixed him, and so he just lay there awake studying the ceiling for a long time, *pretending* he was asleep. Pretty soon he heard sounds in the room next door, so he got up, sneaked out the back door, went around the house, and crossed the street and found himself a lookout behind a tree. What he saw was a whole parade of firemen in and out of his house, so finally he woke up to what had been going on all this time. But he controlled himself – he waited for the last one to come out before he did anything. Then he crossed the street and went back in the house."

In spite of the narrator's perverse sense of storytelling, the story had us all by the throat. Even the charismatic lady was holding her fire so that we could come more quickly to the ending.

"Those who were there say that husband was like a madman. They say his face was purple with rage. He threw open that door, stalked into the bedroom, grabbed his wife by the hair, dragged her out onto the porch, and threw her out in the street as naked as the day she was born."

Now nobody was laughing. The abruptness of the finale had taken our breath away.

"So you see, missus," said the narrator without missing a beat, "we men may be false, but women can be a whole lot falser yet."

"Those that are, are," intoned the man from Maunabo in a conciliatory tone of voice, "but most women are truer than we men, you know, my friend, as my mother is, and I imagine your own."

The sentimental evocation of our mothers calmed tempers a bit. The latest storyteller, in fact, was rendered so tender-hearted that he did not even realize that his mother's purity had been called, ever so delicately, into question.

"There's more to the story than that," said the charismatic lady suddenly, and we all turned to look at her.

"You haven't told but one side of it. You've made that poor woman sound like the villain."

The man from Guayama opened his eyes wide and shrugged his shoulders in a guise of total innocence. But the lady in the habit was adamant. She looked him straight in the eye and crossed her arms censoriously.

"Then *you* tell the story, you tell it," urged the driver, his tired eyes taking on new light. The lady considered the invitation, hesitated a few seconds, and then without further ado launched herself into the tale, her fingers fiddling with the rope-ends at her waist, her eye set on the window.

"What happened was that this businessman we were talking about was no saint himself. His idea of fun was to take the ignorant young girls from the countryside around there and carry them to a house of ill repute there used to be in town and have his way with them."

The phrase made the kid with the Walkman smile. But he contritely lowered his eyes when my gaze met his.

"That place was famous for the parties they used to have there – the most degenerate men along the whole southern coast with their mistresses and whores and scarlet women. Orgies was what they had there, orgies that'd put the Roman emperors to shame."

"Well, now . . . " murmured the schoolteacher, who was beginning to be distressed by the turn the story was taking. The charismatic lady, though, was not so quick to relinquish the floor.

"The wife, of course," she forged on, "knew nothing about any of those shenanigans. The whole world knew what was going on, but since her husband kept her all shut up in that great big house of theirs all the time, with no family and no friends, there was no way for her to hear anything about it. So about that time a pretty young girl comes to work in the house. This husband of hers had sent the girl supposedly to help out. The girl was polite and obedient, a real nice girl, and the wife was delighted.

"One day, as she was cleaning, this young maid stuck her hand back behind a bookcase in the room the husband used for an office. And what did she put her hand on, behind a false wall, but a whole stack of books all wrapped up and tied with a cord. Since the poor girl didn't know how to read, she didn't realize she'd come across a collection of dirty books – every one of them, every single one, on that Index, that list the Catholic Church keeps of forbidden books. But she did know how to look at pictures, and since the books had gotten her curiosity up, she started thumbing through one particular big thick album that she found sticking out between two smaller books. Imagine the look on that poor innocent young girl's face when she sees what's in it – all these photographs of the husband and his filthy friends doing terrible things with little girls twelve and thirteen years old, and with negro women and even with animals, oh my God . . . "

"Those orgies must have been something," said the driver, fascinated, and nobody dared to laugh.

"She didn't want to get into trouble, so she kept her mouth shut about what she'd found. *To each his own, I guess*, she thought. But God works in mysterious ways, and what happened was that this businessman we were talking about, he'd had his eye on this girl he'd brought in to help his wife around the house, and around this time he begins to fondle her a little bit every time she'd get within reach. At first she tried to brush his hand away, like this, you know, not too much fuss about it, but the man kept on and kept on, and he'd watch and try to corner the girl whenever he could. The night he tried to get into her room, she drew the line. She packed up her things and the next morning she went in to say goodbye to the wife. But the truth was, she liked the wife, the wife had been real good to her, so when she opened her mouth to tell her she was leaving, she broke out crying like a nine-year-old child. The wife didn't know what to think, of course, so she started asking questions. And she kept asking questions until finally the girl told her the truth. The woman didn't want to believe her, of course, but the girl took her by the hand and led her into the husband's office and showed her the false wall and the album of dirty pictures and everything."

After the requisite pause to let her words take effect, the charismatic lady couldn't resist hammering in one last nail:

"So you see," she said, smiling, "how the story changes depending on who's telling it."

The man from Guayama, though, was not altogether abashed.

"I hope you'll forgive the question," he said, in a tone entirely too polite for the moment, "but where exactly did you get that version of the story?"

Surprisingly, it was the driver that came to the lady's aid.

"From the same place you got yours, and did anybody ask *you* how you came by it?" And he broke the tension with one of his inimitable bursts of laughter.

A comfortable silence fell over us. The driver, as he shepherded us along the Caguas highway, looked bright-eyed and awake now. We'd soon come to the exit for Río Piedras. I knew that by all rights my turn had come, but fortunately the trip was almost over. Then just as I try to corner the girl whenever he could. The night he tried to get into her room, she drew the line. She packed up her things and the next morning she went in to say goodbye to the wife. But the truth was, she liked the wife, the wife had been real good to her, so when she opened her mouth to tell her she was leaving, she broke out crying like a nine-year-old child. The wife didn't know what to think, of course, so she started asking questions. And she kept asking questions until finally the girl told her the truth. The woman didn't want to believe her, of course, but the girl took her by the hand and led her into the husband's office and showed her the false wall and the album of dirty pictures and everything."

After the requisite pause to let her words take effect, the charismatic lady couldn't resist hammering in one last nail:

"So you see," she said, smiling, "how the story changes depending on who's telling it."

The man from Guayama, though, was not altogether abashed.

"I hope you'll forgive the question," he said, in a tone entirely too polite for the moment, "but where exactly did you get that version of the story?"

Surprisingly, it was the driver that came to the lady's aid.

"From the same place you got yours, and did anybody ask *you* how you came by it?" And he broke the tension with one of his inimitable bursts of laughter.

A comfortable silence fell over us. The driver, as he shepherded us along the Caguas highway, looked bright-eyed and awake now. We'd soon come to the exit for Río Piedras. I knew that by all rights my turn had come, but fortunately the trip was almost over. Then just as I

"Goodness gracious," he said, "that's just a trick of mine to get to hear people tell stories . . . "

I walked down Georgetti toward my apartment, and I hadn't got far before I had the eerie sense that someone was following me. Given the all-too-real possibility of a mugging to welcome me to the metropolitan area, I turned around, only to discover that it was the kid with the Walkman. I thanked him for coming to my rescue in the *público* and we walked on together toward Ponce de León. He told me he went to the university days and sold ice cream nights in Los Chinitos.

"Come in sometime and have an ice-cream courtesy of the management," he said, this time with a less ambiguous wink. And then, just as we were about to part –

"Hey, listen, what do you do? Do you work here, or what?"

I just smiled, coyly waved goodbye, and kept walking. I didn't want to break the magic of the moment. My head was full of words, and I could hardly wait to sit down at my typewriter and roll in that first piece of paper.

MISS FLORENCE'S
TRUNK

Slavery per se is not a sin. It is a social
condition ordained from the beginning
of time for the wisest purposes,
benevolent and disciplinary, by Divine
Wisdom.

– Samuel F. B. Morse, *Letters and
Journals*,
published by his son E.L. Morse in 1914.

Folks here pity my loneliness,
but I continue to exist.

– Susan Walker Morse, letter to Mary
Peters Overman,
Arroyo, Puerto Rico, February 28, 1848.

I

On the morning of December 8 1885, Miss Florence Jane (of the honest English Janes) went to her door, took up the *New York Times* that had arrived just moments before, and carried it into her small parlor. Idly she stood and scanned the news, but then, with a searing cry of pain, she flung the newspaper from her, as though it were a white-hot coal. Yet still, from the burgundy-velvet sofa where the journal lay, there continued to burn into her eyes (more accustomed to the softer lights and shadows of the novel) the fiery letters of a headline:

MYSTERIOUS DISAPPEARANCE AT SEA

Though laconic, the words were devastating, for the person who had disappeared, the person whose name the article revealed, had once been Miss Florence's dear benefactress, friend, and employer. It took Miss Florence several minutes to feel strong enough once again to trust her legs, and to go from the room in search of the smelling salts and lemon-balm water.

That night, in spite of the linden tea she sipped in extraordinary amounts, sleep would not come. The fragile, graceful figure of the woman who had once been her benefactress roamed, in a long white wispy robe, the somber hallways of her memory. Toward daybreak, exhausted from her long prayers for the repose of that soul which haunted her nightlong vigil, Miss Florence at last fled the warm refuge of her sheets.

Almost without realizing what she was about, she found herself kneeling on the floor, her back bent low and her head at a precarious angle. A quick glance sufficed to confirm that indeed the thing she looked to find was still beneath the bed, dark, somber and solid. No matter how hard she tried, though, she could not remember what drawer, chest, or nook it was to which she had entrusted the small key to the old lock, the one fragile protector of the trunk's inviolate privacy. Very much to her regret – and even more to that of the sleeping neighbors on the floor below – she determined to force the catch, her accomplice an old rusty hammer.

The smell of things locked away – moth balls and lavender sachets – made her draw her head back, and for a time she fought the compelling urge to sneeze. With a linen handkerchief held to her blushing nose, at last she nerved herself to disturb, for the first time in almost twenty years, the hermetic peace of those *souvenirs*, neatly organized by dates and places.

It did not take her long to find, in the sturdy black box with its lining of red taffeta, the volume whose cover of leather-grained cardboard bore a line of large gold letters:

JOURNAL: PUERTO RICO 1856–59

The yellowed pages clung to each other; they resisted the fingers that clumsily tried to turn them. Miss Florence's eyes nervously skipped about the pages, and as they alighted upon random words here and there, hushed sensations were awakened in her breast. There were moments when some ravelled piece of the past would play the tyrant to her attention, and upon that scrap her eyes would linger as though deciphering the enigmatic handwriting of a foreign manuscript.

LA ENRIQUETA

I am here at last, after a horrendous – nay, hellish – voyage. Many times I thought the sea would receive the contents of my mutinous stomach. The captain that brought us from Saint Thomas must have made a pact with the devil to have tamed such waves. Mrs. Lind's letter and my British passport (much respected in these latitudes) saved me the discomforts of the formalities of Customs. A negro coachman in white livery – a curious colonial custom, not without a certain charm – was awaiting me, as I had been told he would be, in front of Mr. Lind's warehouse.

The hacienda lies some three miles from the harbor. We drove to the end of the main street of the village of Arroyo, and then we took a dusty, bumpy road that ran in absolute assurance to the gates of the estate picturesquely named La Enriqueta.

If the dry monotony of my journey had made me many times long for the English countryside, not so the splendid grounds of this palatial country place. I have used the word "hacienda," but I use it as those who live here use it, to refer not so much to a desert-like ranch such as those in the regions of Mexico and the southwestern territories of the United States (as I understand them to be), but rather to a sort of plantation, a veritable small city more like an English manor house and its many outbuildings than anything else of which I have experience. All is luxury and ostentation, though set in the country. There are artistically designed gardens in which a profusion of exotic flowers bloom. Before the grand mansion of wood and masonry, with wide porches all around it, a fragrant fountain sprays rainbows of water over the finely sculpted heads of nymphs and dolphins. Parrots, monkeys, and even serpents are kept in spacious bamboo cages suspended by ropes and vines from the trees, many of which bear exotic fruit that I know not the names of. Towards the western and eastern boundaries of the immediate grounds, two artificial pools, ringed with Greek and Roman statues and sailed upon by proud black swans, multiply the blinding glare of the tireless sun.

Mrs. Lind, who welcomed me with the greatest cordiality imaginable, urged me to call her simply Miss Susan, as all the servants, she said, do. I could not hide the astonishment caused in me by that voluntary abandonment of wedded title and name. Still, in order not to mar that first impression which is so important to the career of any governess, I kept to myself as best I could my reservations.

Miss Susan's husband is away, travelling, as it appears he pretty often is. His simultaneous responsibilities as man of business and owner of a large hacienda almost constantly require his presence on the neighboring islands and in the nearby towns.

The young Charles – who but fleetingly showed himself – has the carriage and the aspect of any young European gentleman. His skin shows no sign whatever of that underlying yellowish sort of tint which so blemishes the appearance of white persons born in this part of the world. Miss Susan told me that they had just returned from the house of her father – the famous Mr. Samuel F. B. Morse – in Poughkeepsie, where they had spent the greatest part of the summer. One must, she added with a hint of sadness, retire to Locust Grove (as Mr. Morse calls his first fixed abode) in order to repair the harm done the lungs and the blood by the rigors of the tropics.

Before we sat down at table, which bore an impressive display of delicate porcelain and silverplate engraved with the ornate family *L*, Miss Susan took me into the kitchen, where I was introduced to the servants one by one. One of them, Bella, a negress of indeterminate age with sweetly canine eyes, was especially recommended to me. "She has been with me since the day I married," the lady of the house told me, embracing her with a certain unwonted – though sincere – affection.

If the meal had one fault, it was its abundance. Too spicy for my sober taste, the native dishes indisposed my stomach a bit, and so I was very glad indeed when Miss Susan asked Bella to go with me to my room. In this small room, then, on the second floor of the main house, its enormous window opening onto a spectacular cloud-filled sunset, I now sit, and perched as I am, I find that I too am mistress of this empire of sugar cane stretching as far as the eye can see toward the dark-blue Caribbean.

MASTER CHARLIE

My charge seems quite a temperamental child. His favorite victim is poor Bella, who shows him more affection than his own mother does. The boy has learned Spanish like a prodigy, but his accent, in no way befitting a member of his class, betrays the African origins of his school. It is in Spanish that he replies, impudently, when I try to catch his attention for some lesson.

I am not the first – though I hope to be the last – to have accepted the challenge of the domestication of this spoiled little wild beast of the Linds. The unfortunates who preceded me (and there have been, according to information that I believe to be trustworthy, no less than six) lasted but a few months, each one, before being replaced. I was warned by good Mrs. Travers of all this when she asked if she might recommend me for the post.

The boy detests history and arithmetic. Only drawing and singing can keep him at the desk, or even inside the room, on a sunny day. With more craft than patience, I have, however, been able to interest him in reading, thanks to two magnificent volumes of Sir Walter Scott that I found in the house. From the most violent antipathy toward literature, he has swung like a weathercock, and now exhibits the most effusive love for it. What would Mrs. Dayton say if she should see me turn from the solid virtues of the classics to the easy success of the moderns? It was, nonetheless, under her own teaching that I learned to value more the ends than the means. And as for my relations with this rebellious angel, I know not what will be worse: suffering his eternal contempt, broken by intermittent outbursts of childish per-

versity, or awakening his interest, with the uninterrupted
questioning that is sure to ensue from that.

Early this afternoon we went on a little walk to Punta
Guilarte. The excursion, out and back, took us a bit more
than an hour. I used this time outdoors with Charles to
test his knowledge of natural history. To my delighted
surprise, my charge, very much of his own accord, and
almost with pride, ticked off the names (in Spanish,
almost always) of many plants and animals that we
passed, names that I myself, of course, did not know. I
will have to look out for some trustworthy source with
the proper translations.

The sea was so still that one might have thought it a
lake. I removed my shoes to test the temperature of the
water, which shone almost white in the afternoon sun.
As my feet sank into the moist sand, a warm sense
of well-being ran up my legs, which had before been
accustomed to the cruel cold of European waters. So
absorbed was I in those comparisons that I almost forgot
to oversee my charge. I got quite a start, even if only
momentary, when I realized that the boy had disappeared, and without a word to me. But then I saw him
leap, as agilely as a little rabbit, from a dense stand of
sea-grapes. I could not help a cry of alarm at the sight
of his totally naked body. I quickly turned my back so
as not to be exposed more to that very primitive natural-
ness with which he reacted to my distaste. And then,
informing me that he had his father's permission to
bathe as God had brought him into the world, he ran
(without bothering to request my own permission) happily off into the waves.

As Charlie's impetuous quickness had caught me off
guard, I patiently waited for him to finish his impromptu
swim. I did avoid, however, looking into his eyes, so as

not to awaken in him, at such an early age, sentiments of a dubious nature. I supposed that he had acquired this and who knew how many other questionable habits in his contact with the African children who have always been his playmates. Small wonder Miss Susan has forbidden him to frequent the negro quarters.

On the way back to the house, a remark from Charlie satisfied my curiosity as to a matter that I would never have had the temerity to broach. He revealed to me very playfully that unlike Mr. Lind, who is, to all indications, quite given to nude bathing, Charlie's mother generally swam in a petticoat, out of fear of the stings of the men-of-war.

MISS SUSAN:
OBVERSE AND REVERSE

Is one to think that it is the long absence of her husband that has sunk my mistress into these depths of melancholy and idleness? While Charlie demands my attention almost twelve hours in the day, my mistress wanders like a discreet ghost about the house, the prey of an endless tedium. The heat and humidity of the afternoons confine her, as though she had been dramatically stripped of every ounce of *force vitale*, to the hypnotic web of the hammock. Almost nothing can persuade her to go out of the house without company, yet she has confided to me that most of her friends bore her. Her thin face grows every day sharper and more lean, and her waist can be encircled with the fingers of one hand.

Bella's attentions are futile, her mistress's lassitude without salvation. Only the sea-baths, along the beaches that mark the southern boundary of the property, soothe her flesh, which is mercilessly devoured by the legions of mosquitoes that breed in the swampy regions of this coastal plain.

Suddenly, though, I discover that she is capable of enthusiasm. The news of the imminent arrival of Mrs. Molly Overman, a visit confirmed only days ago, seems to have had the power to transform her. Suddenly, the house is magically possessed; the grounds are a hive of feverish activity. Miss Susan directs the operations as though we were to be visited by royalty. Now if she is wearied, it is in bringing to the complicated preparations every nuance of elegance, and it is weariness that seems to vivify her. She has had the guest room redone as though for a princess: Louis XV gilt, Queen Anne chairs, damask bedcoverings and pillows. She has spent hours preparing the menu for the welcome dinner, which will be an impressive and delicious *mélange* of American and native dishes. She has had coconuts, mangoes, and passion-fruits brought directly from the trees for elaborate desserts and drinks. An immense bouquet of tropical flowers, whose names – bird of paradise, *flamboyán*, bougainvillea, shower-of-gold – make my sober head spin, will greet the triumphant entry of the New York guest into the house. Mrs. Molly is not just Miss Susan's niece, she is her best friend.

MY SOCIETY DEBUT

Miss Susan and Mrs. Molly are like two girls, with that disconcerting combination of brashness and innocence so characteristic of certain American young ladies. At night I can hear (not without a certain twinge of discomfort) their gales of laughter. At table, it is Mrs. Molly who monopolizes the conversation with her racy stories. Smiling nostalgically, Miss Susan vicariously lives the sweet frivolity of the city life that her Antillean exile has so pitilessly robbed her of.

Yesterday, at the urging of the two ladies, I found myself accompanying them for tea *chez* Mrs. O'Hara, the wife of the British vice-consul. The grand wooden house of the O'Haras, located on Isabel Segunda Street, where many of the well-to-do families of the small town live, has a sober sort of elegance about it. As we approached it, I found it odd that the sight of the Union Jack snapping in the ocean breeze brought me neither pride for my origins nor longing for my old home. The years I have lived away from England have somehow blurred my pleasant memories of Oxfordshire, and I find that I recall only my father's long illness, his slow decay, and, upon the finality of his death, a deep sense of no longer belonging.

Mrs. O., as her friends and family call her, is a stout woman with wavy red hair, a most pleasant hostess eminently skilled at conversation – though to my taste she is a bit over-curious. In a flood of banal questions, there softly floated forth the inevitable inquiry as to my state of matrimony. "I am a free woman," I answered somewhat shortly, "and for the moment have no pressing reason for not continuing to be so."

When I turned my head to put an end to this interview,

I found myself looking into the merry eyes of Miss Susan and Mrs. Molly, who could not altogether hide their surprise at my sharpness but who were mischievous enough to enjoy it. As the maid served tea and cakes, Mrs. O. returned to the subject, offering to present me to the "few acceptable unmarried men in the region" at the next *soirée*. At that, the providential arrival of two ladies (who turned out to be the vice-consul's sisters) prevented my compatriot's indiscretion from making me forget my manners.

I was relieved when we rose to take our leave, I must admit. The visit, which I had found interminable, made clear to me the reasons for my mistress's reluctance to frequent the salons of the foreign *crème de la société*. Other people's lives are the only thing on the menu: the *plat de resistance*.

ENTER MR. LIND

The heat of this time of year (which is paradoxically called "winter" here) is worse than stifling. The oppressiveness of the weather sometimes makes me wish for a hard rain, a storm, a veritable hurricane to come and lash the countryside around. Fortunately, Charlie spends his afternoons swimming or splashing about in the creek with Miss Susan and Mrs. Molly (whom he adores), and that allows me to take refuge in the only cool place I have been able to find: the rear veranda. The roles have been unexpectedly reversed: Miss Susan bustles about while I languish in the hammock.

Tonight during dinner we heard a horse gallop up into the front garden of the hacienda. My mistress rushed euphorically out to the veranda as Bella scurried to set another place at the table. Charlie surprised me by remaining calmly in his chair, a miracle I attributed to his obvious fascination with the effervescent beauty of his cousin. Mrs. Molly went on eating imperturbably. For some reason, a growing nervousness evidenced itself in my hands, and I had to put down my fork in order not to betray the agitation caused in me by the sudden and unexpected arrival of the owner and master of La Enriqueta.

Miss Susan and her husband were a good while coming into the dining room. By a curious effect of the mirrors of the house, however, we could see their silhouettes as they embraced in the semi-darkness of the passage. Mr. Lind's arms passionately encircled his wife. I turned to the boy in order to distract his attention with some silly question, but as I turned back, I saw with some confusion that Mrs. Molly's eyes were brazenly fixed on the scene, the contemplation of which, I should have thought, even the most elementary sense of modesty would have prevented.

In spite of his penetrating green eyes, Edward Lind is not what the world generally calls a handsome man. His nose is too long and his lips too heavy to raise him to the plane of aesthetic harmony, not to mention the fact that when I first laid eyes on him he had not trimmed his beard or shaved for several days. He does, however, possess qualities capable of impressing certain women. His forthright manliness, his playful smile, and his slight foreign accent combine to give him a *je ne sais quoi* that a woman like Miss Susan must surely have found difficult to resist. Descended from a family that has lived for many years in St. Thomas, and of excellent Danish lineage, his conversation is varied and he has a sharp sense of humor, two qualities not a little surprising to find in a man accustomed principally to the society of animals and Africans.

After eating and drinking very well, not to say in abundance, he sent Charlie, who had remained pretty cool to the effusive greetings of his father, off to his room. Neither the pleas nor the heated protests nor, finally, the tears of his son could alter Mr. Lind's firm resolve. Neither of the ladies intervened, much less this woman who is but an employee of the family. The tantrum lasted but a moment, however. One word to the boy from my master (his voice, it is true, raised a bit) was all it took to send the child running from the room.

His good humor recovered, Mr. Lind asked Mrs. Molly to sit at the piano and he delighted us with sailors' ditties (if I can call delight that gay confusion that the frankly *risqué* nature of the numbers aroused in us females). As the laughter and the applause died, I could not help observing that Mr. Lind looked at me fixedly, and that Miss Susan never took her eyes off his face.

It must have been almost ten o'clock (an hour at which I could not but wonder at the untiring energy of a man just returned from a long journey) when Mr. Lind was struck by a sudden idea – he would give his guest a ride on his new horse. He has just bought a lovely *paso fino*, as the breed is known, a small horse with a canter that is, they say, as smooth as a rocking chair's.

"You come, too," he said to me with a boyish smile and sparkling eyes. "There's always room for more than one lady on my horse." I could not even raise my eyes for the confusion caused in me by the suggestive nature of his invitation, which I could only attribute to excess of drink. I courteously declined his offer, and, with my mistress's leave, I withdrew to my room as soon as I could. The shrieks of the new Amazon and the hilarious instructions of the experienced horseman have somewhat prevented my concentrating fully on these notes.

A LETTER

The Christmas season here, in spite of the all-embracing papism of the country, is, more than religious celebration, a pagan festival. We have already been treated to several *músicas*, as the tropical sort of carolling is called here in which neighbors journey to each other's houses to perform. La Enriqueta's rum is served abundantly to the carollers, and is accompanied by a great variety of fried delicacies generically known as *frituras.* Miss Susan seems to enjoy these impromptu parties very little. As she stands next the door to the veranda, her expression is one of impenetrable distance, while her husband mingles cordially with the creole visitors and even asks the ladies to dance.

Mr. Lind's sister and brother-in-law have replaced Mrs. Molly in the guest room. The aristocratic bearing of the Salomons, who have come from Ponce with servants and all, is not much to the liking of my incorrigible charge, who has begun to call them, to Miss Susan's delighted shock, "the Royal Couple." Even the dog they have brought along (a majestic collie whose rich coat makes him a pitiable victim of the heat of the tropics) perfectly suits their air of refinement.

Just three days ago it was that in the midst of great

happiness I was delivered an urgent missive sent from St. Thomas. The bearer of the letter was Mr. Lind himself, whose horse had rushed like a black streak of lightning across the front of the house while I was having my five o'clock tea on the veranda. Seconds later he ran up the steps, three at a time, and put the letter in my hands.

"Miss Jane – your last name sounds more like a Christian name," he said, not yet releasing the envelope and looking very fixedly at me with that unsettling calmness that he has, as though he were expecting some happy phrase from me in order to open a long-postponed conversation. I could only produce a weak smile, however, as I lowered my eyes (as usual), now under the pretext of deciphering the illegible name of the sender.

With a rapidity almost feline, Mr. Lind took a step forward, coming so near me that I could very clearly hear, in the afternoon's silence, his labored breaths, redolent of rum and tobacco. Instinctively I took a step back. He stepped once again forward, and it was as though we were in a partnerless dance.

"Shyness is bad company," he softly murmured after a pause that seemed to me an eternity. It was utterly impossible for my paralyzed lips to speak a word. I know not what would have happened had not at that very moment Charlie's lithe figure appeared in the doorway. Mr. Lind took his eyes from mine and, turning to his son with somewhat exaggerated joviality, challenged him to a race to the other end of the veranda.

With a gesture of indifference the boy rejected his father's challenge; instead, he walked toward me, a look of questioning on his young face. It was only then that I realized I was holding the letter.

Once I reached my room, I broke the seal. Mr. Wolf, the Anglican pastor at Christiansted, had sent me the details of the rapid and painless (thank God!) death of my angelic protectress Mrs. Travers. The delay in the Spanish post had put off my grief for two long weeks.

Sitting at my dressing table, my forehead resting against the silvery cool mirror, I cried, tearlessly, for the perfection of my solitude in the world.

AN HOMAGE

This morning as I entered the library a little before eight, I found on my desk a drawing, very beautifully done. It showed me (the resemblance amazing in its detail) walking under the stars in the garden of La Enriqueta with my hair down and dressed in what I must say was very flimsy clothing – a fine lace petticoat and nothing else. At the bottom, there was a verse from Browning.

At first I could only smile at the somewhat over-idealized image of a nocturnal nymph that Master Charlie had drawn of me. Long later reflection, however, caused me to reconsider that smile. Clearly (and in spite of the tantrums that he sometimes still inflicts on us) my student is growing day by day farther from that childhood I continue to envisage him inhabiting, and entering the irreversible road to puberty. The equatorial heat, I understand, favors and accelerates that process. At thirteen years and two or three months, his angular, gangling body betrays the developing maturity that his childishly high and mighty airs sometimes deny. What silent transformations must be secretly at work in that mind so recently tender! White girls of his own age are conspicuous by their absence from these parts, and that is no doubt the explanation for this unhealthy attraction to adult women. Beginning today, and in spite of my natural affections, I shall have to keep a greater distance between us.

THE TABLEAU

The arrival of a new physician, come to take over old Dr. Tracy's practice, was the occasion for a reception that the Linds attended today. Though more than a bit reluctant to involve myself in social activities that hold so little interest for me, I was obliged to accompany them if I was not to risk committing an "offense to the British community," as my mistress was kind enough to tell me, quite ceremoniously.

In a dress from Miss Susan's vast collection, and selected and fitted by herself, I felt more inadequate than ever. Charlie, the insolent little imp, confirmed my fears; he made merciless fun of the high hemline of my dress, out from which peeked not only the toe but the entire top of my black lace-up shoes. He laughed so hard that Bella had to scold him, though that did not prevent him from making faces at me from behind her ample skirts.

As we were about to leave, with the buggy waiting in the drive in front of the house, I was witness to a most deplorable scene. Mr. Lind, who had been hearing with good patience the boy's insistent pleas to be included in the party, suddenly grew angry at Charlie's refusal to stay at home, and grabbing up the buggy-whip that stood beside the front door, he lashed out at the boy in rage. I could not speak, so great was my horror at the exaggerated violence of his reaction. The fury in the man's eyes made Miss Susan cry out and Bella take a step back, both women utterly terrified. The boy tried in vain to fend off the attack with his forearm. Impulsively, I stepped forward and before the father could bring the lash down again on his son's reddened skin, I seized the child and drew him to me and walked him, without a word, to his room.

Upon my return, the Linds were seated in the buggy. The driver helped me up, and I took my seat in silence beside Miss Susan, who discreetly squeezed my hand. Mr. Lind, his face turned away from us, spoke not a word during the trip, or even deigned to look at us.

In the entrance hall of the O'Hara residence, the butler awaited us, and this sight made my master exclaim, in an attempt to leaven the atmosphere: "There are two things the British never forget when they pack their bags for the colonies – their tea and their butlers!" I suppressed the smile that came to me, trying at all costs to keep my expression impassive, however falsely so.

The physician, it turns out, is a Frenchman some thirty years of age who has already been living for a short time in Arroyo. His name is Fouchard, and his English is very correct, though marked by the inevitable guttural *r* of the French. He seemed to me not only courteous and handsome enough but also somewhat shy, and of more than average intelligence.

As we talked, a young creole man with an extraordinarily long nose and an amazingly square chin came up to us and was at once introduced to me. His name is Alvaro Beauchamp, the son of a French father and Spanish mother, and his cordiality is quite disarming. In a few moments his sister Ernestina joined us, a young woman as affable as he. Almost at once, without a word from me, she began to tell me details of "our Dr. Fouchard." Her brother and the doctor had been introduced to one another in Paris, where they both studied medicine, by a mutual friend, a young man from Cabo Rojo (a town here in Puerto Rico) studying in France also. This young man Fouchard had known since his school days in Toulouse. Fouchard's interest in tropical diseases had brought him as far as the island of Guadeloupe (a French island, *naturellement*), and from there he had come on, at Beauchamp's urging, to Puerto Rico. The sparkle in Ernestina's eyes and the frank enthusiasm of her voice when she spoke of her brother's friend made me think at once that the presence of that friend on the island could mean but one thing.

As we sipped our drinks and enjoyed the hostess's good *hors d'oeuvres*, the conversation turned to the far-off events in Saint-Domingue (now Haiti) and the not-so-far-off French Antilles. The planters and men of business in the group could not hide the uneasiness they felt at the possibility of an African uprising, though it was a threat which the men of business preferred to make light of. With the greatest tact, Fouchard avoided being drawn into the discussion, an attitude I thought very prudent in one so recently arrived.

"God save Queen Victoria and deliver us from political and natural catastrophes," the vice-consul said, raising his glass in a toast. The guests most feelingly seconded him.

Mr. O'Hara's sisters had set up a stage for a *tableau*, and to carry it off enlisted the aid of their guests. I shrank into my armchair, hoping no one would conceive the misguided idea of including me in the cast. My fears, unfortunately, were not unfounded.

The protagonist of the plot, a predictable and (if I may confide my opinion frankly to my own notes) puerile one, was a very wealthy widower who publicly advertised for the "sincere and disinterested" love of a woman. Given such a premise, the candidates for the gentleman's wife were, predictably, not few. With his son's assistance, the gentleman managed to eliminate the female pretenders one by one as they revealed their venal flaws. As the discouraged gentleman (played by poor Dr. Tracy) is about to give up the search, he addresses the distinguished ladies present, among which – he has been told – is the Pure and Incorruptible Ideal Wife. In the starring role of the son, Mr. Reed (captain of one of Mr. Lind's ships) thereupon proposes that the young unmarried women of the company (six, including myself) pass one by one across the "stage" in order that we may be interviewed and appraised by the widower, with the kind collaboration of the other gentlemen as spectators and jury.

I was tempted to stand and, under any poor excuse that might occur to me, leave the room before my turn came. But my cowardice was greater than my sensitivity to ridicule, and so, in unspeakable misery, I awaited the fatal moment. To my misfortune, I was the last candidate to pass across the stage, after Miss Buckmar, Miss Balestière, Ernestina Beauchamp and Mrs. O.'s extroverted sisters-in-law, Lorna and Diana, had had their own opportunities to exhibit their many stunning talents.

With trembling hands and lips, I yielded myself up to the torture of the public eye. Dr. Fouchard, who looked even more uncomfortable than I, gave me a little wink of support, for which I showed my thanks with a sickly smile.

"Perhaps it should be our new *petit docteur* who inter-

rogates Miss Jane," the ever-inopportune Mrs. O. quickly shrieked. I could have murdered her without a second thought had the moment allowed it. But to my profound dismay, before the shy Fouchard could react to our hostess's suggestion, we were addressed by the deep voice of Mr. Lind, which echoed above the gay chatter of the room:

"Let us declare winner by acclamation a candidate who does not have to speak to justify her victory."

A surge of boiling blood rushed to my head, and I thought for a moment my legs would fail me. General applause brought this vexatious episode to a close and enabled me to seek asylum once again in my deep armchair. As I received the effusive congratulations of Fouchard, I felt on the back of my neck the heat of a glance which I had not the courage to return.

THE MUSE

Taking advantage of his father's absence, and in open defiance of his mother's orders, Charlie went off today to see Carolina, the negress who suckled him until he was three years of age, and who is, it seems, in very delicate health. Fearful of the consequences, Bella came to tell me of Charlie's escape. I refused to intervene in the affair. My failure to act, however, was interpreted as tacit consent, and may earn me my patrons' censure. The risk of becoming the accomplice of a boy so given to disobedience should not be underestimated.

I devoted the free time given me by Charlie's escape to classifying the books in the library; they had been shelved by their only reader, Miss Susan, solely as her whim dictated. There is an impressive collection of French and British literature. Almost all the covers bear the initials SWM that Miss Susan has not wished to abandon. Some are gifts from Mr. Morse and have long dedications, signed, in every case, "Your most affectionate father."

As I opened one of the books – a volume by Mary Wollstonecraft on the equality of the sexes – there fell onto the table a pencil sketch. It showed the slender silhouette of Miss Susan dressed in the Greek robes of one of the nine Muses. Miss Susan often boasts of having once posed for a similar portrait, now famous, painted by her father.

How absurd seemed to me then the life which fate has given my mistress! How justified her *mal de vivre*, her indifferent surrender to the tedium of her days! She has abandoned modernity, the stir of the city, the intellectual ferment of her upbringing in order to pass her time, like the mockingbird her husband gave her on her wedding-day, in the perpetual lethargy of a golden cage. How powerful must be the magnet that holds her within it, and that weakens more and more each day the futile beating of her wings!

Although I am greatly moved by the sacrifice implied by that renunciation, a more obscure sentiment runs parallel to my pity, for I too am a prisoner, and likewise by my own will, though the loss of my freedom obeys causes much less sublime.

An emotion almost like envy steals from time to time into my soul.

THE SEQUESTRATION

Today I was the victim of a strange practical joke played on me by Charlie. I did not find it amusing. The two of us were in the garden, sitting on my favorite bench in the shade, when, suddenly taking my hand in his, he said with great urgency in his voice, "Come, come with me, I have something interesting to show you." Curious, I followed him at once. He took me to a little brick outbuilding occupied at night by the watchman, and stepping aside to let me pass, he told me to look inside. I should not have been so guileless, but the desire to find out what it was that was so "interesting" overcame my common sense.

Suddenly, I realized that the door had closed behind me, and that I was confined in that tiny space by thick brick walls. The heat was suffocating; the small openings that served as windows barely admitted air.

Outside there was no sound but Charlie's uncontrollable laughter.

"How do you like your new room?" he asked mockingly, his faced contorted with malicious hilarity.

I tried to keep calm, though I was far from feeling so, and I coldly instructed him to let me out.

"I'm going on a journey," he replied, his tone still insolent, "and when I come back, I want you to have dinner ready for me."

With these insolent words, he left me to my fate for a period of time which rage and impotence made seem immeasurably long.

I know not how many minutes, hours, centuries later, I felt upon my burning forehead a breath of cool air and I saw that the door was opening, little by little, as though by magic. Charlie's tall figure appeared suddenly on the threshold. Ready to box his ears, scratch his eyes out, anything to avenge the humiliating affront to myself, I rushed at him. With a quick, sure gesture he stopped my upraised hands, pulling them behind his back and forcing me by pure brute force to embrace his waist.

In that position, as uncomfortable as it was shameful, he held me for some time. At last, in a very low voice which did nothing to conceal the emotion he was feeling, he said, "Forgive me, Miss Florence, I only wanted you to understand what life is to a prisoner."

His arms dropped to his side. His lips trembled and tears spilled from his eyes. Then, casting aside my own resentments, it was I who held him against my breast.

THE EVE OF A VACATION

They all left yesterday, very early in the morning. Mr. Lind, forever occupied upon his affairs, could not or would not go with them to the harbor. My mistress looked radiant; her wide smile showed how happy she was to be departing for the continent. The serious look my charge put on, however, as he bade me good-bye, gave me pause. Seized by a sudden attack of sadness, Bella refused to come out even onto the veranda.

As the coach pulled away, I went (attracted by the fragrance of good coffee) into the kitchen, where I found Bella crying beside the great cookstove. Drying her tears on her apron, she shoved a letter at me. In it, my mistress very brusquely notified me of the arrangements she had made for me to take "a very well-deserved" vacation in

Ponce as the guest of the Salomons. The coachman had been informed and the date of my departure set. I was given exactly a day and a half to make my preparations.

Miss Susan's decision (taken without having so much as consulted me, and announced this way in writing) took me very much aback. On the one hand, I was of course tempted by the idea of leaving, even for a short time, the narrow universe of La Enriqueta. On the other, the prospect of falling into the satin clutches of the "Royal Couple," collie and all, was not particularly pleasing to me. But as to all appearances I had no choice, I put the best face on things I could.

The torrential rains of the last few days have flooded the low-lying parts of the hacienda, and work has been stopped. Mr. Lind paces, the victim of chronic ill humor and a headache which Bella says can only be cured by two shots of rum and some lettuce tea. I too have felt somewhat indisposed. There is no doubt that the tropical climate, changeable and unhealthful as it is, does not sit well with us.

I was in the kitchen in the evening, helping (more out of boredom than obligation) make some candy and other little things to take with me to my hosts in Ponce, when Joseph, the overseer and Mr. Lind's most trusted employee, called at the window. Bella put her head out and they spoke for a while in the *patois* of the English islands. I saw her cross herself three times before allowing the poor rain-soaked man into her kitchen. No sooner was he inside than the two of them attempted to put upon my shoulders the responsibility of informing the master of the escape of a party of seven slaves. When I vehemently refused, Bella crossed herself again, gave Joseph a look of anguish, and went off to the parlor.

Mr. Lind's outburst of fury could have been heard in

the farthest negro quarters, even above the sound of the rain. And no matter how absurd it was to try to follow the fugitives' tracks in the implacable deluge that was falling, Joseph was commanded to send out two bands along the most probable routes: the coastal region outside Guayama called Jobos and the steep, rugged mountains of Arroyo. Mr. Lind himself went out to saddle his horse, and cursing his blinding headache, rode off at the head of one of the search parties.

My spirits fallen and my body in the grip of a sort of chill brought on by the rain, I retired early. I made a place in my luggage for the jars I was to take to Ponce, and I sat down to finish some socks for Mr. Salomon. The indisposition that I had felt coming on since the morning at last made me put aside my work and lie down on my bed. My forehead was hot and I felt terribly tired.

I must have fallen asleep, dressed just as I was, because suddenly I awoke with a start. The clock in the dining room was striking twelve. The rain continued, and when I went to close my window (which was wide open), a wet, clammy cold gripped my feet.

I went back to sleep, but I was very agitated; I woke often to find my face bathed in icy sweat. In that intermediate state between waking and sleeping, I could hardly distinguish the whistling of the wind from the far-off howling of the dogs and the hoofbeats of the horses. I know not how much time passed before the wooden floor creaked under the slow footsteps that stopped inches from my door. I held my breath, and did not exhale again until the steps went away and I could hear the discreet but unmistakable sound of a bolt shot softly through its eye.

Today I am worse, and Bella has written to cancel my journey.

FEVER

While I suffered under the strange ailment that kept me in my bed for almost a month, and which even as late as yesterday gave signs of not having fully beaten its retreat, it was only rubdowns, herbal teas, and the pious mutterings of Bella that brought relief to my fever-racked body. Concerned by the ill health of his employee, Mr. Lind had sent at once for Dr. Tracy, begging him to make haste, but Dr. Tracy, in spite of his long years of experience, declared himself not competent to deal with tropical illnesses. Dr. Fouchard was away on a journey. Science, then, had perforce to yield to the secrets of homeopathy as practiced here, for which the word is *curandería* – what some might call witch-doctoring, if the "doctoring" part be emphasized.

As the housekeeper's many occupations prevented her devoting more time to the care of her new ward, a new servant, just recently (and upon the master's express orders) come into service in the house, took her place at the head of my bed. Her name was Selenia, and she was a tall, well-built mulatto woman who wore her wiry, disorderly hair long and loose. She would sit silent and sullen at the window of my small room, directly in the salty breeze that toyed with the covers of my bed.

For some reason impenetrable to me, Bella had declared war on this young woman from the outset. Myself unable to lift a finger to beg for silence and a

measure of tranquility, I was forced to witness her bitter
quarrels with my peevish nurse, over any little thing.
Selenia, though, would haughtily bring forth this exasperating and unvarying pronouncement:

"Mr. Lind di'n bring me inta his house for that!"

On more than one occasion Bella had to take herself
out of the room, else she'd have boxed the young
woman's ears, while Selenia would smile to herself
smugly and chill my soul with the icy indifference of
her eyes' gaze upon me. How could so much beauty
and so little human kindness combine in one face? Could
it be true, as Mr. Lind says, that this hybrid race in the
islands has been born without soul?

I had never felt so utterly alone and abandoned to my
fate as during the course of that bedeviling sickness.
Selenia would seize the least occasion to slip away from
my bedside, while I would spend the greatest part of my
day floating between the delirium of the fever and the
agitated dreams of unrestful sleep. The hallucinations
that I suffered swung, with a kind of mad illogicalness,
between the most diverse episodes from my past and
scenes from my residence in these latitudes: a mocking
Charlie come to show me his drawing-pads covered
with scrawls and indecencies, my deceased father seated
beside my pillow softly caressing my fevered brow.

One night, in the midst of the confusion wrought upon
my mind by the dreadful state of my body, I had the
clear impression that I heard the shrill, rising notes of
mad laughter. I turned my burning eyes to where the
familiar silhouette of my caretaker ought to have been.
My room appeared to be empty; yet my ears were still
mercilessly assailed by those annoying shrieks – now
counterpointed by a deeper voice, whispering intermit-
tently. Following the pale track of a ray of moonlight

that shone in through the half-open window, my eyes moved down to the floor and scanned across the shadows at the foot of my bed. As pale and disembodied as a spirit apparition, there glowed in the darkness the naked legs of a woman and a man, tangled in an obscene embrace on the plaited rush of the carpet.

I sank, unresistingly, into the deep waters of unconsciousness. When I came to my senses again, all was silent, and my body was shaking violently from head to toe.

CONVALESCENCE

In time the fever subsided, yet the terrible weakness which was its legacy remained. I had lost a great deal of weight, and all the strength my racked frame had once had. I could hardly move about, and the mere thought of raising myself from the bed brought on nausea and dizziness.

Selenia had found entertainment to fill her time. Taking advantage of my utter inability to form the slightest protest, the crafty slut wandered freely about my bedroom, opening and closing drawers and boxes, fingering the objects on my dressing-table, poking about in the pockets of my dresses and trying on my shoes – which fit her, it pains me to say, perfectly.

"Miss Susan has better taste," she dared mutter one morning as she reviewed the few dresses modestly hanging in my wardrobe.

I witnessed these brazen violations of my little world with total impassivity, not for any lack of firmness of character but simply for lack of energy to make known my displeasure.

The efficacy of the chicken broth sent up by wise Bella soon was demonstrated. Slowly (too slowly for my own likes) the color began returning to my pale cheeks, life began returning to my movements. With the help of two plump pillows I could now sit up in my bed and take refuge in the refreshing world of a Charlotte Brontë novel. And so for brief periods I would withdraw from the calculated insolence of my companion.

So accustomed had I grown to a solitude interrupted only by Bella's sporadic visits and underscored by Selenia's ever more frequent absences, that I was startled one day to hear a decided knocking at my door. To my start was added confusion when, giving the permission my invisible visitor sought, I beheld the imposing figure of Edward Lind standing upon the threshold of my room, with his wet shirt clinging to his chest and his pants splattered with mud. With no further greeting than his smile, he came to my bed and announced in a falsely solemn voice:

"Miss Florence Jane, I hereby declare you survivor of the yellow fever. You've the stuff of an African woman in you – I never thought you would turn out so strong."

His mocking compliment brought the blood to my face. My discomfort increased when I saw Mr. Lind's eyes travel down my body, exposed under its linen nightdress to the curiosity of his gaze.

I turned my eyes away in confusion. From outside, a light mist blew in sidewise through the window. Mr. Lind's grave voice once more claimed my attention, and I found myself falling suddenly into the bottomless well of his dark eyes:

"The devil takes personal interest in the climate of

these islands, you know. If it doesn't rain, we dry up and shrivel away; if it does, we're drowned."

Not knowing how to reply, I smoothed my disordered hair with my hand. Anything I might say seemed to me banal, unnecessary. Mr. Lind leaned over and touched my arm softly with his hand, with no more pressure than the furtive brush of a cat's paw. And then, without losing even for one second that smile, he said as he turned away:

"Take good care of yourself, Miss Florence. We'll see if we can't teach you to ride a horse one of these days."

It was only then that I became aware of the presence of Selenia. She was standing in a corner beside the silk-covered wall, strangely tense and mute. Her gaze was fixed on the door, which now stood wide open.

A VISIT

Yesterday for the first time in many weeks I went down to the garden, feeling as though I had been born anew. I took the precaution of wrapping myself in a shawl, to forestall the danger of a relapse. All seemed different: the rain had enlivened the colors of the foliage, and the sky gleamed clean and bright. The air was cooler, too, no doubt because the shade trees are swollen with sap. Upon my marble bench I let time drift idly by; I was bathed in the coolness of the breeze and I floated in the sweetest lethargy.

Bella came to interrupt my reverie, informing me of the most welcome arrival of a visitor. Moments later, there appeared before my eyes the kind and friendly face of Dr. Fouchard, whose greeting to me was one of his ever-unexpected winks. The frequency of these winks made me conclude that the doctor suffered from some sort of nervous tic, the product of his terrible shyness in the presence of the opposite sex.

"My dear Miss Florence!" he said, his voice trembling, "how happy it makes me to see you so recovered!"

He then explained to me, in a wealth of unnecessary detail, the fact already communicated to me by Dr. Tracy: he had been unable to attend me personally during my illness and long convalescence because he had been called away suddenly to Guadeloupe, to attend a hearing concerning an inheritance he had come into. He insisted so much and so perfectly contritely upon his powerlessness to put off the journey that at last I could only laugh. My thoughtless gesture somehow relieved the tension of our meeting, and likewise eased the flow of our conversation, which then went on for some two hours or more. I hardly noted how the time had passed, absorbed as I was by the fascinating stories of his life that René (for thus it is that he insists I am to call him) so skillfully wove to entertain me.

When the time came to end our talk, René said, in a new seizure of shyness that made him stammer and stumble over his words:

"If I were not afraid of tiring you, I would suggest a walk."

I did not think it prudent to accept his invitation just then, and so I asked that it be put off till the next morning. René agreed at once. He would not hear of my leaving my bench to accompany him to the gate, and he retired as discreetly as he had come.

When nightfall forced me to seek shelter in the parlor, I learned from Bella that more than a week ago Mr. Lind left for Hamburg, where he has both family and business dealings. That night I dined alone in the dining room, oppressed by the silence that reigned now, unchallenged, in the house.

AN OUTING

The doctor drove me in his buggy along a road as narrow as it was beautiful, down to the banks of the Guamaní River where an immense open-air market offers all sorts of merchandise for the daily life of those who live in the country.

My companion seems to know the area as well as if he had lived here for many years. His recounting of the fire that devastated Guayama more than two decades ago and of the cholera epidemic that decimated the population of that town a short time before I came to Puerto Rico so totally claimed my attention that I lost all sense of time and place. Sitting on a reddish rock jutting up in the middle of the river, the current running strong beneath our feet, far from the feverish bargaining going on in the market area, we conversed animatedly as noon came on. Suddenly realizing the time, René motioned me to wait for him while he went off to buy bread, cheese, and fruit for a little picnic lunch.

"What brought you to this island, Florence? What, or who, have you traded away your winters for?" he asked, handing me an orange he had peeled as the French do, and with the sections of it temptingly spread open.

I took the proffered fruit and put an end to his questioning with a shrug of my shoulders. "I do not talk about my past; there is nothing there that is worth remembering."

René's smile disarmed me.

"Let's forget the past, then," he said softly. "I consider it a privilege that you would allow me to figure in your present."

CONFIDENCES

Our outings have become an agreeable routine, a pleasant habit that breaks the tedium. I fear, on the other hand, that for René they may have taken on unwonted importance. Giving signs of total confidence in my ability to keep a secret, he has confided to me that he suffers the affliction of an unrequited love. He has been very careful, however, not to reveal the name of his beloved, and I, of course, have not asked. Something tells me that it is not Ernestina Beauchamp, about whom he speaks rarely, and without much enthusiasm.

Today an incident occurred which showed me another, and until now hidden, side of him. For my solitary walks I had always obeyed Miss Susan's admonitions and never penetrated the hedge of vines and taken the path to the negro quarters – the *batey*, as Charlie calls the little earthen plaza around which the negroes' rude houses are built. I had always chosen the other path, which leads through a stand of extraordinarily tall and graceful palm trees down to the very edge of the ocean. This day, however, at a little past six o'clock in the evening, as dusk was coming on, we took, at René's urging, a short-cut back to the house, and the path led us directly through the area of the negroes' dwellings. Under the pretext of weariness, my companion chose to enter that inhospitable and foul-smelling place about whose true life I knew naught but the echoes of voices and of drums wafted to me on the wind on certain nights.

A strong smell of boiled codfish hung over all. In great iron kettles of steaming water, plantains and green bananas bobbed. A hunchbacked old woman with a red kerchief knotted about her head was slowly stirring the cornmeal concoction that they call *funche*, a dish which, sprinkled with sugar, accompanies many a meal, even in the house of the master.

René's words, previously soft and melodious as he revealed to me his deepest emotions, now were strangely hard. All tenderness had fled his eyes, which looked upon me fixedly, with no flicker of a wink.

"It's curious that they are not called by their true name – slaves. It is as though we insisted upon denying their real condition, as though if we can but avoid naming it we may allow ourselves to be blind to the true horror of their state . . . But what are they if not slaves? They work in the fields from sun to sun; they live like beasts, one atop another, locked into these wretched hovels; they suffer punishments to their flesh that would shame the barbarians; they come, they go, they breathe to a rhythm set them by our mere wills . . . "

We had paused by the side of the road. The harsh expression on my companion's face disturbed me. I opened my mouth to say that I wished to go on toward the hacienda, but I closed it again upon seeing that René had turned on his heel and was attentively gazing into the green-black wall of sugar cane encircling the batey. As though in response to his gaze, a long cortège of ragged men and women, their bare feet, covered with mud, stumbling in the clumsiness of exhaustion, began to file slowly toward us. My heart beat violently in my breast. I raised my gaze to my companion's face, my eyes pleading for an answer to this spectacle.

"Look at them. Look well, Florence," he said, bringing his lips down to my ear, so close I could feel his breath. "These are the men and women who give the sweetness to our coffee."

My eyes clung fatally to those emaciated torsos, those scarred backs, those grim and hostile countenances that looked like faces issued from some dark cavern in the bowels of hell. Eager to erase the painful ugliness of that scene, which the failing light of evening invested with a spectral glow, I quickened my steps along the trail back to the house. René followed, but we spoke not a single word to each other until we were once again inside the magic circle of the gardens.

An odd being, this man capable of baring his heart while remaining shadowed in mystery. The more I try to persuade myself that my suspicions are irrational, the more tormented by uncertainty I am. Can Dr. Fouchard be one of those young idealists who preach the freeing of the black race? His obscure origins, his intriguing comings and goings, his impassioned denunciation of slavery – it all points toward that disturbing conclusion. And if my fears are unfounded, why place at risk our friendship with behavior that threatens not only my position but that of my protectors?

Tomorrow, when he comes for me, Bella will tell him that I am not in.

THE RETURN

Miss Susan has come home again, loaded down with extravagant *bibelots* for her mahogany curio cabinets. There is a new set of china for the table, and two enormous agate vases from Italy. She has been kind enough to bring me two novels by George Sand. I am grateful, though the novels run directly counter to my usual literary taste. Taking the stairs two at a time, Charlie proclaimed to the world his happiness at seeing me again. In his eagerness to deliver my gifts to me, he accidentally tore one of the covers.

Trailing behind the son there appeared, much recovered from her previous thinness, the lady of the house. It was the first time she had deigned to enter my room; I presumed, therefore, that she had come to offer her sympathy for my illness of the summer past. I was not to be so honored, however. She sat for a long while telling me in great detail of her activities at Locust Grove and of her adventures in New York when she went with the Overmans to the theater or the opera.

"One gradually loses one's sensibility, seeing nothing but negroes and sugar cane," she sighed, lying back unthinkingly against my pillows.

With a total lack of reserve (which I found at once shocking and complimentary), she proceeded to disburden upon my ears her afflicted heart. As I am not one accustomed to being made privy to the intimate details of the lives of my superiors, I feared that my discomfort would be all too obvious to her, and I made an effort to conceal it.

Miss Susan revealed, with evident homesickness for the paternal estate, that she had never spent so much time before with Mr. Morse. The constant moving from house to house, the early widowhood, and the somewhat unstable personality of the genius who was her father – these things had conspired to deprive Miss Susan of the consolation of a paternal presence for many years. A real childhood, it could not be said she had had, she continued with a slight stiffening of her lips, forced as she had been to take on (all unprotestingly) the mantle of substitute-mother for her two brothers. The ever-traveling father had not even been present when she and Edward, after the wedding in New Haven, had embarked for Puerto Rico. My mistress paused, barely able to contain her tears.

I remained silent, squeezing between my nervous hands a perspiration-soaked handkerchief which I did not think it prudent to offer her. Then, as suddenly as her words had begun to flow, Miss Susan said a hasty good-bye and abandoned my room. The boy, who had sat in silence through his mother's tale of tribulations, hesitated a moment beside the door, waiting for me to ask him to stay.

During the days that followed, my thoughts went many times over that troubling scene. I could not keep my mind from the image of the sad girl, grown up too quickly and now become, by a cruel twist of fate, an equally sad and solitary wife. Had Samuel Morse had his doubts before he had agreed to that sudden wedding of his daughter and the foreigner she had met but a year earlier at her uncle Charles Walker's house? Had he found unacceptable the idea that Miss Susan should go off to the ends of the earth to live, upon an island subject to earthquakes, hurricanes, and yet other trials? Had he been consoled by the knowledge that she would be the mistress of a prosperous estate of more than a thousand acres, with a windmill, a steam engine, and a hundred-sixty slaves?

I find myself, more often than I would like, reliving pieces of other person's lives – lives often more intense, more vivid, more real than these vapid chapters of my own.

THE INVITATION

It was Miss Susan who decided – without consulting me, as always – that I should attend. She was so intent upon telling me the news that she broke into our lessons, rendering naught my herculean efforts to hold Charlie's wayward attention to the lines of Milton assigned for that day.

"Can you guess who's coming? And coming next Sunday?!" she asked, her voice all animated delight. I immediately thought of Mr. Lind, who should be returning from Europe that same weekend. I let her, however, answer her own question, as had been her intention from the first. All right, she would tell me: the person who was coming was none other than Adelina Patti, the famed diva whose incomparable voice had seduced the entire Continent.

"In the company, of course," she added, her enthusiasm if anything greater, "of the great Moreau Gottschalk."

The little worldly culture I possessed prevented my sharing the intense pleasure which to all appearances my mistress was enjoying at the thought of receiving into her house the man I soon learned to be a famous piano virtuoso, the glory of the state of Louisiana. The information that made my pulse race was other – and contained in the speech she impulsively launched herself upon, no doubt so as not to give me time to prepare my own defensive broadside.

She began by scolding me for my "terrible shyness," which, she claimed, made me avoid parties and receptions "like the bubonic plague." She then proceeded to remind me, most untactfully, that "at one's age" it was never a bad idea to expose oneself to society and the possibility of making new friends. As she spoke, her voice grew more and more firm and her countenance more and more serious. She concluded her sermon with a statement which much resembled a command: She would hear no excuse for my not performing what she considered, without exaggeration, to be my sacred duty – if not out of obedience to the wishes of the family, then out of consideration for them.

I was doubly astonished. First of all, nothing in my mistress's previous behavior would have led me to suspect that she had such esteem for my humble self. In the second place, I was dumbstruck by this authoritarian outburst by a person who had, until that moment, shown me nothing but deference and consideration. When I could at last summon the strength to offer the excuse (a very weak one, as I recognized even as I spoke it) of the austerity of my wardrobe, my mistress produced another triumphant piece of news: she had already ordered me, from her own, quite well-known, seamstress in Guayama, "the perfect gown."

"I hope you won't be upset with me, dear Miss Florence," she said, reverting to her accustomed sweetness, "but in order not to disturb you, we have used

Selenia's measurements, which we believe, as you will soon see, closely approximate your own."

The mere idea of wearing a dress sewn virtually upon the body of another woman, and more so when that woman was the hateful Selenia, was (to put the matter bluntly) repugnant to me. But I judged it inopportune of me to oppose Miss Susan's will just then, and essentially nil the possibility of changing her mind.

All these details disposed of, then, Miss Susan at once led me to her room, where I was given to admire, in all its splendor, the fine craftsmanship and impeccable cut of "the perfect gown." It goes without saying that the kind insistence of my protectress left me no alternative but to resign myself, and to slip the generous folds of that dream in white satin over my shoulders.

"It's made for you!" Miss Susan exclaimed, smiling with mischievous pride at the deed she'd done. "You look like a young bride!"

"The decolleté ... " I began, trying to cover my exposed bosom with my hands.

Miss Susan laughed so spiritedly that she lost her balance and fell back onto the bed. In gales of laughter she buried her face in my pillow. Somehow, her hilarity vexed me more than the obligation to go to the reception.

THE TOAST

At six in the evening, the coaches and traps of the most prominent families of the entire coastal region around Guayama began turning into our drive. In the gardens, a group of the most select of our neighbors, among them more than a proportionate number of French and Englishmen and their families, awaited the arrival of the famous guests.

Shortly after seven, a servant came out onto the veranda and rang a little silver bell. All the guests began filing into the house, as though drawn inside by a power stronger than their own will. In the parlor, their hostess announced unexpected but happy news: the soprano and the pianist were awaiting us all in the dining room, where the event in their honor would begin. They had somehow outflanked all the gracious vigilance for their arrival and entered the house, secretly, through the back door.

From my place halfway down, I could keep my eye on what happened at both the head and the foot of the table. I could also see, thanks to the mirror at the other side of the room, the discreet and diligent attentions of the servants.

Seated between her father and a young Puerto Rican gentleman who hung on her every word and gesture, Patti looked like some pink-cheeked cherub. As to Gottschalk, I am not sure whether it was his voice or his remarkable height that impressed me more. But my gaze was drawn time and again not so much to our dazzling visitors as to that person who, by his rare presence among us, could be considered more a stranger than a member of our own circle.

Clean-shaven, smelling slightly of *eau de Cologne*, dressed in his formal suit and string tie, he was suddenly invested with a gentlemanly aspect that radically transformed the everyday roughness of his appearance. He sat at the table with perfect correctness, inclining his head from time to time to offer another portion to a guest or to reply politely to a question. At the other extreme of the table, flushed and a bit moist, Miss Susan could not be said to show the same composure.

The dinner, lavish in its assortment of wines and exquisite delicacies, was a long one. My immediate neighbors, who happened to be French, ignored me with that combination of indifference and arrogance that so often seems to characterize those from the other side of the Channel. Their affront, which could not be considered a serious one, had its advantages: it allowed me to observe without being observed.

More than once my eyes met those of my employer. I do not know whether from the effects of the wine or from my imagination, or from a secret alliance between the two, but I read in them the same curiosity that impelled my own. Made uneasy by the bold amusement of his gaze, I could not avoid the discomfiting reflex of putting a hand over my breast, which was much exposed by the graceful lines of my "perfect gown." My little trust in the confused perceptions of that moment prevent me from putting a very specific name to the enigmatic smile that my almost-involuntary movement caused the master of the house.

When the time came for dessert, our host called for the champagne, which flowed generously. He raised his glass and gave a long and brilliant toast to the glory of the celebrated *artistes* who were with us. Then he looked in turn directly into the eyes of every woman at the table, and pausing very deliberately (or at least, in my extreme nervousness, so I thought) at my own, he said, his voice suddenly silken:

"And a toast as well to the feminine beauty which, like the sea, surrounds us – and which, like the sea, is the cause of so much wealth and so many capsizings!"

My raised glass shivered a little in the air, and a few

drops of wine spilled upon the tablecloth. Fortunately, the delighted applause that met our host's witty toast pretty much distracted the diners' attention. From that moment on, I tasted not a bite more, and my gaze (blurred not a little by the champagne) remained fixed on the mirror.

When we went into the music room for the concert by our guests of honor, Miss Susan showed me to a chair beside her own.

"Don't you find Dr. Fouchard's absence intolerable?" she whispered softly, not looking at me.

EXIT CHARLIE

As I was finishing breakfast with my charge in the garden that same morning, I had been an involuntary witness of a deplorable scene. The angry voice of Miss Susan came to us through the thick hedge of jasmine in whose shade we were sitting.

"Why did you wait so long to tell me?" she remonstrated, and then, without waiting for a reply from that interlocutor whose identity I still knew not, she went on. "She will leave this minute! Tell her to get her filthy rags together and go to the field hands' quarters this instant!"

Suddenly, I was conscience-stricken at overhearing a conversation so clearly not intended for our ears. About to stand up and walk away and distract the boy's attention, I was interrupted in my plan by the gruff voice of Bella. With her usual good sense, she asked a question which, to judge by the silence it elicited, needed no answer:

"But Miss Susan, what will Mr. Lind say when he finds out?"

I did stand up then and with mock spontaneity ran off toward the pond, challenging my young ward to catch me if he could. And sure enough, Charlie, who never fails to take up the gauntlet of a dare, leapt up and was off like a little deer after me.

"I'll bet you don't know," he said when he caught me, his voice decidedly mischievous, and before he'd even recovered his breath again, "who they're talking about."

"I'm not certain I'm interested," I replied, feigning more indifference than I really felt, and adding for the moral edification of my indiscreet pupil, "Nor, for that matter, should you be."

The boy just laughed, shaking off the dart of my irony and taking my two hands in his own. Then, in a voice of extreme insolence, he said, "Sometimes, my dear Miss Florence, I have the impression that I am *your* tutor."

The heat I felt in my cheeks betrayed me. I quickly pulled my hands away and bent down to the water to touch a water-lily. My pupil leaned against the trunk of a royal palm, and his mocking voice (which was no longer the falsetto of before but rather a grave and disquieting baritone) came to me strong and clear across the morning's calm:

"You should know, even if you would rather *not* know, that Selenia's belly is swelling, and it's not from eating green mangoes."

At that moment there became abruptly transparent to me a fact which (for some reason I still cannot fathom) I was determined not to acknowledge: this skeptical and *blasé* young man had changed – he had ceased to be, for all time, my innocent little Charlie.

HURRICANE

The mournful ululation of the wind upon the cliffs of Dover is pale beside the hellish howl of those gales that threatened to rip the roof from the house. The negroes had been closed up with the animals, under heavy lock and key, in the two strongest outbuildings. The owners of more fragile dwellings came to take refuge behind the solid walls of La Enriqueta, which was by far the most resistant structure in the entire area.

Even so, the house shivered from roof to foundation, and the concrete piles upon which it is constructed rocked. While Mr. Lind directed the neighbors in a constant opening and closing of doors and windows so as to channel, insofar as possible, the blasts of wind through the house, Miss Susan sobbed like a frightened girl in the arms of a proud brave Charlie. The din of shattering crystal exacerbated her desolation. With all the unconsciousness of youth, the boy was thrilled by what he considered this grand adventure.

In spite of the terror I myself was feeling, I distracted my nerves, which were keen to the point almost of temporary madness, by closely following the movements of Mr. Lind. With inexhaustible energy, he seemed to be everywhere, on every front, concerned with the slightest detail. In the midst of the gale, and against the desperate pleadings of his wife, he went up against the wrath of the elements and captured, with his own hands, an escaped horse. Wet to the bone but victorious, he returned to nail boards across the shattered windows of the second floor. Thanks to his able and courageous breasting of the storm, there was no major damage to the main house of the hacienda.

Huddled and cowering in a corner, feeling myself perfectly at the mercy of the elements (and knowing myself useless in the crisis), I watched him stride by me a thousand times. Though his eyes fell upon my body more than once, he spoke not a single word to me, nor did a single sign of recognition cross his features. Who is this contradictory, evasive creature, this unpredictable man at once attractive and repellant? However hard I try, I cannot assemble the jumbled pieces of his life into one true portrait of him. His distance can be glacial; his touch burns like fire. If I draw close, he retreats; if I avoid him, he seeks me out. Only in fugitive moments (as dreaded as desired, and now blurred in the sidelights of my memory) does his ardent flame take on more reality, does his violence clash with my fear.

ADIEU

Mrs. O. and her sisters-in-law, come to the hacienda on virtually an official embassy, can talk of nothing else. The scandalous news of Dr. Fouchard's "flight" has spread like wildfire throughout the entire Guayama area. There is a great deal of speculation – though no foundation whatsoever, of course – as to the mysterious reasons that the doctor may have had for abandoning home and office in the middle of the night, without a word of goodbye for anyone, without a word of explanation for anyone, even his intimate friends the Beauchamps.

"*Cherchez la femme,* I say," pronounced Mrs. O. with a commiserating look at Lorna, the vice-consul's elder sister, whose open infatuation with the doctor had gone neither unobserved nor unremarked.

"No," I blurted out automatically, and without gauging the consequences my clumsy intervention might have. "René is not that kind of man."

When she realized that in my reflexive defense of the doctor I had called him by his Christian name and not his surname and title, Miss Susan looked over at me, clearly intrigued.

Mrs. O. wasted no time in following up on such a tempting clue.

"Oh?" she said mockingly, feigning a lack of interest she was far from feeling. "And what kind of man is he, then, Miss Florence, if you might be kind enough to enlighten us in that regard . . . ?"

I was silent a moment, while before my imagination's eye there paraded a train of unforgettable images and words which I would never have the courage or the right to reveal. My hesitation looked so suspicious, unfortunately, that I was obliged to cover my growing discomfort with a frivolous "Too timid for my own taste," which had the fortune to divert the conversation toward the "lack of boldness in the men of today" and the fateful consequences of that lack of spirit on the "state of matrimony of some ladies."

Having turned Mrs. O. into one of her favorite avenues of conversation, I lowered my gaze and took up the interrupted thread of my own thoughts. Out of the corner of my eye, I saw that Miss Susan followed my every reaction.

As I write these notes, a profound sadness overtakes me, so that I can hardly continue. I have been robbed of perhaps the only sincere friendship I have had in this country. If the causes of Dr. Fouchard's departure are really those that I suspect, it may be for the best – it may be preferable in the long run that our souls, so similar yet so different, have parted.

A BIRTHDAY

How quick time is, and how slow our perception of it! The fourteen years that Charlie observes today mark the beginning of the end. Little more than a year is left of my stay at La Enriqueta, and that year is justified only by the French lessons I give Charlie – the only subject that now seems to interest my restless pupil.

With great solemnity he has announced to me his plans to go off to Paris, where he says he will pursue his great passion – painting. I should be surprised if Mr. Lind allowed his only son to choose such an unpromising vocation. The father has little sympathy for art; his own talents, almost preternatural, are for business. In a very few years he has multiplied the acres of his property many times over, purchasing not only the cane fields of his sister Henrietta but also the adjacent lands of La Concordia. Moreover, the trade in Africans produces enough to offset the occasional loss in the fortunes of the sugar cane. It will no doubt take poor Charlie considerable work – and from what one sees, many tears –

to persuade him. His father's iron will has now, more than ever, a concrete cause for being brought to bear: the future of the estate and of the business.

Miss Susan had asked that a very special meal be prepared for tonight's birthday celebration. When I came downstairs, dressed for dinner, to take my usual place at the table, the mother and son were impatiently awaiting Mr. Lind, who had been told of the dinner beforehand yet still had not come in. While Inés, the girl who has replaced Selenia, was serving the first course, the head of the household at last made his appearance.

His ill humor was evident. He did not even go upstairs to wash before dinner, but rather sat at the table and, sweaty and still panting from exertion as he was, he ordered his meal brought to him straightway, as he informed us that he had to leave again at once. To Miss Susan's questions he replied grudgingly that there was a rumor of a rebellion in don Jacinto Cora's negro quarters, and that the landowners of the area were meeting to take measures against a possible uprising.

Charlie could hardly conceal his disappointment, though for obvious reasons he kept silent. Disregarding entirely the order and etiquette of the dinner, Mr. Lind attacked the main dish before our eyes: a fricasseed goat accompanied with rice and pigeon-peas. No sooner had he so precipitately supped, he passed the linen napkin across his beard and threw it (whether unconsciously or not, I cannot tell) to the floor and strode from the dining room without a further word.

We finished our dinner in silence, and with very little appetite. By the time Bella, in a heroic attempt to save the evening, placed in the center of the table the enormous coconut birthday cake that she had made herself in honor of her beloved Charlie, the party had turned into a wake – a strange wake without a corpse.

NEWS

Two letters arrived today. The first, brought by Mr. Lind, announced that Mr. Morse would soon be coming to Puerto Rico, and it has put Miss Susan into a state of absolute delight. The second has come into my hands through more secret means.

It was about four in the afternoon when, to seek a saving coolness, I started out onto the veranda for air. Just as I reached the door, Bella came into the room behind me with the unexpected announcement of a visitor. Moments later, Ernestina Beauchamp was shown in, looking much thinner than was her wont.

"I know you'll be surprised to see me, Miss Florence," she said weakly, and then without another word she put into my hands a sealed envelope, addressed to me. I hesitated a second before opening it. Suddenly I felt her hand, fragile and very cold, on mine.

"You must read it in private," she said, smiling sadly.

I offered her a chair, which she gratefully accepted. Her drawn and emaciated features revealed a most dolorous state of health, and this appearance was confirmed by her next words.

"I shall be only a short time longer in Puerto Rico. My brother has made arrangements for me at a sanatorium in the French Alps. I have come to say goodbye."

Her revelation surprised me less than the fact of her visit. Our meetings had been few, and our relationship somewhat superficial. The only thing we shared in common was our friendship with René Fouchard. I impatiently waited, letter in hand, for an explanation to justify her unusual action in coming to visit me this way. My wait was not long.

"He always spoke of you. He admired you."

I did not have to ask whom it was she referred to; her eyes, brimming with tears, told me. It was I, then, who put my hand upon hers, and that small gesture had the power to calm her. I sent for tea, and we made no further mention, during the rest of her brief visit, of the illness that afflicted her or of its cause. Her coachman was waiting for her in the drive; I accompanied her there, and stood on the veranda until the cloud of dust raised by the horses as she went had settled again.

I went to my room to break the seal on the letter. It was, of course, from René. The date – some months earlier – was an indictment of the Spanish mail service, or perhaps bespoke the reluctance of its more proximate messenger to deliver it. The sender apologized for our abrupt separation, and he attempted to explain his disappearance (an event as disconcerting as it was mysterious): "By the time you have consented to read this letter, I will be far from Arroyo, on my way to meet a destiny which I myself dare not predict. With a celerity that would not allow me the consolation of a goodbye, I had to leave – my continued presence on the Island, and the nature of the activities which, in the conscience of a fair and freethinking man, justified it, would sooner or later have compromised the welfare of my friends and contributed to the pleasure of my enemies."

His words throbbed with the force of the most authentic emotions, awakening in my own thoughts echoes, in spite of the unbridgable chasm that separated our two minds: "My dear friend – if I have any counsel for you, it is that you save yourself, that you flee that luxurious and pleasant prison in which you live, a prison built on the bones of so many of God's creatures. For if you do not, the brilliantly glittering lie of that rotten world will undermine your spirit and your will and turn them into the crushed and desiccated fibers of the sugar cane from which all the sweet life-juice has been squeezed."

The letter ended with a farewell which moved me greatly: "I send you, then, assurances of an affection blasted before it could bloom. I will never lose the hope of seeing you again."

The strident chords of a dizzying waltz resonate in my brain. Ernestina's desolation would drown my heart.

THE CHARLESTOWN PRODIGY

On the ship *Estelle*, of Long Island, and accompanied by his wife and the two children from his second marriage, the famous Mr. Morse has arrived from England, where he was vacationing. From the coast of Arroyo watchers might make out in the distance the American flag snapping in the wind atop the roof of the Lind mansion. The town doctor, a good-natured Irishman who turned red with pride upon shaking the inventor's hand, accompanied the family in the Ministry of Health launch to the place of disembarkation. There, a coach, crowned for the occasion with the imposing figure of an eagle admirably prepared by some remote taxidermist, awaited them, and in it a radiant Miss Susan, clapping her hands in delight, along with the slightly stand-offish Charlie and myself, filled with emotion.

The temperature was so oppressive that Mr. Morse could hardly believe it was December. He was fascinated, in spite of the suffocating heat, by the vision of those 1,400 acres of white-tasseled sugar cane swaying in the breeze that softly blew from the mountains down to the ocean. "A princely estate" were his precise astonished words as he contemplated the grandiose architecture of the house which for some months to come would be his home.

The Christmas festivities have taken on a special brilliance with the presence of the genius of Locust Grove. The inevitable Salomons have come from Ponce with a musical group – guitars and the smaller island *cuatro*, so named because of its four strings, plus the rhythm accompaniment of gourd-players – to initiate the visitors in the delights of the local folk traditions. The O'Haras, the Fantauzzis, the McCormicks, and the Aldecoas, among numerous other neighbors who wish to pay their respects to our international celebrity, frequent the house these days as never before.

To Miss Susan's grateful surprise, Mr. Lind has been the model husband and host. He has insisted on personally escorting his father-in-law about the estate, and about all the neighboring parts as well, taking him wherever he is invited. To reciprocate – or perhaps out of an inborn indisposition to leisure of any sort – Mr. Morse has promised to take upon himself the task of building a telegraph line between La Enriqueta and his son-in-law's warehouse on the docks.

Between overseeing all the many activities of the kitchen and attending to her step-mother and her half-siblings (who have fallen prey to an embarrassing infestation of head-lice), Miss Susan barely has time left over for a daughter's conversation with her father. And much less time, I suppose, to broach a subject as difficult as the little wrinkles that continue to furrow themselves into the terse skin of her happiness.

MELANCHOLY

The efforts of these three months have born fruit: the promised telegraph line is now complete and today Arroyo celebrated the occasion.

The authorities have spared no expense in impressing Mr. Morse. Baskets of flowers and fruits fill the veranda. A most *soigné* luncheon has mobilized the principal citizens of the town. The main orator was – as it must have been – the gentleman from Poughkeepsie, who, standing proudly between the flags of Spain and the United States, posed for a photograph to memorialize the day. I have all these details from none other than Charlie, who (thanks to the irresistible urging of his grandfather) accompanied the group through every minute. We women remained at home upon the hacienda assisting in the preparations for the domestic festivities.

In spite of the diversion that the presence of our famous guest means for Charlie, there is a melancholy, unseen by all but me, that has come over my pupil's spirit. I can guess its causes although I cannot be sure of them. Neither the comfort that surrounds him nor the granting of his every wish can fill that bottomless chasm that has opened in his heart. His loneliness, imperceptible to those who lack sensibility, is only comparable to that of this slave, who though not in chains finds her happiness dependent upon the caprices of a master who is forever absent.

THE ENCOUNTER

The departure of the Morses has left a terrible void in the house. Dispirited and aimless, Miss Susan drags herself about again. I would not be in the least surprised if she should fall ill, as she always does at this season. I miss Charlie's impish laughter. When I invite him to go with me on some outing, he makes absurd excuses.

My employer seems to have been swallowed up by the earth. No sooner had his distinguished father-in-law boarded the boat that would take him away than Mr. Lind disappeared into the cane fields as though desperate to regain a freedom that had been long withheld from him. Can the dimensions of this enormous house be too narrow for the adventuresome restlessness of his soul?

Today, determined to change my own habits and escape the tedium of this household, I went out on a walk by myself. Rising from the great cauldrons, the smell of molasses that permeates the atmosphere when the harvest of cane is ended followed me no matter how far I went. I took the road to Cuatro Calles, which I rarely take, so as to avoid the constant greetings in town. As I was walking back, late in the afternoon, I had a surprising and unpleasant encounter.

When I came to where the road to Guayama crosses

Isabel Segunda Street, I recognized an unmistakable silhouette, tall, straight, and elegant in spite of the fact that
upon its head there sat in perfect balance an enormous
basket of fruit. It was Selenia, the woman cast out of our
garden, and she had lost none of her beauty – or her
arrogance. Slung from her back there was a baby, its skin
lighter than her own, wriggling restlessly.

We came face to face, and inevitably we looked at one
another. But neither of us showed the slightest sign of
recognition. Seemingly oblivious to the most elementary
principles of courtesy, the two of us walked on with the
haughty indifference of two duchesses. The child turned
its head to look after me. The open curiosity in its vivid
green eyes brought me, almost in spite of myself, a smile.

What secret poison feeds dislike? What generous river
brings the water of life to our affections? That wretched
woman that fate set in my path has the power – though
our lives have barely brushed against each other – to
strangely disquiet me. What is this rude and obscure
language that hunchbacked and wizened envy whispers
into my ear now?

A CONFESSION

I could never have imagined that my pupil's
moroseness owed less to his grandfather's absence than
to the powerful influence of Cupid. Yesterday he came to
me with a confession. Her name is Carmelina, she is a
creole, and she lives in town. Her father, a small
businessman and a widower, keeps watch over her as
he would a wife. She cannot so much as walk out upon

her own balcony. It is truly remarkable that the two young people have even met.

Charlie's effusions, while those of one his age, are yet the product of a pretty indiscriminate taste. The girl (if one can call a person of twenty-one years still a girl) is far from his equal not only in age but also (and above all) in condition. Unless I err (and I will have to find a way to confirm this) I believe I have heard Mrs. O. – who knows everything and keeps back nothing – say that there are stories in Arroyo about the doubtful nature of the ties that bind her to her father.

Oh my poor innocent Charlie! Your blessed lack of experience may well yet be a curse!

A WAKE

Last night Carolina, Charlie's old nurse, died of dropsy – or if Joseph is to be believed, from chewing tobacco. Stunned, the boy ran straight for Bella's comforting arms. Miss Susan did not dare try to stop him from running out to the negro quarters.

A group of men and women came later to ask permission to celebrate the event. Africans do not share our sense of mourning; death for them is a state akin to recaptured freedom, a final return to their homeland.

I was in the parlor giving the last touches to a violet shawl I was knitting for my mistress. It was almost eleven, and Mr. Lind had still not honored us with his presence. Through the open door, I heard Miss Susan's impatient voice; she was fearful of giving the negroes permission without first consulting with her husband.

She therefore called for Joseph and sent him to look for Mr. Lind.

When she came back into the parlor, Miss Susan tried, with obvious effort, to smile at me. A profound uneasiness veiled her countenance. Strangely echoing her distress, I too sensed, as she did, that some misfortune loomed. And in fact that obscure intuition had made me postpone for upwards of an hour the moment of my retiring for the night. I had the feeling that Miss Susan was grateful to me for that, and that her laconic "Still up?" was less a question than a recognition.

I do not know how much time passed, but the wait seemed interminable. Miss Susan's restless silence paradoxically irritated me. As though the long-drawn-out wait for Mr. Lind were tacit consent, the drums now were beating in the batey.

Unable to control the trembling that had come over my hands, I put down my needles and got up with the false mission of bringing in the linden tea that Bella was preparing in the kitchen. More to hide my uneasiness than to make conversation, I shared with Bella my indignation that the men sent to find Mr. Lind had still not returned with any news of him.

"Oh, Miss Florence," the housekeeper exclaimed, her big eyes now almost starting from her head in fright, "somebody saw him at that woman's house, there in town. Who's going to dare go there and pull him out?"

Shaken by the compassion in her voice, and by its fatal certainty, I neither wished nor was able to ask more. By the time Bella went into the parlor bearing the silver tray with its two cups, I had bade good-night to Miss Susan and gone up to my room.

With the Margaret Fuller book I had taken from the library untouched on my night table (though the kerosene lamp glowed softly in the darkness), I spent the night unsleeping. The secret eruption of my fury kept me awake. I sat for hours thinking, remembering, going over the hopes and regrets held deep within my spirit. Little by little, reason began to comfort me, to make me understand the absurdity of dreams and illusions. I swore to myself then to advance the day of my departure, to escape forever from this accursed greenhouse existence in which, before they can bloom, hopes wither.

Very early in the morning, before sunrise, the sudden silence of the drums, the reddish glow in the sky, and the familiar sound of hoofbeats made me run like a madwoman to the window.

BLACK CLOUDS

As summer nears, I have thought it imprudent of me to keep my decision from Mr. and Mrs. Lind. I have completed the three years of my commitment to the education and moral upbringing of Charles Walker Lind, and nothing now holds me here. My pupil will depart soon for the United States, where (as his father expressly requires of him) he will study engineering. I too will take that northern route. And (should my mistress's generosity of spirit not extend to recommending me for some employment there, similar to my position here) I will place an announcement in a New York newspaper offering my services as tutor or lady's companion, and in the meantime take lodgings (with the savings I have been able to make) in a modest hotel.

I have told Charlie before anyone else. But his heart

is the prisoner of new emotions which prevent his being stricken very much by the news. Perhaps I chose badly the moment to confide my plans to him. He had just vented his spleen at the "mute intransigence" of his father. He was sure, though he could not support his conviction with any proof, that Mr. Lind had discovered his infatuation with the famous Carmelina, and that that was the reason for his forced exile. In vain I assured him that the idea of sending him abroad was simply part of the normal expectations not simply of any father concerned about his son's future but in fact of every young man brought up in the narrow confines of the colonies.

What happened then has been a source of deep consternation for me. Not since those first turbulent months of my stay here have I seen Charlie so beside himself, so incapable of containing or even moderating the expression of his anger. Openly accusing me of having betrayed his confidence, he said such hurtful things to me that it was only my sense of decorum that allowed me to tolerate them. He threw in my face my supposed "prejudices," my "double standard," my position as a "paid spy." Rendered utterly speechless by the torrent of insults (which I knew myself far from deserving), I could only listen in silence. When the storm subsided at last, I picked up my books and papers with deliberate calm and left him alone with his conscience in the dimness of the library.

Miss Susan was less expressive but kinder. Not only did she assure me of her full protection and that of her friends in New York, but she promised me a letter of recommendation from Mr. Morse himself.

I had originally planned to sail in July on the same boat that Charlie sailed upon, but now, for obvious reasons, I have had to reconsider. I was greatly relieved when Miss Susan herself asked me to stay on until mid-August, when she once more expected a visit from Mrs. Molly Overman. The dull and lightless gaze that accompanied the kind words of my mistress told me that Miss Susan's desperation was even greater than my own.

LETHARGY

Charlie's last weeks in Puerto Rico have passed with maddening slowness. Relieved of the responsibility of his lessons, freed from the routine imposed by some fixed purpose, my days drag out like some long blank roll of parchment.

Mr. Lind is in Ponce, and is not expected back until Friday. Will it matter to him that I too am leaving, that I am leaving forever the protection of his house?

My ex-charge, now more the mutinous boy than ever, roams the gardens listlessly. Sometimes I see him walking pensively toward town. I know where he is going – to pay the bitter tribute of a love without future. Under the weak excuse of some vague indisposition, he hardly eats with us any more. It is as though he were already gone from us, while the ghost of his body has remained behind.

Most of my resentment has now dissipated – perhaps I should say my indignation. The romance between Charlie and Carmelina has reduced me to the sad role of a rival banished and without rights.

July is here, with its heat and mosquitoes. The preparations for Charlie's trip are going apace. His father has ordered a huge trunk for him, so that he can comfortably travel with all the wonderful clothes that his mother has had made for the young scion.

THE RECONCILIATION

Attended by Dr. Tracy, the O'Haras, and other neighbors that in some cases affection and other cases courtesy made it necessary to invite, this evening the intimate farewell party took place.

"Master Charlie is already teaching us how much we shall miss him," remarked Dr. Tracy affectionately when at six o'clock the guest of honor had still not made his appearance. Perplexity was on every face but two: mine, for I knew the causes behind the effects, and that of his father, less confused than angry.

In an attempt to dispel her husband's obvious ill humor, Miss Susan had tea and cake brought in, a habit of the house since the arrival of this humble British subject. But the strategy did not have its hoped-for effect. Mr. Lind got up and took the stairs three at a time up to Charlie's room, where he burst in the door. Miss Susan sat utterly unmoving, her eyes fixed on me in clear but mute supplication.

I waited for Mr. Lind to find that his son was not in the house (a fact I had known from the first) and then before I could repent of my plan I intercepted him at the foot of the stairs. His green eyes interrogated my own with absolute coldness.

"I know where he is, let me go for him," was all I could manage to say, though I did have the temerity to brush his hand with mine. Miraculously, the tension fled his features.

"Go, then," he said with that softness that I had thought lost to me.

I went out into the garden without the slightest idea of where my steps ought to take me. What I wanted more than anything was to flee the oppressive air of that parlor. As I approached the gates, though, and was about to confront the decision as to which road to take, I came upon the overseer, returning at a gallop from the fields. When I asked where my pupil might be, he pointed down the Punta Guilarte road and said, "Down there."

Only the desperation of knowing how far away he was would have induced me to accept the bold invitation that came next. Impulsively, without thinking, I took the hand gallantly offered me and I mounted the horse in front of the overseer.

During that foolish race through the jungle of tall palm trees to the shore, I could feel my skirts flying and my hair come loose in the mad wind. And yet I felt I was safe. The veins on Joseph's arms swelled with the effort of holding me. My unruly fantasy made me close my eyes, change the horseman's name, the color of the skin of the hands that were tight about my waist.

The sun was low, and its sidelong rays tortured our eyes, but then suddenly the unmistakable figure of my dear Charlie appeared against the sky. He turned his head upon hearing the horse's gallop, and then came slowly toward us, though he did not return our greeting. Sliding carefully down, I asked Joseph to return to the house and send back two men with horses – a chore he could not have enjoyed doing but which he rushed off to perform.

A dense silence enveloped us after the sound of the

horse's hooves had died away. We looked at each other, and the murmur of the waves drowned the beating of our anguished hearts. It was Charlie who with a single gesture cured all the hurt, all the pain of the wounds. My clumsy words were hushed by the close, warm embrace of his arms. We sat on a fallen treetrunk bleached by the waves and waited for the horses' return, remembering that day when, naked and innocent, he had shown himself to eyes that did not want to see.

FAREWELL

Today, very early in the morning, while the servants lashed the trunk to the roof of the coach, Bella took down my message: Miss Florence was indisposed. From my room I was the invisible witness of the impassive farewells of Charlie and the flowing tears of Miss Susan. The father, who had still not forgiven the terrible social affront committed by his son, showed his stubbornness by his absence.

Just as he was about to step into the carriage, the young voyager looked up toward my window. I waved my handkerchief softly. He blew me a kiss. And thus were separated Charles Walker Lind and his tutor: without promises and without tears.

The same route taken by my Charlie would lie before me in two weeks. Like a pain that sears my breast is the burning desire I feel to flee this little island forgotten by the world, and inhabited by none but birds of passage.

THE GRAND FINALE

With her habitual courtesy, Miss Susan offered me a wonderful dinner, and she set beside my plate an envelope swollen with money. Bella had made my favorite dish: roast turkey with minted rice stuffing. The master did us the supreme honor – all the more eloquent for its infrequency – of dining with us at the table.

After the delight of the superb dessert (*omelette norvégienne flambée*), Mr. Lind adroitly opened a bottle of his best champagne and raised his glass in an astounding toast – "To happiness."

"Does such a thing exist?" I asked, joking to hide a sudden access of anger.

Miss Susan smiled her approval and proposed another toast, this one less pretentious: " 'To serenity' would be more like it, don't you think, Miss Florence?"

At that I raised my glass too, and inspired by some strange spirit of mockery (from my Celtic ancestors?), I drank "to chance, to ever-possible chance."

I refused to acknowledge the darts from his eyes nor to allow them to find their mark in the warm moistness of my own.

Tomorrow the boat will sail, and I will be taken forever from this bitter island. It is late, and my candle gutters. I have taken the latch off my door.

Miss Florence held the closed diary to her breast a moment before she put it carefully back into the small black box with its lining of red taffeta. Then she reached into the old trunk again and took from it a package of envelopes neatly tied together by pink ribbon. When she pulled one of the loose ends, the envelopes spilled onto the carpet like old playing-cards in a game without rules.

The French postage-stamps with the stern image of Napoleon III caught her eye at once. Opening one of the envelopes that had fallen a little apart from the rest, she recognized with a smile the long cursive strokes that invariably marked the handwriting of one of her own pupils.

The letter was not easy to read. Doubtlessly because of a scarcity of paper – or perhaps because of that incorrigible desire to mystify that he had always shown – the writer had covered both sides of the paper with horizontal and vertical lines superimposed upon each other.

Paris, May 24, 1866
10, rue du Roi-de-Rome

My dear Teacher,
You will surely wonder at having news of me after so long. Not a day, however, since we lost sight of you, now more than six years ago (almost a quarter of my life), has your memory ceased pursuing me. I will not say that I have deliberately thought of you every day of my tedious life. That would be to deceive you or, worse, flatter you – both of which your example always taught me to abhor. But I have frequently had the occasion to miss your witty British irony (which so often mortified me) and that constant disposition for indignation (which never failed to amuse me). Not to mention, of course, our infinite walks in quest of crabs and hibiscus flowers, or the inevitable five-o'clock tea in the garden of flesh-eating plants.

I take the liberty of recalling those sweet memories without even contemplating the possibility that you

have cast all those years into oblivion. Is it true, Miss
Florence? Can you have been so cruel, so strong?
Have you erased from your mind those years of my
innocence (and your own) in Puerto Rico?

Finding where to write you was more difficult than
(if I do not misremember) obtaining your acquiescence
to my childish afternoons when I wished to escape
the school-room. No one knew anything about *la
petite Anglaise*, save that she had arrived alive and
well in New York and then had disappeared into
thin air. No one, that is, except a good friend of the
family (whose name I will not reveal) who had had
the enviable fortune to come across you in the streets
of Manhattan in the company of your current
employer, one Mrs. Weston.

Why did you never write? What reasons did we
give you (did *I* give you) to make you wish to
uproot us in this way, so utterly, from your heart?

But I will not waste good time in recriminations,
not when I have so much to tell you. (For you
should know that you are even unto this moment
my only, and exclusive, *confidante*. It is quite simple:
I have never told anyone, nor ever will tell anyone
else, my ridiculous "sorrows of young Werther.")

The last time we saw one another (I on the step of
the carriage, you at the window of your dovecote),
my sadness was my only baggage. Is one's first love
the only one, or at least the most memorable? In
that case, I am not certain who it was harder for me
to abandon – the captive princess of Arroyo or the
captivator of princes of La Enriqueta. Would that I
possessed the gift of ubiquity, so that I might be
witness at this instant to the color that has just come

into your cheeks. I must content myself,
unfortunately, with imagining it.

As to that dark and melancholic chapter of my life,
only one piece of information is left me to tell you,
the piece of information that paints this so-
predictable fairy tale a dreadful red: the death of
Carmelina a few months after my departure, a death
by her own hands. Time passes, Miss Florence,
though not so the tracks left upon us by the wounds
that cut too deep.

It is not my intention to weary your nights with
stories that will steal your sleep away. You are no
doubt asking what a great engineering-fellow, who
was graduated (and the passive tense of that verb is
more than intentional) by force and against his
natural inclinations, is doing wandering now about
the streets of Paris. Well, I have returned to the
calling that you yourself so wisely helped me
discover -- the vocation of art. I follow in the footsteps
of my illustrious grandfather (who, as you well
know, not only sent telegrams but also painted
paintings) and more literally than you might think.
At this very moment, for example, I am staying in
the eleven-room apartment which Mr. Samuel F. B.
Morse has just rented, a few steps from the Bois de
Boulogne and not far -- a bracing walk -- from the
Champs de Mars. Here my grandfather can enjoy, in
the company of his wife, his children, and his parvenu
relatives, the Grande Exposition Internationale, that
material hymn to the technical and scientific glory
of the Second Empire. Even Mrs. Goodrich, his sister-
in-law, is here -- with her entire southern clan -- in
order to spare themselves the "horrors of
Reconstruction" after the Civil War that has left

them virtually in the street. And where would we be without Mr. Prime, that excellent newspaperman in search of material for a biography (not mine, certainly).

As you will recall, I am not one for what might be called family reunions. I think, therefore, that I will be here on the rue du Roi-de-Rome for no longer than the time strictly needed to find a flat and a position as an apprentice in the *atelier* of some famous painter (M. Courbet, perhaps: I have ambitions). Mrs. Goodrich finds me a bit unsociable for her taste, and has said so to Mr. Morse, who (in defense of the family honor) unceasingly sings the praises of my venerable father. So you see, not even in France am I able to be anything but "Mr. Lind's son," that magical phrase which on the Island had the curious effect of simultaneously opening doors to me and shutting them.

But all is not as tragic as my telling of my tale might make one think, for my outlook has I'm sure been contaminated at least somewhat by the *esprit romantique* that infuses this nation. No, for there are amusing things as well, such as the vision of that wondrous patriarch Father Samuel (so republican in his convictions) dressed in the style of the French aristocracy, with a sword about his waist and all, climbing up on a chair with his wife Sarah in order to see, over the heads of the ten thousand citizens invited to the grand reception in the Hôtel de Ville, the Emperor in person.

I revel as you cannot imagine in the sheltering anonymity of this city's effervescent life, with all its multitudes and its overwhelming spaces. It makes me feel a kind of lightheadedness, almost a dizziness, like drinking too much champagne. In the narrow cobblestoned streets of this city where all is possible, I recover the faculty I thought lost – the faculty of trusting in the merits of my own decisions.

As I know you will judge harshly one who would dare close this epistle without one word about the elder Linds, I will send you *four* words, with my most cordial respects: *ça va, malgré tout.*

Is it too much vanity to hope for a reply? No matter – one can be arrogant with impunity at the age of twenty-three (precisely – my birthday is today).

Believe me, my dear Teacher, your most loving and grateful

– C.W.L.

By one of those frequent caprices of fate, or of the postal service, Miss Florence's reply never reached her nostalgic former pupil. More than a year later, a second letter from France revealed at least part of the reason: the young man's address had changed.

Paris, September 16, 1867
39, rue de Douay

Ungrateful heart of ice –
Once again I dare offend you with a letter. I put aside the pride that has made me continue to await an impossible letter, and allow myself the hope that the most gratifying eventuality is in fact the true one – that you never received my first.

This one shall be much briefer. Speaking to an imaginary interlocutor is not the favorite pastime of a mind which, in spite of the overwhelming

evidence against it, still aspires to the state of sanity.
One simple anecdote will perhaps most efficiently
serve to communicate to you how complex (and
absurd) my current *état d'esprit* really is.

A French friend of mine took me a few days ago
to the studio of an artist whose specialty is the fruits
and vegetables of the tropics (in paint, I mean).

"I understand he is Puerto Rican, like you," my
enthusiastic cicerone told me, and only my fear of
offending him restrained me from laughing in his
face. Puerto Rican? What does this new epithet
mean, whose syllables never once assailed my ears
in all the time I lived in Arroyo? Geographic
proximity is surely not sufficient reason for
bestowing adjectives of birth and antecedence so
cavalierly, much less when one's parents have always
behaved as though La Enriqueta were the displaced
center of an eternally foreign universe. My
upbringing, as you well know, only accentuated
that distance. The summers in Poughkeepsie or
Europe, or in the ancestral mansions of the Linds
and Overmans in St. Thomas, served to remind me
each and every year of my essential foreignness,
my ancestry so little rooted in the land whose
generous fruit nourished my family's wealth.

Yet, my dear friend, curiously, that word which I
found so absurd had the power to shake me to the
core. What has my life been but one long wanderlust
without destination or compass? Where will it be
that I, should that day come, plant my roots, however
aerial they may be? When I stepped into that studio,
the pineapples, the papayas and mameyes of the
tropics, hanging in effigy and exile upon the walls,
made me feel that I was once more close to the sea,

feeling the cordial embrace of the sun as I lay upon the sand with you.

As for my artistic work, it saddens me to admit that my father's astute prophecy is very near coming true: "If you don't come back a second Delacroix, you'll have shamefully wasted your time and my money." After several unsuccessful attempts to be taken into a prestigious studio, I see that I cannot do without the letter of introduction that my famous grandfather so kindly handed me upon my arrival. I have discovered that in Paris, as in all cities, one must have a godfather if one is to be baptized.

One piece of encouraging news – which, in seeing the address above, you will have already noted: I live alone. I am renting a small room "under the roof," as the saying goes, with skylight and all, in a modest building just steps from Montmartre. Wouldn't you like to come back to Europe? (Oh, forgive me, I know that England is another continent. . .) You could walk with little Charlie along the mysterious Seine. This last mad sentence will have shown you that I am still capable of daydreams (at least).

Please, madam, receive the imperishable, though unrequited, affection of your ever-faithful

– C. W. L.

The day had long dawned upon the city, and the morning's gray light was dripping thickly down the walls of the buildings, when the shutters of the little room on Bleecker St. were drawn open and a window raised. Inside, the stove cracked and ticked, and it gave off a smell of gas that stung the nose. A freezing gust of air blew into the room. Miss Florence Jane closed the window, yet she stood for a long while looking down at the streets filled with dirty snow.

When she turned back, she saw the newspaper spreading its wings like a black and white butterfly across the sofa and the open trunk, which suddenly was as unsettling to her as a coffin without its corpse. While the water whistled mockingly in the kettle and clouds of warm steam filled the room, Miss Florence strode without the slightest hesitation to the wardrobe.

II

"It is the same sea, the same waves; their rhythm has not wavered or abated in all this time. The smooth surface of the ocean does not change like the fickle heart of men. And that blue drapery! How could I have forgotten how intensely blue a sky can be which fears no winter? The pelicans and sea gulls wheel and dive, heralding the land. It is difficult to believe that with that same grace they rip and devour their submarine prey – as mercilessly and relentlessly as, secret and terrible, the very sharks."

With those words Miss Florence Jane began the diary of her return to Puerto Rico. She followed the same route as on her first voyage, twenty-seven years before. The cargo ship on which she had sailed dropped anchor, as it had that other time, a prudent distance from the dock. A little dinghy rowed her and the few other passengers to the shore. There, an absent-minded customs officer, black-uniformed, motioned that she could proceed.

Presenting herself at the hacienda without notice, her baggage slung over her shoulders as it were, seemed to her the most flagrant sort of breach of courtesy. Not even the respectable pretext of a visit to pay her condolences would justify such a violation of the rules of etiquette. With the aid of a small fistful of dollars, she persuaded the porter to take her bag – and her request for a room for the night – to a run-down-looking hotel on the main street, visible from the docks. The porter's hints as to the doubtful reputation of the place were in vain. To calm the man, Miss Florence finally had to assure him that she would not be staying there for any length of time at all.

As soon as I had taken a room at "El Marino" – whose reality only confirms the porter's apprehensions – I took off my hat in order to retouch my hair, which had been much blown by the wind. A mirror encroached upon from all sides by blotches gave back to me an image, in the stale shadow of the room, of a face much wearied by journeying. While I awaited the arrival of the coach-man – who was taking his time, one might add – a whim made me change the sober gray dress that I had chosen for my voyage and put on one of pink silk whose cut favored me better. I then sat, nervously, upon the sway-backed cot which was to be my bed, if fortune smiled upon me, for but a single night.

The coachman's expression was one of perplexity when I asked him to take me to Mr. Edward Lind's residence. I repeated my request, attempting to Hispani-cize my pronunciation of the name as best I could, but it was not until I mentioned the name of the hacienda that we could at last drive out toward Cuatro Calles – much more slowly than suited my impatience.

January was in its full tropical splendor. The white silk crown of the sugar cane swayed in the wind, and the deep green of the trees, thick with leaves, were a sign of benediction upon these lands of erstwhile drought. The warm wetness of the air, and the perspiration it provoked, bathed my face, and I was constantly obliged to mop my forehead and throat with a kerchief.

Up until that moment I had acted as though in a dream. I had been as though propelled by hidden clockwork springs, by irresistible winds blowing this way and that across the geography of my desires. Now, so near the truth, so near my destiny, I was assailed by the full violence of my consciousness of what was about to take place. What was I to gain from this absurd and unreasoning leap backward in time? Would I even be recognized by that person who for so many years had, alone, inhabited the shadows of my memory? Would I recognize him, who would have been tattooed, weathered, and scarred by life's storms? His features took on life once more, they sprang up again, lighted by sudden lightning-glare, and then once more faded, like a footprint in sand, under the cruel tide of my presentiments.

At last I saw the baronial gates, now gnawed by the salty air's erosion. Impelled by a need to step of my own power across that threshold of the paradise lost, I had the coachman stop the horses there. I felt it better to keep the secret and the surprise until the last. With more curiosity than good will, the man offered to wait for me. Handing him his money, I sent him off with an impatience I could not conceal.

Nature had made such incursions into the drive that

my bootlaces tangled in the overgrown grass. Led by habit, I made my way, slipping and tugging, up the drive toward the house. The troublesome little burrs that I now again remember pulling from young Charlie's socks and pants-legs stuck to the silk of my dress, making a yellow fringe that mercilessly scratched my legs.

I rehearsed in my mind the impossible speeches of my return: the dutybound condolences, the hidden motive. What would be the new mask under which I faced anew his presence? Would time have tamed his old impetuosity? Would he, as he had of old, fall silent and withdraw his gaze? Fear whispered in my ear that a mere knock at his door would not suffice to undo the tight knots of unhappiness.

When I reached the turn in the drive and stood for a moment in the thick undergrowth that obscured what had once been the perfect design of the gardens, I suddenly caught sight of the spectral outline of the house. The mid-afternoon sun lit the scene, revealing to me the desolating vision that my incredulous eyes in vain attempted to discredit: Its roof sunken, its woodwork fallen and rotting, its regal staircase mutilated, its doors and windows hidden by enormous boards, the princely mansion of La Enriqueta stood, its death-throes long past, like a soulless body amid the green of the trees. What diabolic curse had spewed its poison over the glorious palace of my youth? What evil planet had now eclipsed the triumphant rainbow of my hopes?

Of what happened next I have but the vaguest memory. The blood rushed boiling to my brain; my knees buckled, my legs failed me. My breast, shaken by the commotion produced upon my senses by the spectacle of that ruin, struggled to breathe the suddenly rarefied air. A black curtain fell over my eyes, and I slipped, unresistingly, into the bottomless abyss of unconsciousness.

The first thing she felt as she regained consciousness was the warm touch of hands under her head. She tried futilely to rise, but she realized, with some alarm, that her body was as though hanging in the air. With the abrupt return to sensation, her blurred vision made out the distant lighthouse of a pair of green eyes looking with concern down upon her.

"What happened to you?" asked the voice that accompanied the eyes. Without waiting for the improbable reply of that pale woman borne in his anonymous arms, the green-eyed man deposited her very delicately in the grass.

At first, Miss Florence was frightened by that dark visage that leaned over her own bloodless one. If she did not get up, it was because her legs, still unsure, would not permit her. The open smile of the young mulatto, however, the rare color of those eyes observing her with a mixture of curiosity and compassion, little by little disarmed her mistrustfulness. At last she was able to murmur words of gratitude for his help, and even to make a weak attempt to open her purse, still hanging from her wrist, and offer him a few coins, which he would not accept.

As reply to the mute questioning reflected in the intense gaze of her rescuer, she asked with many gestures and few words about the whereabouts of the hacienda's owner. The man answered in Spanish, though his interlocutress could not decipher the meaning of his long explanation. After another such exasperating exchange, he courteously offered Miss Florence his arm.

Leaning upon that arm, she walked toward what had once been the batey of the negroes, now a clearing circled by little wooden cabins with thatched roofs. As she walked, she felt her strength gradually returning to her. In the earthen plaza that was the center of the rustic settlement, a group of children were noisily playing chase with pods of the locust tree.

The young man stopped before one of the cabins and signalled to her that she should wait outside. She leaned against a breadfruit tree and closed her eyes a moment. Almost immediately, her rescuer stuck his head out the door of the cabin and motioned for her to come inside. Timidly, Miss Florence approached the open door.

Her eyes had to accustom themselves to the dimness. The single window, open but a chink, allowed one thin ray of light to penetrate the room. It illuminated the white head of an old negro woman ceremoniously sitting in a rocking chair, rocking.

"What a sight for these sore eyes, miss! I thank heaven for letting me see you once more before I lose my sight forever!" The words, in the musical English of the islands, were immediately recognizable to me. Opening her arms, smiling an almost-toothless smile, she gave me the warmest reception I have ever received. The tears I had so far been able to contain ran freely now down my cheeks, mixing with Bella's own.

"Oh, Miss Florence, Miss Florence," were the only words her trembling old lips seemed capable of speaking. Moved and surprised, the young man who had brought me to Bella stared at us from the hammock.

When she recovered herself, Bella introduced me to Andrés, whom she insisted upon calling her grandson. This surprised me no end, as I knew that Bella had never had any children, and that when our lives diverged she had been a woman of some fifty years of age. Naturally I said nothing, accepting her statement as one accepts a mystery of the faith.

More restored now after the constant siege of emotions, I sipped the bitter coffee that Andrés, at his "grandmother's" bidding, served me, and I sat down on a low stool that the young man offered. I did not have to initiate the conversation (as I had rehearsed so often in my mind) with questions. Bella forestalled me by launching herself almost at once into a detailed accounting of the events that had so drastically transformed our respective lives. Andrés, smiling, listened attentively to the monologue, though his ignorance of English kept him from understanding much of it. His green eyes' insistence inexplicably disturbed me, and it required some effort on my part to avoid his glance.

"You know, Miss Florence, that we are free now?" Bella announced proudly. When I nodded, she went on without further interruption.

"Well, then ... Mr. Morse, rest his soul, had died, when all of a sudden from over there, from Spain, came the news that we were free. No sooner had we heard, than Domingo and Juan Prim jumped on their horses and rode off down the coast yelling and carrying on to spread the word. You should have been at La Enriqueta that night! There were people from every hacienda in Arroyo, Patillas, and Guayama. The torch-lights lit up the place like it was high noon, and the drums beat till daybreak. Miss Susan and Master Charlie – the sweet boy had come back by this time – sat on the veranda and watched. He looked happy – he even pulled me out of the kitchen and made me go down to the batey, and he stood off and watched me, he waved at me to dance, and shake myself, and cast off all the shackles on my soul. Mr. Lind had gone to bed early. And the expression on his face ... Things were not going well for him you know – money things. He had more debts than acres of land, and the government kept throwing monkey wrenches into any plan he invented to get a little ahead. They wouldn't even let him bring over an engineer from England so he could pipe water down from Ancones Creek so the cane fields could get some water. It was just too much for him, you see, to have to pay the folks that used to work for him for free."

My patience began to wear a bit thin, but fearing to show any too-forward (if not totally unjustified) interest in the family's private matters I kept my questions to myself and did not mention the name that trembled upon the threshold of my lips. Somehow Bella must have caught the silent plea in my eyes. Her next words seemed an attempt to satisfy my longings:

"You cannot imagine, Miss Florence, the things that a person heard in that house. They were like dogs and cats, the father and the son all day rowing and arguing, shouting at the top of their lungs at each other, right at the dinner table, over the crazy ideas that Mr. Lind said Master Charlie had brought back from France. Mr. Lind said he rued the day he'd ever wasted his money on such a trip as that. The child had always loved to paint – you know that better th'n anyone. But the master of the house wanted to put him behind the counter in the store, you might say. And Master Charlie more than thirty years old, while Mr. Lind was treating him like he was still a child. Until one day the poor thing could take no more . . . "

Bella paused, clearly affected by the vivid memories awakened in her by this emotional retelling of the past. But then with a deep sigh she went on with her distressing tale:

"Miss Susan had sent me to make up the room that used to be yours, the little one upstairs, remember? She didn't sleep with her husband anymore now. In fact, she kept so to her room that you almost never saw her anywhere else in the house anymore. It broke my heart to see her that way, so all alone, so shut up inside that room, inside herself. I even took her favorite parrot up to her so she could hear a human word now and then. Mr. Lind was never in the house, and when he did come home, the arguments with Master Charlie would drive him outside again in no time."

Andrés had closed his eyes, and his chest was rising and falling regularly; the hammock gently swayed. Bella smiled when she saw the direction my indiscreet gaze had taken.

"Young people aren't interested in these old folks' stories," she said. The words seemed to give new strength to her nostalgia, for she then continued.

"Well, then, Miss Florence – things were bad, and then all of a sudden they got worse. As though he hadn't made his father mad enough at him already, Charlie fell in love again. But don't misunderstand me – that wasn't the worst part of it. Mr. Lind did want to see the boy married, for it was his hope that his grandchildren would raise up that plantation again. But he didn't want him marrying the woman Master Charlie picked out, if you'll forgive me calling him Master Charlie still – it's that that's the way I always think of him, Miss Florence.

Anyway, to keep himself occupied and to earn a little money now and again, Charlie would paint the portraits of the better families, you know, in the towns around, in Arroyo and Guayama especially. And that was how he came to meet Brunilda, which was the daughter that don Jacinto Cora had had by a servant girl. Brunilda was light-skinned, lighter-skinned than Selenia, if you remember her, Miss Florence. Her skin was as olive-colored as a gypsy, and she had big eyes the color of honey, and a nose that looked like somebody had whittled it down, it was so fine and narrow. The only thing that gave away her birth was her hair, which was just like mine, kinky, even though she wore it in a kind of a bun that favored her face wonderfully.

"When I say that Charlie fell in love, I'm not telling the half of it. The poor thing was like a puppy – he would send her flowers, he would take her candy, he would give her books to read, he would draw her . . . Every day on God's earth he would go out for a buggy-ride with her. The horse finally got to know the way – it never had to open its eyes after a while. And that girl's family, you can imagine, just delighted, delighted – why, they were the ones that would come out ahead in the match, of course.

"But I haven't mentioned the hurricane that was brewing in the *other* house. Mr. Lind did not approve of his son's intentions. Marrying a mulatto woman was not the same as sowing some wild oats with the negro girls. Oh, Miss Florence, like father, like son . . . But how could two men be so alike in their pleasures and so different in every other way?"

Instinctively I touched my forehead, a gesture that betrayed the discomfort brought me by such indiscreet words. Bella laid her rough hand over mine and went on, her smile full of wisdom:

"Master Charlie wouldn't budge. The more his father opposed the match, the more determined he was to marry the girl. In town it was all anybody could talk about – the vegetable-peddlers pushing their carts around town talked about it, and even the black share-croppers made jokes about it, laughing over the way Mr. Morse would be spinning in his grave the day his dark-skinned great-grandson was born."

She sighed again, and her expression became grave. One would never have been able to predict that expression from the lightsome tone she had used to tell the story so far.

"Well," she said, crossing herself, "you know how the story ended. Let's not disturb the dead anymore than we have to."

These last words shook me from my previous reticence to speak, and I assured Bella of my total ignorance of the events to which she so mysteriously alluded. Her face underwent a transformation that made my blood freeze. A dry, cold knot gripped my throat.

"Then . . . you don't know?" she whispered, as though to convince herself of what was now a palpable reality. And in the face of the anguished silence that met her question, she broke into uncontrollable sobs, and cried out in pain, "Oh, Miss Florence! My God! . . . he's dead!"

At Bella's outburst and the cry that escaped my lips, Andrés sat up in the hammock. I could not move; I was seized with horror and astonishment, yet I would have postponed forever the moment of the bitter revelation. The tears refused to come. My dry eyes remained fixed on old Bella's face.

When I had gathered my little strength to mutter a few confused and incoherent words, I at last learned my poor ward's tragic ending. Five years had now passed since that fatal night, but Bella remembered the precise date and hour. It was exactly eight o'clock at night when the father and son, after bitter words of recrimination at the table, went off together into the darkness of the gardens. Perhaps they had wanted to spare the mother their angry shouting. Or perhaps, wishing to keep their differences between themselves, they had simply withdrawn out of earshot of the servants. Of what was said, no one was witness. How they offended one another, no one knows. All anyone ever knew was that without a backward glance, and as fast as the wind, Charlie fled his enchanted garden forever. Pale and wounded, he went to his room. His father dropped onto a marble bench, his head between his hands, and he did not lift his head again until he heard the shot. That was the beginning of his own death-in-life.

The day dawned gray and dreary. Haze floated heavily over the greenish sea around Arroyo and low black clouds smudged the far-off line of the horizon.

The town was still half asleep when Andrés gave a tug at the cord of the doorbell. He hadn't long to wait; the door opened almost instantly, and a small figure swathed in mourning emerged. The woman followed in the young man's quick steps with all the darting nearness of a shadow.

The town began to stretch. Some early fishing boats had already returned to the dock. A tramp sat up in his burlap bed to look with unconcealed curiosity upon that astonishing vision of a young mulatto man carrying a bunch of flowers followed by a phantasmagoric white woman dressed head to toe in black.

They made their way down San Fernando until they saw, from a curve in the street, the white wall upon whose dirty top there arose, like apparitions gauzed in mist, the enormous stone heads of two angels. The man and the woman stopped before the closed gates. The legend above them, encircled by a leafy crown that embraced a cross, proclaimed its hopeful yet mournful message:

THIS, A GARDEN OF SILENCE AND CALM IS,
WHICH NONE BUT THE SINNER NEED FEAR.
BODIES ARE LAID IN THE EARTH HERE,
WHILE THEIR SOULS TO NEW LIFE HAVE ARIS'N.

To Andrés' summons the gravedigger soon responded, slowly and laboriously dragging his bad leg. He leaned the shovel he had been carrying against the guardhouse wall and without so much as a good-morning told the waiting man and woman that this was no decent hour to be visiting the dead. Andrés lay the coin discreetly passed to him by his companion into the calloused hand of the growling Spaniard that tended the place, and without more ado the rusted chains parted.

While my guide asked for the exact place, I went on ahead, walking down between the two rows of stones and funerary monuments that formed the long main avenue. Suddenly I stopped and, led by blind intuition, traced my steps backward a few feet. The ill-humored gravedigger's directions were unnecessary. There, before me, but a few feet from the entrance to the graveyard, there rose a low house of red bricks, like an altar — my poor Charlie's last dwelling-place. The letters of his beloved name, cut into the sober marble gravestone, burned into the dry fibers of my eyes.

I knelt on the wet ground to murmur a prayer for the eternal rest of his afflicted soul. I lowered my eyes and called up the image of the mischievous child with round, rosy cheeks that he had once been. Sobs shook my body, and they somehow eased the pain in my breast, which had been wounded by a grief that I knew would never end. Confounded by the intensity of my tears, Andrés laid in silence, beside the tomb, the bunch of flowers so lovingly prepared by Bella for her dead babe.

I gave myself up to cruel reflections, which could only nourish my suffering. Again and again I remembered, though I had never lived, that terrible night that had cut off happiness forever. Had Charles Walker Lind sensed, two hours before dusk began falling, that that was to be his last sunset? When had there begun to germinate within him, like some black flower, the idea of death? Had he perhaps unknowingly sowed the design in his indifferent and mocking father's mind, so that in that distant and alien ground the burning seed would sprout? What was the angry fear, the cruel derision that crowned his daring? What fatal words dissolved the bonds? Who ripped, with a single slash, the placid canvas?

A sudden blinding flash of lightning cut the sky, and the thunder resounded in the desolate cemetery. The Spaniard crossed himself and limped off in search of shelter.

Andrés extended a hand, to help her to her feet. Before Miss Florence laid her trembling hand in his, however, she bent to leave a kiss upon the cold stone of the tomb. Needles of mist played their melancholy mazurka upon the wet marble.

It was true, horribly true – my own senses, oddly sharpened by suffering, had confirmed it. Now, no matter how hard I tried, I could never again deny it. My Charlie was – and I had to say the word – dead. His mortal body would never again tread the fertile earth. Only his memory, destined to suffer the slow fading of the emotions, would live with me.

Stricken with a grief that defies all attempts at description, I turned my back and covered my face. Long I stood like that. Thinking me disoriented, Andrés courteously showed me the path back to the entrance. I shook my head and asked him to leave me alone. He retired a little way, while I wandered down those paths flanked by imposing mausoleums. I do not know how long I walked, what miles I must have covered, how many hours passed, how many epitaphs with their futile cortege of surnames filed past my unseeing eyes. My black calico dress stuck wetly to my body, and a sharp wind mercilessly lifted the folds of my cape, cutting me to the bone. Almost as though in a trance I wandered, like another ghost in that precinct of the dead, breathing the fetid and poisonous air of the graveyard.

Exhausted at last from so much aimless wandering, I retraced my ever more lagging steps, leaving behind this place and returning, without happiness, to the world of the living. But a mute, deep voice drew me wordlessly once again to the scene of my previous weeping. If I had been able then to conquer the silent impulse, to break that macabre spell, my feet would not have returned to circumambulate the beloved remains of my rebellious angel and my wretched eyes would never have come to rest upon that stone which sealed forever my affliction – identical in cut and style, like a twinned bed, the red tomb of Edward Lind stood mutely confronting his son's, even after death.

The clouds opened then, emptying the rivers of the heavens. The dull scream from my very soul flooded my throat with fire.

Everyone wants to see the white lady, whose figure has floated like a virginal lay-sister through the cane fields. But Andrés has bolted the doors and windows of the cabin. Bella rocks in her rocking chair beside Miss Florence's cot, for Miss Florence is stricken with a fever that will not yield even to poultices and herbal teas. She speaks incomprehensible words to her dead loves. Tearful, downcast, the old servant blames herself for this, and day and night she sits with her rag, scented with eucalyptus, and wipes away the icy sweat that pearls the sick woman's brow.

How can one count the eternal nights of fever? Bella swears it was two nights, and that on the third I opened my eyes to ask what country I was in and if winter had never come. Her chicken broth and saintly patience saved me from the black pit my life had slipped away into since my pilgrimage to the cemetery.

Andrés would allow no one to talk to me of the past, yet the past was all I wanted to know. I had so many questions to ask, if I was to be able to go on living. As my strength grew, Bella gave in to me. Her cruel story filled the void of time with death.

"At first, Mrs. Lind refused to believe that Charlie was gone. She locked herself up all day, calling him and talking to the walls. At night, we'd see her walking through the gardens, looking for him behind the trees, crying and moaning like a soul in purgatory. Mr. Lind would send me out to get her, so she wouldn't get a mind to do somethin' crazy. Sometimes we'd be walking through the cane fields as the sun was coming up ... And then when the sun was up, she would let me bring her back to her room ... "

"No matter how hard anybody tried, Miss Susan didn't understand. All she wanted to do was tell us that waking nightmare that had tormented her since that night, tell us how it repeated itself over and over and over again ... She kept seeing herself as a child in Locust Grove, sitting like a little lady at the long dining table there. She would be chatting as she served herself with the big copper ladle that her grandfather Jedediah had given her – pouring thick rivers of delicious-smelling sauce over a slice of glazed ham. So nobody would think she wanted to eat that whole sauce-boat of sauce herself, she would gracefully hold the sauce-boat up and then go to offer it to the rest of the guests. But when she would turn to her neighbor, her cold hands would drop it, and it would fall to the floor with a great crash. Horrified, she would look down to see the warm red lake spreading on the floor, bathing her bare feet, and as she looked up, apologizing, she would find nothing but two long rows of empty chairs.

"Little by little she got calmer, and then she would let me feed her. I would feed her with a spoon. In no more than a few months, she had dried up, she had got so old that it was almost hard to recognize her – a woman that had been so beautiful. . . "

"What about Mr. Lind?" I timorously whispered, both desiring and fearing the reply.

Bella paused, as though waiting for the right word to come to her. Her face hardened, and she took a deep breath before coldly pronouncing her next words.

"He never even wore mourning. Six months hadn't passed since Charlie's death, and he brought a black woman to live in the house."

Bella's voice now sounded distant. Though the tightness of my chest revealed how heavy upon me lay the anguish of this story, a curious sense of lightness possessed my brain, blunting a bit the knife-blade that probed the open wound of my emotions.

"She came in like a queen. She ruled the roost, all right, and she sat at the table and slept in Mr. Lind's bed. It was like Miss Susan had already died. I stayed there a while so as not to leave Miss Susan alone – the poor thing had nobody to take care of her. But one day I packed my things and went to town. I wasn't going to be no maid to a black woman. And the punishment was not long in coming, either, because the heavens are not deaf. Not long afterward, Mr. Lind fell sick, and his black mistress left him, and she took Miss Susan's jewelry and dresses with her. She went off to live the good life in Guayama . . . "

Hidden away on that dying hacienda, hounded night and day by debt, consumed by god only knows what inconfessable remorse, the father survived his son barely two years. It was Bella who had to see to the details of the funeral; no one else was left. She ordered the cedar coffin, mended the threadbare frockcoat he was buried in, notified the friends and neighbors, and made arrangements with the sacristan for the mass. It had been a quiet service: few mourners, no family, one or two of the official personages of the area. With no pomp or circumstance, his body had been lowered into the ground – and darkness had descended upon my soul.

From my cot I listened, eyes closed and my mind peopled with specters, to the melancholy story of Miss Susan's last days. The images of my fantasy mixed with those that Bella painted with the sure brushstrokes of her memories. Her emaciated face like that of a starving orphan, wearing the rent veil of a widow, Miss Susan rose from her own ashes.

Little by little she had given away everything: the damask bedclothes, the Persian rugs, the mirrored silver tray. There was many a visitor who came through the gates of La Enriqueta, which were now always open, to leave loaded down with little treasures, from rock-crystal doorknobs pulled off the mahogany doors to linen pillowcases embroidered with the manorial L.

She would sit alone at her dining table. The dining room windows would be closed tight, to maintain that unchanging dusk. And Susan Walker Lind *née* Morse would play with invisible knives and forks upon cracked plates. From the other side of the table there would come, like the cawing of excited crows, indecent words and libertine laughter. Two voices clashed in feverish counterpoint: the deep, harsh tones of his and the strident falsetto of that other woman's. Miss Susan, thank god, could not see them. The screen painted with a scene of a woman sitting beside the ocean – painted one day by her now-dead son – fell, like a final curtain, between that inhuman *tête-à-tête* and her eyes now dry from so much weeping.

The image of that man who had so long dictated the

rhythm and direction of my thoughts grew more dim to me with each word Bella spoke – like a shadow suddenly deprived of sun.

Slowly – all too slowly – my mind returned to what people call reality. Bella's unwearying dedication once more returned strength to my exhausted body. As soon as I could walk, Andrés took me down to the ocean, where the salt air and the hypnotic rhythm of the waves might restore to my spirit, at least in some measure, tranquility.

An inexplicable peace fell over all. Sitting beside me, my companion did not move. He knew, without understanding why, that his silent presence was balm to my wounded heart.

Suddenly Andrés raised his head and with curiosity followed the erratic flight of a sea gull. The wondrous light of morning kindled the startling beauty of his eyes, so astonishingly green against his dark skin. An unexpected revelation, blindly intuited, and as blindly stifled, struck me with the cunning speed of a bird of prey. Those green eyes, powerful, and so odd in one so dark – what indelible tattooing did they leave upon my soul?

A wind from beyond the grave blew through the corridors of my memory.

On January 30, 1886, Miss Florence Jane stood beside her luggage on the dock in Arroyo, awaiting the dinghy that was to take her to the boat. Leaning against a wall, the tall man with graying hair and moustache never took his eyes off her. His indiscretion unsettled her so, that she took a few deliberate steps, so as to put between herself and her impertinent observer a more marked distance.

Unaffected by this, the man smiled a conciliatory smile (which was not reciprocated) and quietly approached the traveler's bag, reading there, stenciled upon it, its owner's name. Then, smiling again (and this time with greater confidence), he spoke.

"Pardon me, Miss Florence . . . I had to be sure it was really you before I dared say hello."

Though the face, transformed by years, was not the same, the voice still had that youthful timbre of old. I instantly recognized, under the disguise of age, that long nose, that small square chin.

"*Monsieur*," I replied, offering my hand. Alvaro Beauchamp (for that was who the impertinent stranger was) promptly kissed it. "Fate never ceases to surprise me."

He still had the instant charm and manly sweetness that had always distinguished him. Having been recently widowed, he was on his way to St. Thomas, where he was to take the steamer that would bear him away to France. His two sons had returned to the land of their forebears – one was now living in Toulouse, the other in Aix-en-Provence.

"And Ernestina, how is she?" I inquired, taking for granted that she was still in France and that M. Beauchamp intended to visit her there. He lowered his eyes, which suddenly clouded, and in a voice breaking with sorrow told me of the death, many years ago, of his unhappy sister. I murmured a few words of condolence, though I felt them terribly inadequate. Ernestina's name was barely an echo in my past, while for him it still embodied a beloved human presence.

The conversation seemed to flag, freighted as it was

by the weight of the dead. The formulas of courtesy had deserted me, and I knew not how to go on, what to say. What possible interest could this profoundly grieving person have in the absurd story of my own journey to the depths of suffering? My lips wavered at the question that we both awaited, the name that neither of us could bring ourselves to speak. At last it was he who – knowingly or not – released me from my quandary.

"I have an appointment in Paris with a mutual friend of ours."

I could not pretend that the allusion went uncomprehended. After the loss of so many of our friends from those distant years, René Fouchard was the only remaining link that joined our lives. The conversation was coming to its end. The dinghy was approaching the shore and the passengers were moving toward the dock.

"Please give him my regards," I said, "and the assurance of my pleasant memory of those days."

The words tumbled out a bit clumsily as I violently signalled to a porter to help me with my bag.

M. Beauchamp kissed my hand again, and holding my gaze with almost fatherly tenderness, he whispered something.

"Place des Vosges, at the *Marais*. You can write him there."

The porter had already thrown my bag over his shoulder and was impatiently gesturing for me to follow him.

"14 Bleecker Street, New York," I replied, as I began to move away, and making the supreme effort to smile.

From the dinghy, I raised my hand in farewell. My cheeks burned under the stifling heat of the sun. The glare off the sea made my eyes water, and in a final act of mercy, the outlines of that island which I was now, truly forever, leaving, were softly blurred.

At two o'clock in the morning, the rearing and pitching of the waves has at last abated, and the sea is calm. Only a few hours remain before the boat, the *City of Santander*, reaches port in Havana. There, after unloading the mail sacks, it will remain at the dock only as long as necessary for the captain to be reassured as to the state of its engines. The few passengers it carries will then await the arrival of the ship that will take them to the United States.

On deck, up toward the bow, there is a woman, her gray hair in disarray, watching time pass. She trembles from head to foot, though the air is warm. She pulls the corners of her shawl around her and knots them upon her chest. She has not been able to sleep; she has been driven from her berth by an inconsolable wailing that comes from the sea and by a pale face, peering in the porthole window, that floats bodiless alongside the ship.

The moon illuminates the trail the ship leaves as it passes. In that trail I see the debris of my life. It was upon this very ship that, light with baggage but heavy with memories, my sad mistress set sail upon her own sea of exile, which soon became her bed of rest.

Perhaps just at the verge of a leap into the sea, fear made her waver, kept her, for one moment, from her desire. Perhaps she leaned gracefully over the rail, as though noting down a familiar name upon her dance card. Behold her there now, at last, the woman un-wed – with her crown of starfish, her scepter of seashells, her long mantle of seaweed, she is cleansed now of all foul betrayal, free now of her impossible love. She lies now at peace with herself. Her hardened features have felt the rest of softness; her withered skin has become smooth again. Once more she has become the pensive, beautiful Muse of the painting she once posed for, for her father.

Far away, in the distance, an identical moon shines over the darkness of the wild sugar cane. Its cruel rays wound the palace in ruins that no one now beholds with wonder. In the cracked mirrors of that solitude, in the desolate hallways of that nameless place, two wandering souls blindly seek each other through all eternity.

And what of me? Will I resist the dark temptation? Will I wear that widow's weed that has come so far to find me? Who will read these mute lips? Who will exhume my thwarted story of love and give it words?

III

It is a warm March day. Too warm to have the stove lighted. With the eager avidity of a starving animal, the flames devour the crumbs fed them by Miss Florence's hand. There is not much left: a foxed and faded drawing of a nymph in the moonlight, a napkin, stained with champagne, pressed between the pages of a book, and a yellow-striped rag that once tried to be the perfect dress.

Stripped of its erstwhile contents, the trunk now shows its naked lining. A thick cloud of smoke issues from the open window, up toward a sky traced by the first swallows of spring.

The War of the Saints
Jorge Amado

The image of Saint Barbara of the Thunder is being shipped to the city of Bahia. As the boat that will deliver her is docking, she comes to life to save Manela, a young Bahian girl whose flirtatious behaviour has offended her pious family. At the heart of *The War of the Saints* is *candomblé*, a religious cult that represents the fusion of African, Indian and Portuguese cultures in Brazil — the book is a celebration of racial impurity. Saint Barbara of the Thunder is destined to become a mythical character of Latin American literature like Dona Flor.

The Flight of the Tiger
Daniel Moyano

A powerful tale of house arrest in the Argentina of
the sixties, when the military juntas ruled, *The Flight
of the Tiger* chronicles the peasants' struggle to
overcome the tyrants and the forces that have
brought them into their homes. As in all his writing,
Moyano uses music as a metaphor for freedom.
When the despots ban one musical key, the people
change their pitch, and so multiply their powers to
resist. Rich in irony, black humour and satire, Daniel
Moyano's portrayal of political oppression —
influenced by his masters Kafka and Pavese — exposes
oppression everywhere.

Open Door
Luisa Valenzuela

'Luisa Valenzuela is the heiress of Latin American fiction. She wears an opulent, baroque crown, but her feet are naked.'

CARLOS FUENTES

'The style throughout is terse and taut, often with the staccato immediacy of the present tense and one-word sentences. All the greater achievement, then, to have created a world in which fantasy outweighs fiction and reality remains insidiously pervasive.'

TLS